Fish & Sphinx

Fish & Sphinx

Rae Bridgman

Great Plains Publications
420 – 70 Arthur Street
Winnipeg, MB R3B 1G7
www.greatplains.mb.ca

Great Plains Publications gratefully acknowledges the financial support provided for its publishing program by the Government of Canada through the Book Publishing Industry Development Program (BPIDP); the Canada Council for the Arts; as well as the Manitoba Department of Culture, Heritage and Tourism; and the Manitoba Arts Council.

Design & Typography by Relish Design Ltd.

Printed in Canada by Friesens

Library and Archives Canada Cataloguing in Publication

Bridgman, Rae
Fish and Sphinx / Rae Bridgman.

(The serpent's chain)
ISBN 978-1-894283-81-6

I. Title. II. Series: Bridgman, Rae. Serpent's chain.
PS8603.R528F48 2008 jC813'.6 C2008-900493-0

My thanks to Carol Steer for her ever enthusiastic and inventive assistance in translating the sayings at the beginning of each chapter into Latin, and to Gabriele Goldstone for assistance with the German translations.

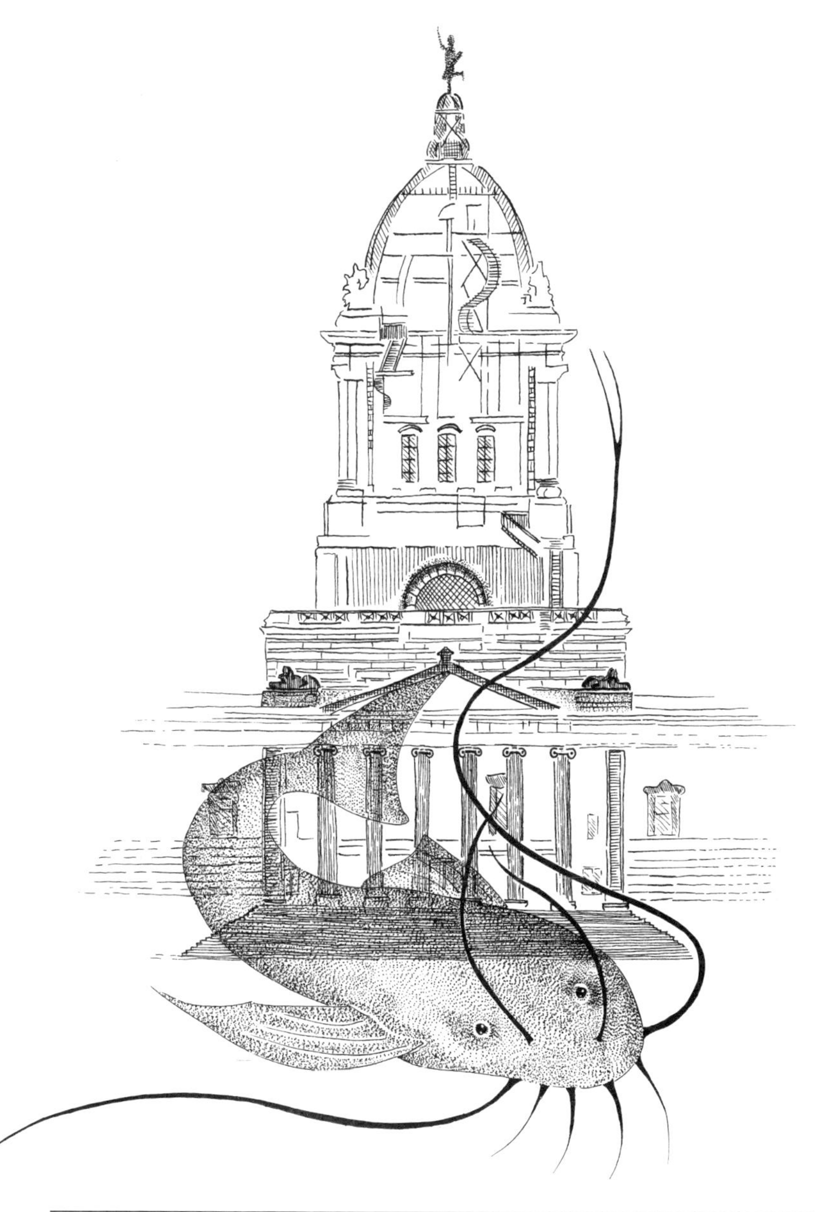

LATENTIA SAEPE PATENTIA.
HIDDEN IN PLAIN SIGHT.

…until everything
was rainbow, rainbow, rainbow.
And I let the **fish** go.

– From *The Fish* (1946) by Elizabeth Bishop

What the dead had no speech for, when living,
They can tell you, being dead: the communication
Of the dead is tongued with **fire** beyond the
language of the living.

– From *Little Gidding* I (1942) by T. S. Eliot

Truth is a torch that gleams through the **fog** without dispelling it.

– From *De l'Esprit,* Preface (1758) by Claude Adrien Helvétius

The Sphinx spoke only once.
It said, "A grain of sand is a desert.
A desert is a grain of sand.
So, let us all be silent again."
I heard the **Sphinx**. I did not understand."

– From *Sand and Foam* (1926) by Kahlil Gibran

Contents

Prologue

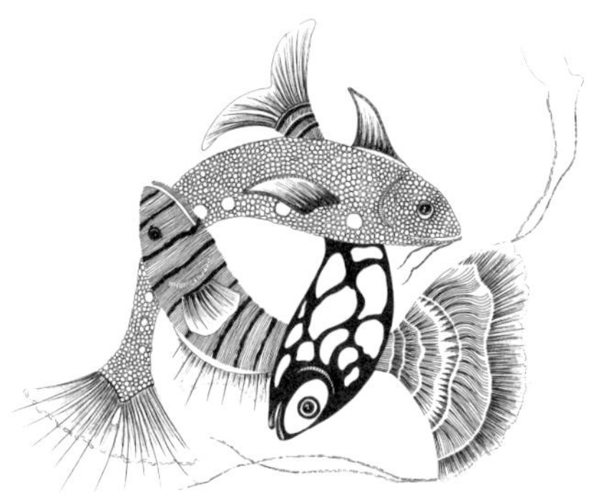

Whisker, whisper, lark and chase.

TEMPUS VENIT, ICTALURUS INQUIT,
LOQUI MULTAS RES:
PISCEM, SERPENTEM, HORROREM ATRUM,
ASTRUM, ALAM, SPHINGIS VER.
EST FABULA FORTIS, PLENA SUSPENSO—
NEGATUR HOC ACCIDISSE SOLUM CASU
CUM TEMPUS FLECTERET SUAM CAUDAM,
TEMPUS FLECTERET SUAM CAUDAM.
THE TIME COME'YSH, CATFYSH SAY'YSH,
CARP'YSH ON MANY A THING:
FYSH, SNAKE, SHADOWED DREAD,
STAR, WING, SPHINXEAN SPRING.
A STORY SO BRAVE, BRIMFULL SUSPENSE—
NONE O' IT, SAY'YSH, MERE COINCIDENCE,
TIME SWYSH'YSH ITS TAIL, TIME SWYSH'YSH ITS TAIL.

The statue of the Golden Boy atop the Palace of the Blazing Star's great dome basked in the fire glow of the setting sun—torch soaring high in his right hand and golden grain splayed in the curve of his left arm. The Golden Boy could have been Hermes himself, that ancient messenger of the gods, if his feet had been graced with winged sandals. Resolutely facing the North Star, The Golden Boy's gaze followed the winding path of the river's muddy waters northward.

Far below the statue, on a large, flat rock by the riverbank, huddled a woman. Her bare and muddied feet kicked idly at the darkening waters. The shifty, muggy fish-tail winds picked up, bringing no relief from the autumn heat, and waves slapped against the rock. Pulling her dull, stone-grey robes more tightly around her, the woman swayed back and forth slowly as if she were rocking a baby to sleep.

The laughter of couples and young families strolling along the gravel footpath dwindled, and then died at the sight of the woman; passersby quickened their pace. No one stopped to offer the woman help, but pitying whispers floated on the air and condensed in a remorseful puddle of momentary guilt and grateful forgetfulness—"Depressing to see somebody homeless, isn't it?" "Crazy as a loon, muttering to herself." "But she must be somebody's mother or sister…or somebody's aunt." "She reeks of fish." "There but for the grace of God, go I." "Poor soul—you'd think somebody would do something, wouldn't you?"

"Mommy, why is that lady sitting there?" asked a small child.

"Come along, dear," replied the mother. "And watch, your ice cream cone is dripping down your shirt."

"But I want to hear that lady's song," wailed the child, who was now pointing the dripping ice cream cone at the woman.

At the child's words, the woman's robes glimmered and shimmered with a pearly translucence.

But the mother only tightened her grip. "Don't point, Sidney," she muttered. "How many times have I told you, it's not polite to point at someone?"

The woman smiled, blew a quicksilver kiss on the wind after the child and whispered, "Time swish'ysh its tail." Her whisper was no louder than the soft creaking of tree branches above.

With a whiskered grin, the woman continued singing, if singing it could be called. For the hoarse words caught in her throat, like mute fishes snagged in a frayed net, struggling to free themselves, to be heard… if only someone would listen.

O
Whisker,
Whisper, lark and chase.
Lahore, Timor, Ulan Bator to
Singapore, Labrador, El Salvador.

Goby, Gudgeon and Wrasse galore.
Perch and Pike, Luce and Hake
Carp and Cod, Herring, Sole and Skate
Sawfysh, Sunfysh, Swordfysh, Angelfysh,
Goldfysh, Batfysh, Flatfysh, Devilfysh.

And even Humuhumunukunukuapua'a.
Name's much longer than that brave little Fysh!

And the greatest Pisces, wherever the port
Blue moon spit, barbel-jaw snort
Nematognathi, hear'ysh my Catfysh Tales.

So if all Catfysh have'ysh shiny, briny scales...

Whisker, whisper, lark and chase.

O, children, hear'ysh me closely.

The stories be'ysh true.

Follow'ysh
My Story
Just-So
For
You.

I A Whiff of Things to Come

"Did you ever see that fish before?"

ABSIT OMEN OMINOSUM.
MAY IT NOT BE AN UNFORTUNATE OMEN.

"Too bad your friends Phinneas and Beatriz couldn't come with us tonight," said Aunt Rue, as she hurriedly pinned up a coiled braid on top of her head. "But they must be very excited the rest of their family has finally arrived in MiddleGate. Children, why don't you run on ahead to the library? Aunt Violet and I will meet you there just as soon as I finish up the last of the dishes."

"See you later..." said Aunt Violet, her voice trailing off. She was sitting at the kitchen table and rummaging through her purse. "I was sure they were in here," she said, sounding puzzled.

"Alligator," quipped Sophie.

"Here they are," exclaimed Aunt Violet. "Wretched things, always hiding on me." She smiled broadly and held up a pair of purple-rimmed eyeglasses, which matched her purple dress, purple shoes, purple earrings and purple hair perfectly. "After a while—" she said.

"Crocodile!" Wil grinned.

"See you soon, you big dragoons," said Aunt Violet, gazing fondly at both children. "Now scat, the both of you."

"Bet a snake's kiss, you can't catch me," said Wil. He tapped Sophie on the shoulder and dashed out the door.

The frames of Sophie's eyeglasses, which had been covered in pink polka dots not a moment earlier, turned snapping red. "Can too," she shouted, "and snakes don't kiss!" She sprinted after Wil down Half Moon Lane.

By the time they reached the Brimstone Snakes monument in Grunion Square, both of them were panting. They slowed to a walk and Sophie felt a steamy trickle slither down her forehead.

"Remember how cold and delicious the triple icicles were at Winterlude Festival?" she said, her mouth watering at the mere thought of them. "I'd love to have one of those right now."

"Or snowcandy," said Wil.

As they drew nearer to the library, they could hear the sound of bagpipes. The pipes only played on special, official occasions in MiddleGate. Their wrenching, aching, haunting sound stirred the hairs on the back of Sophie's neck. Despite feeling hot and sticky—for the summer evening's heat sat on her head like a fuzzy tea cozy—she shivered.

⁜ ⁜ ⁜

MIDDLEGATE LIBRARY ~
THE FISHER RARE BOOK COLLECTION

The large letters—so highly polished they mirrored the orange fire of the setting sun—dazzled Wil's eyes. The doors of the library had been flung wide open and dozens of people were milling about at the top of the stone steps.

The MiddleGate Library, finally open again!

With the arrest of the head librarian, Miss Heese, the library had been closed the whole summer. MiddleGate's entire collection of books, more than anyone could ever hope to read in an entire lifetime, had been locked away so the Firecatchers could complete their investigations. They were the ones who enforced the laws in MiddleGate; they wore distinctive, long red cloaks and were known to probe people's minds. Wil always felt anxious around them—as if their magical smoke might force him to reveal things he did not want them to know.

Miss Heese had turned out to be none other than Rufus Crookshank, the notorious *Snake in the Grass*, a genius at disguise and escape, who had evaded capture for years. But Wil and his pet snake Esme, together with Sophie, had foiled Crookshank's plans to kill hundreds more of the snakes of Narcisse for a magical potion promising everlasting youth.

Remembering all that had happened, Wil smiled to himself and then marvelled, as he always did, at the library's stately columns and arched entrance. The two griffins on either side of the massive doors—one had a lion's head and the other, an eagle's head—had been waxed and polished to perfection for the occasion.

He thought back to his very first day of school at Gruffud's Academy the previous year—how nervous he had been and how the sight of the library had given him some slim hope that moving to MiddleGate wouldn't be so bad after all. With the death of his grandmother, Wil had come to live with his only remaining living relatives, Aunt Rue, Aunt Violet and cousin Sophie. Relatives he had never met and had not even known existed. Official investigations never proved that the fire in which his grandmother died had been set deliberately, but Wil knew his grandmother had been murdered by Rufus Crookshank—for Crookshank had taunted him just before his arrest. *Your stupid grandmother refused to relinquish it. The Serpent's Chain does not take no for an answer, silly boy.*

The "it," of course, was the black medallion that Wil had inherited from his grandmother along with a gold ring. The ring, worn and scratched, was still much too big for him to wear, even though he kept trying it on, hoping that it would fit; and the medallion was a strange coin-sized disc hanging from a crescent moon. On one side of the medallion, the outline of a silver triangle glimmered on the black matte surface. On the other side, a tiny gold serpent and a golden bee sparkled inside the outline of a silver arrow. And whenever the disc spun round quickly, the golden outline of a five-pointed star glimmered like magic, with the serpent and the bee shining brightly at the corners of the star.

The medallion seemed almost to have a mind of its own at times. In the past, it had flashed brightly when Wil was in danger. But Wil's and Sophie's adventures with the snakes of Narcisse and the magical bees of MiddleGate had brought Wil and Sophie no closer to understanding the medallion's mysteries nor why the Serpent's Chain wanted the black medallion so badly. What little the children knew was that the Serpent's Chain had been some sort of ancient and magical secret society; it had been outlawed centuries ago on charges of unorthodox practices.

Although his grandmother had raised him to distrust heartily anything magical—which the black medallion most certainly and assuredly was—Wil had flourished in the secret magical city of MiddleGate. And now with Mr. Bertram's coming to MiddleGate and becoming head librarian, Wil could not imagine living anywhere else.

Mr. Bertram was an old friend, who had owned the antiquarian bookstore below the apartment where Wil had lived with his grandmother. After she was killed in the mysterious fire and Wil moved to MiddleGate to live with his aunts and cousin, he discovered Mr. Bertram had once been a good friend of Sophie's father Cyril Isidor. Sophie's father had mysteriously disappeared eleven years ago, after being accused of murdering MiddleGate's head librarian, a man by the name of Oswald Persimmons. Aunt Rue still lit a candle every night for her dear brother Cyril, hoping against hope he would return some day.

As for Sophie's mother, no one ever knew exactly her fate. She had apparently turned quite strange after Cyril's disappearance and was accused of covering up for her husband; and but a short time after Cyril disappeared, she too vanished. She had never been heard from since. Wil's parents were also dead—according to his grandmother, they had died in a car accident when Wil was scarcely a year old. Thus it was that the two cousins, both of them now orphaned, had come to live with their only remaining relatives, Aunt Rue and Aunt Violet.

"Did you see that?" asked Sophie, interrupting Wil's reverie. She pointed at something, as they walked slowly up the library's stone steps.

"What?" asked Wil. "What did you say?"

"There's a fish," said Sophie. "Did you ever see that before?"

"No, where?" asked Wil.

"Right there. Hiding in the griffin's coil," said Sophie, looking at Wil as if he were hopeless. "Can't you see anything?"

Strange he'd not noticed it before. The fish seemed to be staring right at him. As he was being pushed through the library doors by those coming behind him, he turned to look back; the bulging eyes of the fish seemed to be following him.

With the crush of so many people in the library, however, Wil quickly forgot the fish. The library's high, vaulted ceilings and thick carpets muted the excited chatter. Sophie melted into a crowd of girls, who all giggled when they saw Wil. He quickly glided behind one of the columns and pretended to look at a book lying open on one of the library tables. Hardly noticing what he was reading, something or other about the history of MiddleGate, Wil caught sight of Mage Terpsy, his favourite teacher at Gruffud's (she taught verbology) and Mage Radix, the botanicals teacher and school beekeeper. They were standing with several other teachers, including Mage Adderson (she taught numeristics and was easily Wil's least favourite teacher, due in large part to her sour temper), Mage Tibor (the cartology teacher, whose classroom was peppered with maps of every conceivable part of the world—Sophie's favourite teacher) and Mage Quartz, the gamesmaster. All of them were talking earnestly with Mr. Bertram.

Under normal circumstances, the library was a place of utter quiet, save for pens scratching on paper and pages of books turning and, of course, the occasional squawk when someone discovered Peeping Peerslie, the library's resident ghost, had already filled in the answers on their study sheet or hidden their pen, notebook, bag...

The library air had always seemed heavy and dim, even murky, a feeling only reinforced by the great chandelier, which hung suspended like a bulbous, brooding spider. But this evening, the library seemed to have shrugged off any sense of gloom and doom. The books reminded Wil of soldiers standing on parade.

"Finally!" said a familiar voice in Wil's ear.

"Peerslie?" said Wil. He turned quickly, hoping to catch a glimpse of Peeping Peerslie, but he was, as always, quite invisible.

"Of course, 'tis I," said the voice, sounding offended. "Just because the MiddleGate Library was closed all summer doesn't mean I disappeared from the face of the map."

Wil felt a book fall into his hands.

"Good to see you, Peerslie," said Wil. Then he corrected himself hastily. "I mean, to hear you." He glanced at the book, which had a picture of a nasty-looking fish on the front.

"I've been saving it just for you," said Peeping Peerslie, sounding very pleased with himself. "No mean feat with the Firecatchers swarming everywhere."

"Thanks, Peerslie," said Wil. "What's it about?"

"About?" repeated Peeping Peerslie. He sounded disappointed that Wil was not jumping up and down with glee at his find. "Cannot you tell from the cover?"

Wil looked at the cover again. The fish really was one of the ugliest creatures he had ever seen. It had long whiskers and watery, unfocused eyes, which were swivelling in their sockets. As Wil stared at it, the fish's whiskers bristled, and it glared at him. An old, rancid, fishy smell wafted up from the book. Wil's nose wrinkled. Unnerved, he turned the book over.

"So, where did you find this?" asked Wil, but Peeping Peerslie didn't answer. "Peerslie, are you there?" When there was still no answer, Wil turned the book over. The fish's eyes were now dull, glazed, its whiskers dried, shrunken.

Why would Peerslie keep a book about fish for me the whole summer? thought Wil. I don't even like fish—especially when they're on a plate and decorated with parsley and lemon slices, and those baked, gelatinous eyes stare at you. Thankful Peerslie had left, Wil quickly slid the book onto the nearest shelf and wiped his hands on his shirt. The smell of fish, though, still haunted his nose.

"Fresh air," he muttered, feeling suddenly as if he could hardly breathe. He pushed his way to the library entrance and saw Aunt Rue and Aunt Violet standing at the top of the stairs talking with their neighbour Mrs. Oleander. Wil wondered what they were talking about, for Mrs. Oleander was an ill-tempered woman who had scarcely a good word to say about anything. He jostled through the crowds just in time to catch part of their conversation.

"What a marvelous turnout," said Aunt Violet, as she fanned herself vigorously with her handkerchief. "The board members of the MiddleGate Library must all be very pleased."

"Taking their chances, I'll warrant," said Mrs. Oleander, her voice grating on Wil's ears like long fingernails scratching a blackboard. "You don't find it a little strange that eleven years after the murder of my dear friend Oswald Persimmons, they're hiring his murderer's friend and accomplice?" Mrs. Oleander looked pointedly at Aunt Rue as she said this.

Aunt Rue's face turned pale, while Aunt Violet stared wildly at Mrs. Oleander and held her handkerchief to her mouth.

"And I hear you've got a new scheme on the go, Violet," said Mrs. Oleander, seemingly unaware of the crippling effect her words had had on Aunt Rue and Aunt Violet. Her sharp nose pointed at Aunt Violet, as if it were the beak of a chicken about to peck at a tasty grub. "Fortune-telling, I've been told. I do wish you the very best with it, I'm sure, even though most fortune-tellers, as we know, are charlatans preying upon people's uncertainties and fears. And I certainly hope you're not planning on having a parade of people coming to your door. No commercial enterprises are allowed to disturb neighbourhood peace and quiet."

Aunt Violet's eyes widened above her handkerchief.

Aunt Rue finally seemed to collect herself but two faint pink circles stained her cheeks. "Wil...ah...why don't you find Sophie," she said hastily. "First day of school term tomorrow. Better get the children home. All this excitement, I don't know how they'll wake up in the morning. Good evening, Mrs. Oleander," she added stiffly.

⁜ ⁜ ⁜

As they all walked back home in silence past the Brimstone Snakes, Aunt Violet's tongue finally loosened. "By serpent's blood!" she spat. "Such a pooty, poisonous woman I've never met in all my life! The lady's rule of being *unfailingly polite* is...is...simply pointless, as far as that woman is concerned."

"Aunt Violet, such profanity!" said Aunt Rue in a shocked voice. "Think of the children."

Wil smiled inwardly, for he himself had cursed *snake's blood* on more than one occasion—when he had found himself back in human form from Bee Queendom, for example, and Portius had remarked wryly, "Of course you're human. What did you expect? You would have wings forever?" *By serpent's blood* was a much more serious curse, though, one of the nastiest anyone could possibly say.

"Well, I don't care, Rue. It's far worse for the children to hear such indecency!" snapped Aunt Violet. "Elvira Oleander, what we've had to put up with all these years from her! Imagine calling Cyril a murderer—as if he had been proven guilty...and then...and then...on top of it all...be-be-beslubbering Bartholomew Bertram's good name," she spluttered, sounding as outraged as a steaming tea kettle.

Wil wasn't sure exactly what *beslubbering* meant, but he had a very good idea it probably had something to do with mud, muck and slime.

ii Questions

Everywhere Sophie looked, there seemed to be another fish.

BENE NATANT RES ET BONA EST NATATIO
SED CUM DEMERSERINT, TOTA EST TURBATIO.
WHEN THINGS GO SWIMMINGLY, THEY SURELY GO WELL,
BUT WHEN THEY DO NOT...ALL TURNS PELL-MELL.

September 1st was a warm, sunny day, but the walls of Stone Hall were as cool to the touch as a toad hiding under a rock. The murmur of hundreds of voices filled the hall, as Sophie and Wil filed slowly to their seats under Mage Quartz's watchful eye.

It was already Sophie's and Wil's second year at Gruffud's Academy for the Magical Arts. Sophie felt much older than the grade fives, many of whom were looking scared and bewildered. They had not yet received their first sashes from Mage Agassiz, the principal of Gruffud's.

Sophie and Wil were wearing their brand new sashes, which Aunt Rue had purchased for them several weeks ago. Their grade five sashes had been striped yellow and white, but the grade six sashes were orange and white. Each year had its own special colours. Sophie gazed around Stone Hall and marvelled at how beautiful all the sashes looked. The most beautiful, by far—at least as far as she was concerned—were the sashes worn by grade elevens in their final year at Gruffud's. Those sashes had dramatic black and white stripes; they reminded Sophie of a skunk. No one fooled around with a skunk.

As everyone filed slowly to their seats, Sophie stared at the stone gargoyles lining Stone Hall. There could not have been a more ferocious collection of gargoyles anywhere, she thought. Sharp horns, hairy pointed ears, gnashing teeth, leers, jeers and grimaces—all meant to persuade the students to study hard and to keep the school safe from prowlers and intruders—at least symbolically, Sophie supposed. Just above her head a gargoyle with long, clawed fingers was clutching a book. Sophie squinted at the cover of the stone book. It had a fish on it, just like the fish hiding in the griffin's coils by the entrance of MiddleGate Library. She couldn't believe it. What in snake's name was going on? Everywhere she looked, there seemed to be another fish.

She was about to tell Wil, when she overheard Sylvain's strident voice behind her. There was no love lost between Sylvain Sly and his twin sister Sygnithia, and Sophie and Wil. That pair did their very best to make Sophie's and Wil's lives miserable…all because of the suspicions surrounding the Isidor family. Many people in MiddleGate had still not forgotten, even with the passing of eleven years.

Sophie turned around to find Sylvain and Sygnithia chatting with Phinneas and Beatriz. Her stomach lurched when she saw Sygnithia put her arm around Beatriz's shoulders as if they were old friends.

But Sophie's worst fears were realized when she heard Sygnithia say, "Gruffud's is one of the best schools in the world for magical training. Sylvain and I, we're actually descendants of the founders. Why don't you eat lunch with us and we can show you around the school a little."

"Thanks," said Beatriz, "but we're eating with our friends Sophie and Wil."

"Really?" said Sygnithia, her voice suddenly cold.

"Maybe tomorrow?" said Beatriz, seemingly unaware Sygnithia was now looking at her as if she had sprouted a third arm.

Sophie felt her cheeks flush and saw Wil's ears turn bright pink.

But before Sophie had a chance to say anything, Mage Agassiz stepped forward to the front of Stone Hall.

"Welcome, everyone, to the start of the new academic year at Gruffud's Academy for the Magical Arts. I am certainly anticipating one of our best years ever. Those who are returning will know the original Gruffud's was started 495 years ago in Britain. And this is the 120th year for Gruffud's in MiddleGate itself. In only five more years, MiddleGate will be hosting a historic celebration of the original school's 500th anniversary.

Discussions and arrangements have already begun and distinguished alumni from all over the world will be coming to MiddleGate.

"I will exhort you all to do your very best in your studies this year and bring honour to our school. As always, we shall begin the school year with Gruffud's Chant."

Hundreds of feet shuffled as everyone stood up from the stone benches.

Mage Agassiz raised her hand. As she brought it down, all the voices soared into the air

Um-bris nos de-da-mus.
Um-bris nos de-da-mus.

Give ourselves to the shadows, murmured Sophie to herself. The rounds of the voices echoing back and forth sent shivers up and down her spine.

Finally, the last note of the chant died away and silence filled Stone Hall. It was as if the voices were etched deep into the cracks of the stone walls.

⁜ ⁜ ⁜

As they filed out of Stone Hall to their classes, Sophie heard Sylvain whispering to Sygnithia. "All we've got to do is tell them what her father did. There's no way they'll be friends after that. A piece of cake. Easy-peasy, snakey-wakey."

Sophie rounded on Sylvain and Sygnithia. "Don't you dare!"

"What's your problem, Is-she-a-bore Isidor?" Sylvain retorted. "Mind your own business. What makes you think you've got the right to eavesdrop on a private conversation between me and my sister?"

"You leave Beatriz and Phinneas alone!"

"You don't honestly think they'll be friends with you, do you?" said Sygnithia. "Besides, it's a free country. We can be friends with anyone we want to."

"Just wait and see," said Sophie.

"That's what you say," said Sylvain. "I think we've got an obligation to warn them about you, right, dear sister?"

"We can't have new students falling in with the wrong crowd," said Sygnithia, patting her brother on the back. "It's a miracle you two are allowed to attend Gruffud's Academy for the Magical Arts at all—given everything that's happened, don't you think, bro'?"

Sophie felt like a balloon filled with too much air—she was about to burst. Rather than let the Sly twins see how upset she was, though, she turned her back on them both.

"Better count to ten, Missy-Issy," said Sylvain in a mocking voice. "Did you know the frames on your glasses are the colour of slimy canned oysters?"

At this, Sygnithia and Sylvain both laughed.

Sophie scowled and stared up at the ceiling in Stone Hall. She pretended to be looking at the gargoyle atop the nearest column, but she was now seething inside like a...like a...volcano, its molten lava brimming over. Her eyes strayed back to the gargoyle's clawed hand and the cover of the book it was holding. To her surprise, the fish on the book seemed to melt into the stone cover.

"Impossible," she whispered to herself.

A stone fish couldn't just disappear like that; but the cover of the stone book looked as if it had always been just a plain old cover, nothing special.

Sophie felt her anger ebbing and giving way to panic. What if Sylvain and Sygnithia swayed Beatriz and Phinneas? And what if Beatriz and Phinneas didn't want to be their friends anymore? The thought was so utterly, utterly depressing, that Sophie felt like crawling underneath a rock and crying.

iii Serpent Tails

MiddleGate is not alone in revering snakes.

DISSIMILES FABULAE SED SIMILIS NUNTIUS.
THE STORIES MAY BE DIFFERENT
BUT THE MESSAGE IS THE SAME.

Their first class was with Mage Terpsy, the verbology teacher. She was a short, plump woman with watery eyes—one a brilliant blue, the other muddy brown—greatly magnified by her triangular eyeglasses. She was fussing with a pile of papers on her desk and looked startled when everyone trooped into the class. She seemed to have quite forgotten they were coming.

"I hope you all had wonderful summers," she said, as she quickly shuffled the papers into two piles. "And I do look forward to reading about your adventures in your journals.

"We shall be continuing our work on magical grammar and incantations this year. But I also have a very exciting project for you. The *Serpent Tails* Project—with a small play on the word *tails,* of course! We will be studying serpent myths from around the world. I'll be dividing you into groups, and each group will study one myth in-depth, then do a class presentation about what they've learned." Mage Terpsy picked up a small sheaf of papers from her desk. "I devoted a good part of my summer to studying these myths," she continued, "and there is much to learn from the stories. They speak about fantastic things, things that seem parely bossible but reveal dunderful, weep truths."

The class snickered, but as usual, Mage Terpsy seemed completely oblivious to the fact that she had just reversed her letters; she was known for her many slips of the tongue, often quite humorous. Sophie glanced over at Wil to see if he had pulled out his small notebook yet—the one in which he kept a careful record of Mage Terpsy's many slips of the tongue—what everyone had taken to calling *tipsy-terpsies.* He was madly scribbling down the latest examples...*parely bossible* (barely possible) and *dunderful, weep truths* (wonderful, deep truths).

"Why, just this morning," said Mage Terpsy, "I was reading a marvellous Norse myth about a wolf monster named Fenrir. Fenrir is so dangerous, that he is held captive by a chain, but not just any ordinary chain. A chain as fine and smooth as a silk ribbon, and made from very strange things: the sound of a cat's step, the spittle of a bird, the breath of a fish, the beard of a woman. All these things don't really exist or are very rare, yet Fenrir struggles in vain against the chain."

How could such a flimsy chain be strong enough to keep down a creature like Fenrir? thought Sophie. The chain must contain very powerful magic, or Fenrir would break through it immediately.

"And there are so many interesting terpentine sales," said Mage Terpsy.

The class snickered again, for Mage Terpsy had made yet another slip on *serpentine tales*; but Mage Terpsy continued on blithely.

"We here in MiddleGate are certainly not alone in revering snakes," she said. "People all the over world have thought of snakes as special and even divine. And so, I have chosen ten myths for you to learn more about.

"Group 1, you'll be learning about a legendary Mohawk war chief and shaman."

At this, a piece of chalk on Mage Terpsy's desk rose into the air and scratched on the board:

A-T-O-T-A–R-A-H

Mage Terpsy pointed to the chalkboard. "*Atotarah* is known for the snakes writhing upon his head. His very presence causes birds to fall from the sky.

"Group 2 will tackle an old Norse tale about *Jormungand*, the terrible and frightening World Serpent, whose body coils tightly around the Earth. Group 3 will be studying a West African myth from the Fon people about the great python *Dan Ayido Hwedo*, which encircles the Earth and grips its tail in its mouth for all eternity. There are many such tales about a gigantic serpent clasping the Earth."

The chalk paused, apparently waiting for Mage Terpsy to continue.

"Now, Group 4, what will you be doing? Ah yes, *Medusa*. Have any of you heard of her before?"

Sophie glanced around the class surreptitiously. At the blank looks on everyone's faces, no one else knew who or what Medusa was either.

"You'll find out soon enough," said Mage Terpsy with a broad smile. "She too has a head of snakes. Look deep into her eyes and she will turn you to stone with a single gaze."

Sophie began to doodle a head with lots of snakes coming out of it, while Mage Terpsy described an Aztec feathered serpent creator god named *Quetzalcoatl*, and two serpent-women—the Chinese creator goddess *NuWa*, who came to live on Earth, and the *Naga Kanya* of India.

"Let's see. What else do we have?" said Mage Terpsy and she consulted her sheaf of papers. "Oh, yes, the Balinese World Serpent *Antaboga* that created the World Turtle. On the Turtle's back lie two coiled snakes and a black stone marking the entrance to the Underworld. Group 9—*Yurlunggur*, the Rainbow Serpent, which stretches across the sky...as a rainbow. This snake threatens to cause a great flood to wash away the entire world.

"And finally, Group 10, will travel to Egypt—not literally, of course—to learn from *Meretseger*, an Egyptian cobra-goddess of Thebes. She appears as a snake with a human head and punishes wrongdoers with her deadly, poisonous bite."

By now, Sophie's notebook was completely covered with drawings of strange half-human, half-snake creatures, and there was only an inch of chalk left.

"We have so much still to learn from the ancient Egyptians," said Mage Terpsy. "Think of their ability to construct such wonders of the world as the Great Sphinx of Giza. And their system of hieroglyphics or picture writing contrasts so with our own writing system. Truly fascinating. I hope to visit Egypt one day.

"But I am rambling. Yes, to the numbers...the numbers." Mage Terpsy fumbled in her pocket. "Now, a number will land on your desk—a number from one to ten—that number will tell you which group is yours."

Mage Terpsy drew out a small red bag from her pocket and threw its contents into the air. Numbers swirled in the air for an instant, shimmering like snowflakes on a sunny winter's day. The number four zigzagged down onto Sophie's desk and she looked around the room to see who else had a four. With horror, she saw Sygnithia had just picked up the number four from her desk, and even worse, Sylvain was holding one in his hand.

We can't be in the same group, thought Sophie. We just can't. The spectre of having the Sly twins in her group was more than she could possibly bear. In desperation, she looked over at Wil and almost burst out laughing at his unhappy expression. He looked as if he had just been forced to swallow a mouldy bit of cheddar cheese. There was a number four on his desk too.

Wil held out four fingers under his desk and jabbed them in the direction of Sylvain and Sygnithia, then mouthed the words, *Do something!* to Sophie.

I know, she mouthed back. She scribbled something down on a piece of paper and passed it underneath the desk to Wil.

MIXUSFIXUS?

Wil understood immediately and nodded.

It was a long shot, thought Sophie, but if it worked, they'd be saved from utter torture.

Together, Sophie and Wil and stood up.

"Yes, Mr. Wychwood? Miss Isidor?" said Mage Terpsy, looking surprised. "Do you have questions?"

With a quick glance at each other, Sophie and Wil each drew a circle counter-clockwise in the air and shouted, "MIXUSFIXUS!"

In an instant, all the numbers swept off the desks, flew out of hands and danced in the air.

Mage Terpsy's eyes widened. Regina Piehard shrieked and tried to catch her number nine as it whisked from her fingers. Everyone else, their mouths open, stared up at all the twinkling numbers, which were hovering just above reach.

Then, one by one, the numbers slowly settled back down onto the desks.

"It's not fair," shouted Sylvain. "I had Group 4 before, and now I'm in Group 3."

"By serpent's grace, Mr. Wychwood and Miss Isidor, what got into you both?" demanded Mage Terpsy. "It's fardly hair for everyone."

"We wanted to practice the *mixusfixus* charm, Mage Terpsy," said Sophie brightly. "I remembered…you said it had many uses."

"True," said Mage Terpsy, sounding mollified. "I did say so, and your coordination certainly was impressive. Class, you can see what happens when an incantation is invoked by more than one person at a time. The incantation is, of course, reinforced by the intense concentration of two minds at one and the same moment."

Sylvain muttered, "It's not fair. They should be punished."

"In this case I must issue a warning, Miss Isidor and Mr. Wychwood," said Mage Terpsy. "No such trickery again, either of you. But in view of the fact you deployed an incantation you learned in my class, I can fardly hault you this one time for having been overly eager to use it." She smiled as she said this, and from the corner of his eye, Sophie saw both Sylvain and Sygnithia scowl.

"Thank you, Mage Terpsy," chimed Sophie and Wil together, and Sophie shot a quick look of triumph in Sylvain's direction.

Sophie sat back down in her chair. With all the excitement, she had not even noticed what number was resting on her desk. It was a ten—that was the Egyptian group. And there was a ten on Wil's desk too. Even more miraculously, Beatriz and Phinneas also had tens. Sophie had to restrain herself from jumping up and whooping with glee. Instead, she smiled and passed a note to Wil.

fardly hair
~~3~~5 *tipsy-terpsies in one class*
not bad !!!!

"Next class, we'll be going over chapters one to three in volume II of *Magical Palaver*," said Mage Terpsy, as everyone packed up their papers. "I expect you've all had a chance to purchase your books by now. And remember, it's never too soon for a lick quittle quiz."

"I will be giving you time in class to work on your major projects, but your groups will also be expected to meet after school hours. I have placed a copy of the book *Serpent Tails* on reserve in the MiddleGate Library for your use.

"Also for tonight's homework, would you please write a good page or two in your journals about *My Summer Vacation*."

Wil passed Sophie's note back to her.

fardly hair
~~3~~^{5}*tipsy-terpsies in one class*
not bad !!!!!!
6

IV The Lost Book

Wil looked with dismay at the shelves.

LIBER MANET ET
EXSPECTAT TEMPUS RECTUM;
LECTOREM QUAERIT PERFECTUM.
CUM PARATUS ES TUM LIBER TE INVENIET.
A BOOK BIDES ITS TIME.
IT WAITS FOR THE RIGHT MOMENT,
THE RIGHT READER TO COME ITS WAY.
WHEN YOU ARE READY, THE BOOK WILL FIND YOU.

After school, Wil, Sophie, Phinneas and Beatriz gathered on the stairs outside the front entrance to Gruffud's.

"Can you believe how much homework we got in verbology, cartology and numeristics!" exclaimed Sophie.

"And it's only our first day back," said Wil.

"Is there so much homework every night?" asked Phinneas glumly.

Beatriz hoisted her bag to her shoulder. "I sure hope not," she said.

"I guess there's more work in grade six," said Wil. "At least we got the same group for Mage Terpsy's project."

"Yeah," said Phinneas. "That *mixusfixus* incantation was really good."

"You didn't want to be in the same group as Sylvain and Sygnithia, did you," said Beatriz.

"We're not best friends. Let's just keep it at that," said Wil. Not wanting Beatriz and Phinneas to ask any questions, he said abruptly, "We better stop by the library to get that copy of *Serpent Tails,* before everyone else does."

"Actually Sylvain and Sygnithia hate us," said Sophie suddenly.

"What do you mean?" asked Phinneas, looking puzzled.

"Why?" asked Beatriz.

"I guess you had to find out sometime," said Sophie, the frames of her eyeglasses turning a yellowish-white like dirty snow.

"No, Sophie, don't!" said Wil. "Don't!"

"What is it?" asked Beatriz, looking from Sophie to Wil and back again.

"Yeah, what are you talking about?" asked Phinneas.

"Everyone in MiddleGate thinks my father killed the head librarian eleven years ago," said Sophie in a dull voice. "And Sylvain was going to tell you, so you'd be friends with them instead of us."

"Ridiculous," said Beatriz. "We're friends with you two, not with your father. Besides, Mom and Dad said there was never any proof your father was responsible. It was just easier for everyone to think he'd done it, and no one had to bother looking for anyone else. That's what they think anyway."

"So…you knew already?" asked Sophie slowly.

"Yeah, of course we knew," said Beatriz. "And if you ask me, Sygnithia and Sylvain are way too pushy. It's so obvious they think they're the snake's hips. Besides, look how they treat you and Wil. I bet they're just as mean even to their own friends."

"Yeah, snakes can't change their stripes," said Sophie, hardly believing that Phinneas and Beatriz were actually their friends, for she had been so convinced the Sly twins would ruin things.

"Sophie, your glasses are amazing. They've just turned peacock blue and purple!" said Beatriz, staring at Sophie's glasses. "I wish I had a pair."

Sophie laughed. "But you don't need to wear glasses, Bea."

⁜ ⁜ ⁜

As the four of them mounted the steps to the library, Wil looked for the small fish peering out from the griffin's coils. But the fish was gone. "What happened to that fish thing?" he asked.

"What *fish thing*?" asked Beatriz.

"It was right there," he said, pointing to the spot where he remembered seeing the fish staring right at him. "You saw it first, Sophie. Remember the night the library re-opened?"

"Yeah," said Sophie, peering inside the coils.

"Watch out or it'll bite you," said Phinneas with a laugh.

"The Mysterious Case of the Disappearing Fish," said Sophie. "The same thing happened in Stone Hall this morning. I was looking up at one of the stone carvings; it had long, clawed fingers and it was clutching a book with a fish on the cover. But when I looked again, the fish wasn't there."

"Maybe you just imagined it?" said Beatriz.

"I'm *sure* it was there," said Sophie.

"We're seeing fish everywhere," said Wil. "And there was this strange library book about fish. Peeping Peerslie—he's the library ghost—gave it to me, only I put it back on one of the shelves."

Unnerved, Wil followed the others into the library, but paused on the threshold to pull the black medallion out from under his shirt. With all the fish they'd been seeing, he was sure he would see a golden fish gleaming inside the outline of the silver arrow on the medallion. But only the golden bee and snake glimmered there. He quickly stuffed the medallion back into his shirt and stepped into the library.

They had to wait their turn at the counter, as Mr. Bertram was busy helping an elderly man whose hands were very shaky.

Wil overheard the man say, "Nice to have you b-back, B-Bartholomew B-Bertram. "I never b-believed what everyone else was saying. You can't t-trust all the s-t-t-tories you hear, can you?"

Mr. Bertram handed a book to the man and said, "Mr. Drytail, you have no idea how much it means to me, to hear you say that." When the man tottered off, Mr. Bertram looked after him with a strange and sad expression. But at the sight of the children, his face brightened. "Hello, Wil. Hello, Sophie," he said. "And these must be your new friends, Phinneas and Beatriz? What can I do for all of you? Not that I'll be able to put my hands on anything immediately. Still getting my sea legs here, of course, but Peeping Peerslie has been a great help."

"Mage Terpsy told us she put a copy of *Serpent Tails* on reserve," said Wil.

"You're the very first one to ask for it," said Mr. Bertram with a smile and he brought the book out from underneath the counter. "So *Serpent Tails* is yours."

On a sudden impulse, Wil asked, "I'm looking for a book about fish. The cover has a picture of a really ugly fish on it with whiskers."

"Whiskers?" said Mr. Bertram. "Barbels, you mean—like the kind catfish have? Do you remember the title or author?" asked Mr. Bertram.

Wil shook his head, wishing for the umpteenth time he hadn't put the book back on the shelves. Peeping Peerslie must have had a special reason for saving him the book all summer, and now, here he'd gone and lost it.

"Can't remember the title?" said Mr. Bertram. "Well, no matter. Lost books come back, although sometimes it takes years. Do you know how many times I've helped people find that magical book they read as a child? *It was my favourite book, they say. It had an amazing plot. It had wonderful drawings. There was one about a man who sold dreams for a penny.* But for the life of them, they can't remember the title. It may have been a book they borrowed from the library, or their teacher brought it to class, or their grandmother read them the story so many dusty years ago. They may have read it only once, but something about it has stayed with them forever," mused Mr. Bertram.

"Well, enough talk about lost books—as if any book were ever truly lost," he said. "It's merely biding its time, waiting for the right moment, the right reader to come its way. When you are ready, the book will find you.

"Why don't we check in the ichthyology section. Over here, as I recall," said Mr. Bertram, and he lead them to the corner of the library where the pale marble busts lined the top of the library shelves.

They were the sculpted heads of famous people, who had helped to found the city of MiddleGate. Wil had read the plaques underneath them many times before.

Glynnis Gottfried, with a sharp no-nonsense chin, her hair pulled back into a tight bun, had been a famous seer; she had helped choose the sites for MiddleGate and Gruffud's Academy itself. And Erik Gormsson was a haggard man, who looked as if he had carried the weight of the world on his shoulders. Gormsson's life was written in stone wrinkles, thought Wil, for the forehead of the marble bust was as creased as a dried prune. Wil found the whole line of marble heads disturbing; their eyes were, as always, blank and sightless.

"Yes, here we are," said Mr. Bertram. "Fish, fish and fish. As much as anyone could want to know, I dare say, without actually becoming one!"

Wil looked with dismay at the shelves. There must be at least a couple hundred books, he thought.

"What colour was it, Wil?" asked Sophie.

"I can't remember," said Wil. "It was a kind of blue-grey colour, I think, or maybe it was greenish."

He pulled a couple books down from the shelf and leafed through them half-heartedly, still mentally kicking himself for not having looked at the book more carefully.

"More patrons at the counter there," said Mr. Bertram, "so I'll let you look for yourselves. Why don't you ask Peeping Peerslie for some help?" he suggested. "He was here just a moment ago, I think. I'm not sure where he's got to at the moment, though.

"Oh, and before I forget, I'm planning to visit the snakes of Narcisse towards the end of the month, if you'd both like to come with me."

✢ ✢ ✢

That night, Wil snuggled under his covers and pulled out his journal for Mage Terpsy's class. He carefully printed the words MY SUMMER VACATION across the top of the first page. Chewing his pencil, he sat, wondering how to begin.

Instead, his thoughts turned to Narcisse. Did he really want to go back to Narcisse with Mr. Bertram? He hadn't returned there since the spring…since the terrible shadow duel with Rufus Crookshank. But surely, with Rufus Crookshank in the custody of the Firecatchers, he didn't have anything to worry about. And the Firecatchers were keeping the snake dens under tight security too; guards were still patrolling Grunion Square to prevent anyone from using the Brimstone Snakes portal to Narcisse.

At a loss where to begin, he set aside MY SUMMER VACATION and took Esme out of her cage. As always, she coiled neatly around his arm and looked up, almost as if she were waiting for him to say something.

"What do you think, Esme? Should Sophie and I go to Narcisse with Mr. Bertram?"

Esme wound through his fingers, slithered over his notebook and onto his bed, and tucked into a fold of his blanket, where she deftly coiled herself. Only her snout and one eye peeked out.

Wil laughed. "Either you're telling me to hide and not to go…or you're telling me that, it's all right, I should go, because the snakes are starting to return to their caves."

Wil had a sense of dread about returning to the place where Rufus Crookshank had slaughtered hundreds, if not thousands, of snakes. Still, he would have to go sometime, and sooner rather than later was as good a time as any. "That's settled then. We should go."

He cajoled Esme out from her small cave under the blanket. She coiled once again around his arm, and he turned back to MY SUMMER VACATION.

If I were Sophie, I would draw a picture of the big, hairy bees guarding the hive entrance, he thought. He stared down at the blank page, remembering the irresistible and comforting smell of Mother-of-Us-All and the thick, taste of *Sweet*, the noisy hum-buzz of thousands of Bees. He began to write furiously—

This summer, Sophie and I turned into Bees.

Wil thought for a moment. I better change that, he thought, just to be on the safe side. I don't want to get Mage Radix or Aunt Rue in trouble about the bees and their magical honey. He erased what he had just written and started again.

This summer, I dreamt that Sophie and I turned into Bees. We almost got killed by two evil Bees that were chasing after us.

Sophie and I made two great new friends who moved into a house on our street and I wish it was still summer. My Aunt Violet is going scaly over her new crystal ball that she bought, but it isn't going too well. She is still trying to learn how to use it.

Sophie and I did a lot of work with Mage Radix in the summer. We helped him take care of all his bees.

But except for that, it has been an extremely dull, boring and lazy summer. But before I forget, we did go to the Dragonfly Festival this summer and we saw a man completely covered in bees, live ones, and I mean COMPLETELY covered. At first, I didn't know how he could do it. I understand now because the Bees are very gentle, musical animals but if someone tries to hurt them, you better watch out! We tried eating many different insects at the Dragonfly Festival. The grasshoppers were very crunchy. They tasted all right, especially if you ignored the legs and antennas getting stuck in your teeth. But I hope I never have to eat those things again.

Have you ever tried buckwheat honey? It is almost black. It tastes terrible and it smells terrible. You should never, NEVER try it. It is the WORST honey I've ever tasted. It's hard to believe that honey is famous all over the world.

That's enough, thought Wil, his hand feeling cramped.

He yawned and slipped Esme into her cage. His last thoughts before sleep closed his eyes…

What if Peeping Peerslie decides to hide that fish book forever? And how would a book know if I'm looking for it, anyway? And what if my wanting to find it isn't enough? Mr. Bertram said, *When you're ready, the book will find you.* If I can't find the book—but I don't even know what I'm looking for exactly—does that mean I shouldn't look for it? What if I'm not ready for it yet? But what does ready mean? How do you get ready to read a book about fish? But Peeping Peerslie must have thought I was ready or he wouldn't have given it to me.

Wil yawned again, his head spinning.

And what if I hadn't—

V Whispers

High up in the trees, the crows waited and watched.

IMAGO CREPITU
SUSURRUS IMAGINE
VERBA SUSURRU
CRESCEBANT
THE RUSTLES BECAME THOUGHTS
THOUGHTS BECAME WHISPERS
WHISPERS BECAME WORDS

The first three weeks of school passed so quickly that Wil did not have a chance to worry much about visiting Narcisse. The autumn nights had already begun to turn cooler and the robins had departed south earlier than usual. The Canada geese were gathering by the thousands, getting ready for their long flight south, and the trees were half bare, their yellow leaves strewn over the grass.

Everyone was saying, *As sure as snakes sing, it's an early winter this year.* It was a funny expression, *as sure as snakes sing*—obviously, snakes didn't sing. But every time Wil heard the expression, he remembered the day at Narcisse when he had heard the hissing lullaby of thousands of snakes.

Wil woke up early Saturday morning with a jolt. Mr. Bertram would be coming to pick him up soon, for today was the day they were going to Narcisse, just the two of them. Aunt Rue was attending a day-long workshop, Aunt Violet was busy with the MiddleGate Horticultural Society and had taken Sophie with her.

Wil hopped into his clothes quickly and bid Esme good-bye. "See you later," he whispered.

Esme flicked her tongue once or twice, but did not uncoil herself from her small hut.

Aunt Rue and Aunt Violet had left a note on the kitchen table wishing them a good trip to Narcisse. Aunt Violet had scrawled, *Don't forget to take the lunch I packed. And need I say, no going into any of the caves!*

⁜ ⁜ ⁜

By the time the MiddleGate Bus pulled into the parking lot at the Narcisse snake den, it was almost noon. Only a few people were on the bus and the day, which had started out sunny enough, was wet and drizzly.

"I guess we don't have to be concerned about there being too many people today, do we?" said Mr. Bertram. "It's the snakes we're here to see at any rate. But they probably won't be very active without the sun's warmth."

Wil had forgotten how far a walk it was to the first den, but the rocky path that could trip you up so easily had been smoothed over with a layer of gravel. There were new signs up too, with maps directing visitors to the dens, and wooden kiosks along the path featured large posters. Wil and Mr. Bertram stopped to read some of them. There was lots of information about wildlife and plants in the area, research being done at Narcisse and a funny poster entitled *Who's Afraid of Snakes*?

It was certainly a lot easier to walk along the paths; but Wil couldn't help thinking, even though there were lots of interesting pictures of snakes on all the posters, that they hadn't actually seen any snakes yet.

Strangely, the first den was entirely deserted. And so was the second. A sign said no snakes had been seen returning to these dens this season; they appeared abandoned for the moment.

Along with gravels paths, there were also new chain-link fences and wooden viewing platforms high above the caves—all obviously designed to protect the snakes. People wouldn't wander off the very clearly marked paths and no one could climb down into the snake pits easily. There was no sign of the Firecatchers either, but Wil supposed they would keep a low profile, especially since non-mage people would not know who or what Firecatchers were; nor did they have any idea how important the snakes of Narcisse were to those who lived in MiddleGate—or that MiddleGate even existed, for that matter, thought Wil.

One thing had not changed in Narcisse. High up in the trees, a pair of glossy, black crows waited and watched patiently, their raucous caws as piercing as a knife, a knife both sharp and dull at the same time. They were waiting to swoop down, Wil thought. Any snake unlucky enough to be skewered by their sharp beaks—Wil shuddered.

The earthen smells of spring mud filled his nose. A plump black bird, red and white feathers beneath its wings, was following them along the path. Wil had never seen such a bird before; it was much bigger than a robin. And every time its sharp cry sliced the air, he felt his heart race. The bird slashed at the leaves that had fallen to the ground, and eagerly gobbled up a feast of worms and grubs. Wil thought of the amazing buffet of insect dishes he, Sophie, Aunt Violet and Aunt Rue had eaten at the Dragonfly Festival last summer. Still, he didn't fancy a meal of raw, cold grubs-under-leaf.

Still thinking about the Dragonfly Festival, he started making up the names of new dishes. "*Try Our One and Only Grubs Gravy on Your Fried Worms,*" he muttered to himself. "*Worm Cutlets, the Best in the West.* Or how about *Feel Like Biting Something? Got the Munchies? Try our Crispy Crunchy Mosquito Chips. Guaranteed to Satisfy Your Urge to Bite.*" Will giggled. *"A Great New Snack—Leetle Beetles Will Sweeten Your Day—"*

"What's that you're saying?" asked Mr. Bertram.

"Oh, nothing," said Wil.

"Well, I'm getting a little hungry, aren't you?" said Mr. Bertram. "Shall we stop soon and see what Aunt Violet packed for us?"

"Sure," said Wil, his visions of grubs gravy, worm cutlets and mosquito chips evaporating, as he eyed several bits of sodden fur by the path. Perhaps they were from some hapless rabbit that had been happily hopping along one day until—

If it had been springtime, that fur would have been quickly snatched to line some nest.

"Everything eats everything else, doesn't it?" he said.

The thumpety-thump of a male grouse beating its wings started to drum in the distance, as if answering Wil's question; the thumping sounded like an old truck motor. It started up then died, started up again and died.

"That's a fair statement, Wil," said Mr. Bertram. "A fox eats a bird, a bird eats a worm and a worm eats you...and so, it goes. *O, chain of life rife with strife, the Red Queen runs yet she stands still.*"

Who's the Red Queen and how can she stand still if she's running? thought Wil. And what does that have to do with foxes eating birds and birds eating worms? Mr. Bertram was always full of such riddles.

They tromped on in silence for a few more minutes, Wil still wondering how someone could be running and standing still at the same time, until they rounded another bend in the path. They were already at the third den. The day's drizzle had started to lighten, and the sun was doing its best to peep out from behind a cloud.

At first, Wil didn't see the snakes. He could only hear them, rustling through the grasses and thistles.

And as he listened...the rustles became thoughts, thoughts became whispers, whispers became words.

Thanks-s-s-s...thanks-s-s-s...thanks-s-s...s-s-save us-s-s...s-s-save us-s-s...s-s-save us-s-s.

The snakes of Narcisse had remembered somehow, thought Wil, as if snake had told snake the story of how they had been saved. So closely was he listening to the hiss of words, he did not see what was before his very eyes.

"Would you look at that?" exclaimed Mr. Bertram.

Startled from his daydream, Wil gasped at the sight of so many snakes in one place. Thousands and thousands and thousands of snakes—knotted, tangled, ropy—had mounded outside the third den entrance. As a burst of warm sunlight danced over them, the snakes stirred from their lethargy.

"A veritable serpentine symposium!" said Mr. Bertram. "I'd forgotten how many snakes there were. What a sight! To think this rite has been happening for hundreds, if not thousands, of years." He leaned on the railing, gazing at the snakes, seemingly transfixed. "Quite beyond human time," he muttered.

Wil stepped back from the platform overlooking the snake den, his mind still filled with the snakish words he had heard. "I'm going to check out the fourth den," he said, and leaving Mr. Bertram still marvelling at the mound of snakes, Wil continued slowly along the path, thinking over all that had happened since last year.

How angry he had been that his grandmother had died in the fire and had never told him he had any other family.

How suspicious he had been when Sophie told him they were a mage family—one, as it turned out, that had been accused of murder.

And how, having unwittingly accepted the black medallion as a gift from his grandmother, he was now its keeper. A black medallion mysteriously linked to the long-outlawed Serpent's Chain society.

How betrayed he had felt when the librarian Miss Heese—someone he trusted, someone he thought loved books as much as he did—had turned out to be the notorious criminal Rufus Crookshank in disguise and a member of the Serpent's Chain.

But Wil brightened as he pictured the old house with the five-pointed stars. It was the magical portal to MiddleGate, hidden deep inside Winnipeg. How amazing that a secret, magical city like MiddleGate exists, he thought...and such a place as Narcisse.

And how lucky I am to have a cousin like Sophie, and friends like Phinneas and Beatriz. I stepped off one path and on to another when I moved to MiddleGate, he thought.

At the word path, Wil suddenly noticed a ragged bit of red ribbon on the path just in front of him. He had almost stepped right on top of it; he bent down to take a closer look.

But it was not a ribbon.

It was a bit of torn flesh.

And there was another scrap further along. This one, a patch of scaly skin.

And then he saw it.

A snake.

Torn, guts ripped, ribs bent, white spine bare. Innards gone. Eyes, no longer shining, only dark smudges.

The snake was dead. Very dead.

Wil took a stick and tried to pick the small corpse up, but to his horror, the body flinched.

"I thought you were dead," Wil whispered. "How can you move?"

The snake's sleek, sinous tail flicked, as if the end of the snake were trying to escape, to hide.

Using the stick, Wil picked up the sorry, broken creature and carried it slowly, sadly away from the open path. He parted dry grasses to make a nest and carefully placed the body inside.

The snake shivered and trembled, its single lung still seeking air...but to no purpose now.

It must have happened only a very short time ago, thought Wil. "If I had come just a moment before," he said, "I would have scared away the crows, and you would probably still be...be...whole."

The snake quivered...then shuddered.

It was still at last.

"Everything eats everything else," Wil whispered, and a single tear rolled down his cheek. He fumbled in his pocket for one of Mr. Bertram's mint candies and placed it beside the snake. It reminded him of a snake's egg. He covered over the nest with more grass, stood up slowly and headed back to Mr. Bertram.

✣ ✣ ✣

Their eyes bright and curious, two crows sitting high in an aspen tree watched Wil walking back along the path. The crows preened, their blue-black feathers glinting in the sun. One polished its gleaming beak against the branch; the other clicked its beak, rattled its throat feathers, then croaked as if to say, "Caw me the end, caw me the end." Then it swooped down to the small nest Wil had made, stabbed at the grass, nabbed the lozenge and cawing loudly, took wing into the air.

Cackling noisily, the first crow swooped after its mate.

VI Grouchy Friends

"And we finally found out what her name means," said Sophie.

PARVA DISCORDIA, MINOR CERTAMEN,
DISCREPANTIA ET DIFFERENTIA SENTIA,
DISPUTATIONES SUAVES—UNA VEL DUAE—
ARDENS CONTROVERSIA, QUERULA QUERIMONIA,
DISCORDIA, CONTENTIO, REPUGNANS DISSENSIO.
ALTERCAMUR, DISPUTAMUS, LITIGAMUS, PUGNAMUS,
RIXAMUR, CONCURRIMUS, CERTAMUS, FERVIMUS, GARRIMUS.
TRISTIS, STOMACHOSUS, DIFFICILIS, IRRITABILIS,
INEPTUS, ACERBUS, MOROSUS, IRATUS—
SODALIS SIT SODALIS NIHILOMINUS.
A SMALL DISAGREEMENT, A MINOR DISPUTE
DISPARITY IN VIEWPOINT, DIFFERENCE OF OPINION
AN AMIABLE DISCUSSION (OR EVEN TWO)
HEATED ARGUMENT, QUERULOUS QUARRELS
DISCORD, CONFLICT, IRRECONCILABLE DISSENT
DEBATE AND WRANGLE, BICKER AND BATTLE
CLASH, SQUABBLE, SPAR, BOIL AND BABBLE.
GROUCHY, PEEVISH, TESTY AND TOUCHY
CRANKY, CRABBY, SURLY AND CROSS—
FRIENDS BE FRIENDS NEVERTHELOSS!

It was now the middle of October; the days were much shorter, the nights much longer. Leaves were turning to earthy mulch on the ground, and Sophie felt as if Old Man Winter were already cradling MiddleGate in the palms of his icy cold hands.

It was late Saturday afternoon, and Sophie and Wil were over at Beatriz and Phinneas's house for a sleepover. All four of them were sitting on the second floor landing of the Bain house, surrounded by a massive mound of books and papers. Their *Serpent Tails* project for Mage Terpsy on the Egyptian goddess Meretseger was due all too soon.

Sophie felt her stomach rumbling. Delicious smells of cooking were wafting up the stairs. She wondered how long it would be before supper, but thought it would be rude to ask.

"I have more pictures of Meretseger," she said, showing the two new drawings she had done. "In this one, she's a cobra with a woman's head, and here's she got three heads."

"Three heads?" said Phinneas. "A woman, a cobra and a vulture—this one's amazing," he said, examining the drawing closely. "I wish I could draw like you do, Sophie."

"It is really good," said Beatriz, peering over Phinneas's shoulder. "But I still like this one you did where she has a woman's body with a cobra's head."

"We've got all these Egyptian hieroglyphics too," said Wil, holding up a small sketch with several hieroglyphics, including a coiled serpent. "These are Meretseger's symbols here."

"And we finally found out what her name means," said Sophie.

"What's it mean?" asked Beatriz.

"She-Who-Loves-Silence," said Sophie.

Beatriz clapped her hands. "That's perfect, isn't it?"

"What's perfect?" asked Sophie.

"Meretseger guarded the sacred tombs of the dead, right?" said Beatriz. "What could be more silent than that? We should start our play off inside a tomb—we can ask Mage Terpsy if the classroom can be dark with just one glowworm lantern, you know, to get everyone in the mood."

"You've got to be kidding," said Wil. "It would be just like Sygnithia to giggle or something stupid like that."

"Or Sylvain would pretend to f---" said Phinneas mischievously.

"Don't say it," said Beatriz. "We all know what you're thinking—"

"All right, both of you," said Wil, grinning at them both, "quit your arguing. We should talk about the Egyptian hieroglyphics part of our presentation. We can draw hieroglyphics on the blackboard. I found a book that has a hieroglyphic for each letter of the alphabet. Then we can have everybody try writing their names in Egyptian hieroglyphics."

"That's a great idea," said Phinneas, looking impressed as he examined the sketch Wil was holding.

"This is going to be a really good presentation," said Beatriz. "The only thing we've really got left to do is the play. Phinn and I thought we could all pretend we were robbers sneaking into one of the tombs—"

"—and then Meretseger could suddenly appear and poison us with a snakebite or turn us blind as punishment for raiding the tomb," said Phinneas.

"Sounds pretty good," said Wil.

"But she didn't just strike people down," said Sophie. "There was another side to her. She used to help anyone who asked for mercy."

"Then we could have a scene where the robbers give back everything they've taken," said Beatriz. "And each one of them can tell a really sad story about why they were stealing in the first place. Maybe one of them had to buy special medicines to cure their youngest child, who's dying from a strange, incurable disease."

"But if it's incurable, how will getting medicine help?" asked Phinneas.

"Well, you know what I mean," snapped Beatriz. "It's just an example."

"And then the robbers all fall down on their knees and beg for forgiveness," said Phinneas, paying no attention to the scowl on Beatriz's face.

"Meretseger hears their stories," said Sophie excitedly, "and her heart is touched."

"She forgives them immediately," said Beatriz.

"And then she gives them each a flower or something that will bring them good fortune," said Sophie.

"Okay, so we have two robbers, who are sneaking into one of the sacred tombs to steal things and it's night-time," said Wil. "Who wants to be Meretseger? She's a female goddess. Sophie? Beatriz? It should be one of you."

"I get too nervous," said Sophie, shaking her head. "I'll forget my lines."

"Me too," said Beatriz. "I'd rather be one of the robbers and cover my face."

"But Meretseger doesn't have to say very much," said Wil. "The robbers do most of the talking. Meretseger likes silence, remember?"

"You be Meretseger, Wil," said Sophie. "You'd make a great snake goddess. I can draw a mask, and with you looking through the eyeholes, it will look really creepy."

"I can't be Meretseger—for obvious reasons—and neither can Phinneas," said Wil.

Phinneas laughed loudly, while Sophie and Beatriz frowned.

"It wouldn't work," continued Wil. "Can't you see? Everyone would just laugh at us."

"Look, Wil, you're the one with a snake," said Sophie. "Here's your chance to finally be one. And we can make a snake for you to hold, a snake with fangs—too bad we couldn't bring Esme in, but that probably wouldn't be a good idea. And anyway, she doesn't have long fangs."

"But Meretseger is a *female* goddess," protested Wil.

"Hey, I've got another great idea," said Phinneas. "Why don't we make a snake, and then we can attach a string to it, and I'll drag it along the floor. It will look really realistic. Regina Piehard would probably scream."

"Since when did being a boy stop anyone from playing the part of a girl?" demanded Beatriz, ignoring what Phinneas had just said. "Don't you remember Mage Terpsy told us long ago women were banned from playing any dramatic roles at all?"

"That was then and this is now," snapped Sophie. "Come on, it'll be fun," she coaxed. "You know you'd both love to have the main part, wouldn't you?"

Wil and Phinneas looked at each other and crossed their arms. "No way!" they both said.

With no solution in sight, the argument was brought to a standstill by the tinkling of a bell coming from the first floor.

"Supper time," said Beatriz.

"I'm famished," said Phinneas.

"Me too," chimed in Sophie, secretly very pleased that they could stop working on the project.

It was fun to work in a group, but always way more work than doing a project on your own. Every time they worked in groups, someone was always trying to boss everyone else around. Or someone would begin to whine, *Why am I stuck doing all the work and you're doing nothing*? Or whoever was assigned to bring three hats, a belt and their grandmother's gloves for the costume, forgot to bring them on the actual day of the presentation. Or, worse yet, someone—usually the someone who was supposed to write up the good copy—got sick at the last minute, leaving the whole group in a lurch.

✣ ✣ ✣

"How's your project going, children?" asked Mrs. Bain, when Wil, Sophie, Beatriz and Phinneas appeared on the first floor.

"Pretty well," answered Phinneas, wrinkling his nose as he looked into the pot of soup that was bubbling away on the stove.

"Good," said Mrs. Bain. "Why don't all of you help carry the food to the table? We're just about ready to eat, I think. And Beatriz, could you set an extra place please."

"Why do you have to set an extra place?" asked Wil. "Are you expecting more company?'

"It's for the ghost," said Beatriz. It keeps making bumping noises and opens doors at night. Mom's decided it will be happier if there's a place set for it at the table."

"But ghosts can't actually eat real food," said Wil uncertainly, "can they?"

"No, but Mom thinks it's angry at us," said Beatriz. "I think it's just a plain, old, angry ghost. It wouldn't matter who bought the house. The ghost would be just as angry."

Sophie's mouth watered at the sight of all the dishes. There were bowls of steaming potatoes and carrots drizzled with honey glaze, three different kinds of salad and a platter of roast chicken. There seemed hardly enough room on the table for all the bowls and platters and plates, and it was some minutes before everyone was finally seated and had served themselves.

Mr. Bain sat at one end of the long table and Mrs. Bain at the other.

Mr. Bain raised his glass. "Here's to everyone's health. Elenie, who will soon be moving out west to work on a farm growing magical herbs. A wonderful opportunity to study with the best in the field—can't resist a small pun, my dear. We're very proud of you."

Elenie, who was the spitting image of Beatriz—only a slightly older Beatriz with twice as many freckles on her face—looked very pleased.

"And Olly, only one more year to go. Got that scholarship almost in the bag. I've spoken to your uncle, and he thinks you have a very good chance at it." Oliver, whom everyone called Olly, grinned. He was as freckled as his brothers and sisters, but had recently started to grow a beard.

Sophie, who was sitting beside Beatriz, leaned over and whispered, "Scholarship to where?"

"He's planning on going to Middlebury in England for his AMS diploma—advanced magical studies," whispered Beatriz.

"And Luther, we know you're looking forward to your summer internship at the Cranliver Institute to do research on infectious magical maladies—despite your dear mother's misgivings."

Luther's face reddened and he glanced over at his mother, whose face had clouded slightly.

"But we know your heart is set on it," continued Mr. Bain, "and I can't think of any more important work, what with magical terrorism on the rise here and overseas.

"And Phinneas and Beatriz, how wonderful that you've both got such good friends—here's to Sophie and Wil—living just down the street to boot."

"Dad, can we please eat," said Phinneas. "We're starving."

"And our dear little Ziggy—" said Mr. Bain, ignoring Phinneas's plea.

"Don't forget Alfred the Rat, Dad," said Ziggy, the youngest Bain, who was holding up a brown rat with white paws—they made the rat look as if it were wearing long white gloves, thought Sophie. The rat was wriggling so much that Ziggy was having trouble hanging onto it. "You can't forget, Alfred the Rat," Ziggy repeated.

"Er, Alfred the Rat, right," said Mr. Bain, with a twitch of his mouth, as if he were trying not to laugh.

"Ziggy Bain," said Mrs. Bain, "how often how I told you not to bring Alfred the Rat to the dinner table?"

"But he gets lonely," said Ziggy. With a guilty look on his face, Ziggy tried to stuff Alfred the Rat into his pocket, but Alfred the Rat was not interested in going into anyone's pocket. Instead, he squirmed from Ziggy's grasp and scuttled under the dinner table. Ziggy dove under the table in hot pursuit.

"Alfred the Rat, you come back here right now," muttered Ziggy from underneath the table.

"Alfred's trying to run up my leg," squealed Beatriz.

"That rat's more trouble than it's worth," said Luther. "I don't know why you let him keep it, Mum." He peered under the table. "Ziggy, did you know rats carry lots of diseases, including bubonic plague which killed millions and millions of people?"

"Luther, stop it," said Mrs. Bain. "You'll give Ziggy nightmares. You know how attached he is to Alfred the Rat. I had a pet rat when I was growing up too."

"Wasn't it the fleas the rats carried," said Elenie, "that cause the bubonic plague to spread?"

"Can we please just eat," said Phinneas plaintively. "If I don't eat, I'm going to die."

"Bea, don't kick him!" screeched Ziggy from underneath the table. "You'll hurt him."

Sophie looked under the table. All she could see was a sea of legs. In the middle of the legs was poor Ziggy trying to catch a rat too frightened to be caught. She quickly took off her shoe and put it down on the floor. The frantic rat scurried right into it.

Sophie quickly scooped the shoe. "Here you go, Ziggy," she said.

"Thank you, Sophie," said Ziggy in a singsong voice, peering up at her from underneath the table. "You're my best friend. You're Alfred the Rat's best friend too."

"Alfred's the best rat in the world," declared Sophie. She had to laugh, for the rat's tiny, pointed face with large ears above, was peeking out of her shoe, his long whiskers twitching violently. Sophie wondered what it would be like to have such long whiskers on her face. Probably very ticklish, she thought.

"May I suggest we eat," said Mrs. Bain, "before everything turns stone cold. I don't know why we can't just sit down and eat quietly like a normal family."

"Yes, why don't we eat," said Mr. Bain, "but I do have a very good piece of news I wanted to share with you. I guess it'll just have to wait until after supper."

All eyes turned expectantly to Mr. Bain. Luther quickly swallowed the spoonful of potato that he had snuck, and Phinneas put down his fork.

"Not only has your mother embarked on a new phase of her career here with the MiddleGate Sanatorium for Magical Maladies," said Mr. Bain.

"What is it, Dad?" asked Elenie.

"I just got word this morning that I've received a rather substantial grant to begin a very, very interesting project," said Mr. Bain beaming as he ladled steaming hot carrot soup into his bowl. "The Secretariat of Public Works has given me permission to access their files and, of course, there are extensive archives in the MiddleGate Library."

"But what's the project?" interrupted Olly.

"I'm documenting Septimus Parsimus's plans for Neacosmos," said Mr. Bain, his eyes bright. "A magical city that was never built—extraordinary ideas though. It's a pity they were never implemented."

"What this means, everyone," said Mrs. Bain, "is that your father's work is finally being given the recognition it deserves."

Amidst the general hubbub of congratulations, Mrs. Bain exclaimed, "It is all very exciting. But if we don't start to eat this fine meal—"

"Say no more, my dear," said Mr. Bain, lifting his glass high in the air to her. "Bless the hands that prepared this food."

Amidst happy chatter and the clatter of forks and knives against plates, the mounds of food disappeared quickly. And when supper dishes had been cleared, out came a tray of small iced cakes and gooey cherry tarts. And, to top the feast off, there was a large bowl of crushed raspberries with frothy whipped cream. Mrs. Bain regaled everyone by the roaring fire with a story about a ghost that appeared every twenty years to the day. It was the perfect end to a good day.

⁜ ⁜ ⁜

"Come on," said Beatriz. "Let's go upstairs. We're going to sleep in the spare room on the third floor. There's a big pile of pillows and blankets there."

Sophie, Beatriz, Wil and Phinneas raced up the stairs to the third floor. Phinneas was the first to arrive and slammed the bedroom door shut.

"Open the door, Phinneas," said Beatriz and she knocked loudly, until the door opened very slowly, with a loud creak.

Phinneas was nowhere to be seen.

"Phinneas?" said Beatriz and she stuck her head in the doorway.

"Take that!" shouted Phinneas from behind the door and he swung his pillow at Sophie's shoulder, narrowly missing her when she ducked out of the way.

"Missed me!" squealed Beatriz. She laughed and swung her pillow high above her head and down onto Sophie's back.

Sophie yelped and wriggled under a big pile of blankets.

Phinneas's pillow caught Wil on the shoulder and sent him flying. "There," shouted Phinneas. "Got you!"

"You wish!" spluttered Wil. He was about to swing his pillow at Phinneas, when a pillow winged him suddenly from nowhere.

He fell backwards onto the floor. "Ouch! That hurt." He sat up and rubbed his nose. "Not funny, Phinneas. You didn't have to throw it so hard."

"But it wasn't me," protested Phinneas, still clutching a pillow tightly in his arms.

"If it wasn't you, who was it?" asked Wil, looking over at Beatriz suspiciously.

"Don't look at me," said Beatriz. "I didn't do it."

"It's the ghost," squealed Sophie, peeping out from underneath the covers. "It must be the ghost!"

"Why would the ghost throw a pillow at me?" he asked. "That's if it even was the ghost," he added, looking sideways at Phinneas again.

"I swear, it wasn't me," said Phinneas.

"I thought your mother said the ghost only came out when the house was quiet," said Sophie.

"Yeah," said Beatriz. "And it's never actually really done anything that I know of. Just makes a few bumping noises. And doors open and close at night, but no one is there."

"Mom and Dad are waiting for the ghost to tell us what it wants, but it hasn't yet," said Beatriz.

"But if it doesn't talk, how is it going to tell you?" asked Sophie.

"Mom says it will communicate another way," said Beatriz, "when it wants to."

"Maybe it just did," said Wil, still rubbing his nose ruefully.

VII Unfinished Business

There were dark shadows against the wall.

EST NEGOTIUM IMPERFECTUM
OPUS EST POSTERIS PERFICERE.
YET, THERE IS UNFINISHED BUSINESS—
WHAT ONE GENERATION CANNOT ACCOMPLISH
FALLS TO THE NEXT.

Wil woke up with a start at the sound of footsteps in the room. He struggled to open his eyes. By a slim shaft of light from the hallway, he could see dark shadows against the bedroom wall. They seemed to loom larger and larger, as if they were about to pick him up and carry him away.

"Phinneas? Beatriz?" he whispered. "Is that you?"

There was no answer.

"Sophie?"

But Sophie, who was next to him, only turned over and muttered in her sleep.

Whoever, or whatever, it was, seemed to have gone. It must have been the Bain's house ghost. Or else he had imagined the whole thing. His ears tingled with the sound of faint scratching in the walls...probably a mouse. He yawned and shuffled his covers, which were all bunched down around his knees.

Other people's houses always make different sounds than your own, he thought. Creaking water pipes, stairs groaning, wind blowing against the windows, a squirrel running across the roof, branches of a tree grazing the house, the ticking of a strange clock—no house ever makes quite the same sounds as any other, just as no house has the same smell as any other.

Wil remembered his first several nights in MiddleGate. The sound of the grandfather clock in Aunt Violet and Aunt Rue's house chiming every hour had woken him several times in the middle of the night. After a week had passed, he barely heard the clock any more—even when he listened for it. Its sounds were now as much a part of him as his own heartbeat.

Maybe that's why I woke up, he thought—because I miss the ticking and whirring and chiming of the grandfather clock. At the thought of the grandfather clock's moon face staring down at him as he slept, he snuggled deeper under the covers. But with a groan, he realized he had to go to the bathroom. He threw back the covers and shivering in the cool night air, tiptoed across the room, trying not to step on Sophie or Beatriz or Phinneas. He slipped through the door, his eyes blinking in the hall light, and padded down the hall to the bathroom. On his way back, he looked down the stairs. There was a faint, wavering light on the second floor landing.

He was about to slip into the bedroom, when he heard someone call his name very faintly.

"William."

The voice cracked, as if it were coming from someone who was very old.

Wil stood stock still, his hand frozen on the doorknob of the bedroom.

"William," said the voice again. This time, the voice sounded impatient or annoyed that Wil was not responding.

"Y-y-yes?" said Wil. "Who's there? Where are you?"

"William," said the voice a third time.

"What do you want?" asked Wil.

"I have come to speak with you," the voice whispered hoarsely.

At this, Wil's heart leapt. The voice sounded like his grandmother's.

"Gran, is that you?"

"Come," said the voice.

The faint light on the second floor landing flickered down the stairs. Wil followed and crept down to the first floor, which was dark, but for the glowing embers of the fire. A crackle of sparks shot up as Wil entered the living room.

"Gran," said Wil, "are you…are you…here?"

At his words, the fire burst into dancing blue and orange flames.

Wil recoiled in fright from the fire.

"Do not fear, dear William," said the voice. "The flames will not hurt you."

"G-G-Gran?" stammered Wil.

Out from the fire stepped the flaming figure of a woman, long licks of flame dancing around her head. The woman's eyes turned to him and with a shock, Wil recognized his grandmother's face.

"Gran!" cried Wil. Mesmerized, he stepped towards the awful flames.

"Do not touch the fire, Wil," said his grandmother, and Wil was horror-struck to see blue flames shoot from her mouth as she spoke. "They will not burn you—yet they are icy."

"There are so many things to tell you about, Gran," said Wil, his voice trembling.

"Many things, Wil," she replied, "but we do not have much time."

Wil watched the flames shimmering against her face and remembered how Portia and Portius, the two-faced stone Gatekeeper at Gruffud's, had worn veils of fire last Hallowe'en. He shuddered, for he felt like screaming.

"There is great danger," she said. "I had no choice but to pass the black medallion and gold ring to your keep. And what's done is done. Do you have them?" she demanded, her voice urgent. "Are they safe? Tell me. Are they safe?"

"Yes, yes, Gran," said Wil. He groped at his shirt and pulled out the chain with the gold ring and black medallion. "Here they are. See? They're right here, with me."

His grandmother sighed deeply, and her flaming fingers reached out as if to touch the chain.

Wil felt an icy cold around his neck. The blue flames were not hot; instead, they carried the touch of deepest winter.

"You are the keeper of the last remaining black medallion, William," she said. "Nine there were. But through greed, the others have been destroyed. There is unfinished business—what one generation cannot accomplish falls to the next. It is your turn to right the wrongs of those who have gone before you."

"What are you talking about, Gran?" asked Wil, his teeth chattering. "The k-k-keeper?"

"The task has fallen to you," said his grandmother.

"That's what Rufus Crookshank said. And he said that I would have to do the black medallion's tasks and that I would join the Serpent's Chain…and the black medallion would kill anyone who doesn't belong to the Serpent's Chain," Will blurted out all at once. "But I don't want to belong to the Serpent's Chain. I don't want—"

But his grandmother raised her hand. "You, together with your cousin Sophie, have already completed two of the secret lessons. The third is about to begin. I dare say no more or I endanger you both. " She looked at him sadly and stretched out her flaming hands. The flames began to flicker and sputter, and his grandmother's eyes closed.

"Don't go," cried Wil. "Gran, don't go. You've got to help. Come back. You can't go. You always said there's no such thing as magic, didn't you? Didn't you? Gran?" he whimpered. "Gran?"

But the flaming figure of his grandmother began to dissolve before his very eyes. The flames guttered, burned bright for a moment more and then dimmed—utterly extinguished.

Only his grandmother's voice quavered still. "Keep them safe. For they are yours…yours…yours…yours…love…you…love…you…love…"

His grandmother's voice faded to a whisper, then to nothingness… leaving only the soft, spluttering lament of the fire's dying embers.

VIII A Decision

He had the uneasy sensation that something or someone was watching them.

QUAMQUAM HORRIDUS, HORRIFICANS, HORRIFICUS, HORRIFER,
HORRIPILANS, HORRODORATUS ET HORRISONUS,
HORROR NOCTIS VINCITUR
UBI DIEM REVOCAT ROSEA AURORA.
THOUGH HORRIOUS, HORRIFYING, HORRIFIC, HORRIFEROUS,
HORRIPILANT, HORRODOROUS, HORRISONOUS THEY BE,
NIGHT'S TERRORS ARE VANQUISHED
WHEN BECKONS ROSY DAWN.

Wil woke the next morning to loud giggles and felt himself being dragged along the floor.

"What? What's going on?" he mumbled, trying to open his eyes, which did not seem to want to open at all.

"Come on, Wil," said Sophie.

"We're going to make pancakes for everyone," said Phinneas.

"What…what time is it?" Wil asked groggily.

"It's a freckle past a hair," said Beatriz. "And it's time to make pancakes, before everyone else gets up! It's a surprise. Get up, sleepyhead."

Wil groaned, turned over and pulled the covers over his head.

But someone yanked the covers off and tickled his feet.

"All right, all right," Wil protested. He sat up and felt his head swimming. All that had happened the night before came flooding back.

"You look terrible," said Sophie.

"You won't believe what happened last night," said Wil, rubbing his eyes.

"Don't tell me you had an adventure while we were sleeping," said Sophie, her eyes bright with excitement. "Of all the luck."

"Yeah, tell us what happened," said Phinneas. "Did our house ghost get you?"

"Not exactly," said Wil dryly.

⁜ ⁜ ⁜

"Sshhh, don't make so much noise," whispered Beatriz, as they crept down the creaky stairs.

It must be really early in the morning, because the house is still dark, thought Wil. He tiptoed over to the fireplace while the others went into the kitchen.

Only grey ashes and charred logs remained from the fire of the night before. Papers and books were scattered on the table and the floor. Mrs. Bain's sweater was still where she had left last night, thrown over the back of the sofa. Several cups with the remains of hot chocolate in them sat on the table, along with a drawing of Alfred the Rat by Ziggy. Everything looked so completely ordinary, that Wil began to think that he had imagined the whole thing.

But then he saw two marks on the floor beside the fireplace, right where his grandmother had been standing—the dark outlines of two footprints. He bent down and touched one of the footprints. It smeared as he touched it, and he looked at his finger, which was now covered with dark blue soot.

It really happened, he thought.

"Wil, are you going to help or not?" said Sophie, who was suddenly standing right behind him.

Wil hadn't even heard her walk across the living room floor.

"Why is your finger covered in dirt?" she asked.

"Do you see these footprints?" said Wil. "They weren't there last night before we went to bed, were they?" he asked.

"I don't know," said Sophie. "Why?"

"I saw a ghost," said Wil, "and it wasn't the Bain's house ghost either."

"You're spooking me out," said Sophie, her eyeglasses turning from bright yellow to slug grey.

"Yeah, I'm spooking myself," said Wil, as he stood up and wiped his hand on his pants. "Let's go crack some eggs."

Beatriz was in the middle of measuring out brown sugar into a bright yellow mixing bowl, when they entered the kitchen. "So, are you going to tell us," she said, "what happened last night?"

"Bet he's going to tell us a ghostie story," said Phinneas, who dashed white flour over his face; but he coughed and spluttered when the flour went up his nose, ruining the effect.

"Serves you right," said Sophie, "because actually, Wil did see a ghost last night. And it wasn't your house ghost."

Phinneas and Beatriz both looked wide-eyed. Beatriz dropped her measuring cup into the bowl and Phinneas wiped the flour from his face on the sleeve of his shirt."

"Here goes," said Wil, and he took a deep breath. "So…I woke up in the middle of the night and had to go to the bathroom."

"Sounds exciting so far," said Phinneas.

"Phinn, be quiet," said Beatriz, "and let him talk."

Wil told them everything he could remember…the voice, his creeping down the stairs, the blue fire, his grandmother's face, how there had been nine black medallions, but only one remained—the one in his possession.

"And then she said something really strange—how there was unfinished business and we had already completed two of the black medallion's secret lessons and there was another lesson, a third one. I told her I didn't want to be part of the Serpent's Chain. But that's when she left. She said she couldn't say anything more or it could endanger everything."

"No kidding," said Phinneas, after Wil had finished.

Beatriz and Sophie were silent.

"What do you think?" asked Wil.

"I thought ghosts could only go where the person had gone when he or she was living," said Sophie. "Does that mean your grandmother actually visited MiddleGate?"

"Only some ghosts have to stay in one place," said Beatriz, "at least I think so. Others can go wherever they want."

"But what I don't understand, is that Gran always said there was no such thing as magic," said Wil. "She was really serious about it. She always said, it was a bunch of hocus-pocus, but here she is, I mean there she was, telling me all this, and I could almost have touched her, only the blue flames were so cold—and she told me not to touch the fire. Then she just…she just up and disappeared."

"And that's all she said?" asked Beatriz.

"That's everything," said Wil. "At least what I can remember."

"And what's this black medallion look like and the gold ring?" asked Beatriz.

Wil was about to pull out the chain with the medallion and the ring, when they heard footsteps coming down the stairs.

They all jumped at the sound.

"Are you making pancakes," asked a small voice. It was Ziggy, who was carrying Alfred the Rat in his arms. "Can we help?"

✣ ✣ ✣

"Good morning, children. What a beautiful day, sun shining. Perfect day for a walk. Why, what a wonderful surprise!" exclaimed Mr. Bain, as he came into the kitchen and surveyed the remarkable mess of bowls, cracked eggshells, maple syrup dripping onto the floor, mixing spoons and spatulas sopping with pancake batter, powdered sugar, honey licks and slicks of sunflower oil and melted butter, two greased skillets…and a platter heaped high with golden (if somewhat misshapen) pancakes.

He looked at the five upturned grinning faces.

"We wanted to surprise everyone," said Phinneas.

"It's almost ready," said Ziggy.

✣ ✣ ✣

It was so sunny outside that after breakfast, Wil, Sophie, Phinneas and Beatriz raced outside down toward the river just in time to see three families of ducks swim by. The ducks quacked loudly as a long V-line of geese heading south flew overhead. It was definitely colder and Wil was glad he was wearing his hat and gloves. A stiff breeze flung the last few remaining leaves left on the trees into the air, and Wil imagined each leaf whooping as it swirled high and sighing as it zigzagged to the ground.

The four children walked slowly along the crazed, dried muddy flats of the river's shoreline, hunting for unusual stones or bits of coloured glass. Wil was glad of the fresh air, for it seemed to vanquish his grim thoughts from the night before. He squatted by the side of the river, took off his gloves and dipped his hands in the muddy water. It was colder than he had imagined. He shivered and quickly shook his hands dry. As he did so he thought he saw a ripple nearby. Something had broken the surface of the water.

"Did you see that?" he asked.

"What?" asked Beatriz and Phinneas, who had collected a pile of twigs and were building a miniature fort from them.

"I thought I saw something in the water," said Wil.

"It was probably just a fish," said Sophie, and she turned back to the mud drawing she was working on.

"What are you doing?" asked Wil.

"I'm drawing a fish with whiskers," said Sophie.

"That reminds me of a fish I saw in Master Meninx's office one day," said Wil. "It had long whiskers and he was dissecting it."

"Yuck," said Sophie.

"Yeah, it was kind of yucky," said Wil.

He picked up a grey stone and threw it into the river and watched the ripples spread until he couldn't see them any more.

What right does my grandmother have to tell me what I have to do with my life? he thought. She's dead. It's bad enough Rufus Crookshank killed her; I don't want the same thing happening to me. The Serpent's Chain will just have to find someone else. Besides, I'm only a kid. And even if two lessons have been completed, that doesn't mean I have to do any more. I can just throw the medallion and the ring right into the river, and they'll sink deep into the mud or rocks, or whatever else is down there—and that will be the end of it.

"Yeah, that's what I'll do," he whispered quietly to himself.

"What did you say, Wil?" asked Phinneas.

"Did I say something?" asked Wil, startled.

"You said *That's what I'll do*," said Beatriz, as she picked up a perfectly round, black river stone.

"I was just thinking I could throw the black medallion and the gold ring into the river, and then I wouldn't have to think about any of this," said Wil.

"You can't do that," said Sophie, sounding shocked. "Not when your grandmother gave them to you. You can't just throw them away. They're really magical."

"What if someone like Rufus Crookshank found them?" said Beatriz.

"Yeah, we'd be in real trouble then," said Phinneas.

Wil's heart sank. "I guess you're right," he said reluctantly. "There's no point in running away, is there."

"Or flying away," said Beatriz.

"Or swimming away," said Sophie.

They continued wandering along the river path in silence, past the grove of cedars to the large, flat rock where they often sat to eat their picnics.

"Let's follow the path further along to see where it goes," said Beatriz, and she ran ahead.

"Wait up," cried Phinneas and Sophie.

Wil followed more slowly, his stomach still feeling full from pancakes and maple syrup. He could hear the others laughing up ahead.

Entire trees had fallen over into the river; thick vines snaked along their trunks. Wil's feet moved slower and slower, as if they did not want to be walking along this path. The rush of the river gurgled in the air, sounding strangled. A mossy tree root seemed to reach up and grab at his ankle, and branches scratched at his face. He almost stumbled over the nub of a round stone. At the sight of a large snail shell smashed in the middle of the path, he called in a choked voice, "Sophie? Beatriz? Phinneas?"

Only the swoosh of wind in the tree branches replied and a grey squirrel scolded him as he passed by. Wil had the strangest feeling that he was not alone. Someone or something was watching him, he was sure of it. He looked behind him but the path was empty, save for a single black-banded dragonfly that darted across the river. It had been weeks since he'd seen any dragonflies; this one must have emerged from the water very, very late in the season.

"Sophie…Phinneas…Beatriz," he called, and he hurried along the path. "Wait up!"

"We're here," answered Sophie, but her muffled voice sounded as if it were coming from very far away.

"Where are you?" he shouted.

Up ahead, he saw a gigantic, old willow tree leaning over the river, the largest willow tree he had ever seen, its bark deeply furrowed and branches thick and gnarled. The ramshackle ruins of a long-forgotten tree house sagged from its branches, creaking with every gust of air.

"I can't see you," he called. "Where are you?"

He could hear giggling, but it sounded as if it was coming from inside the tree. As he neared the willow tree, he saw a hole that was just the right size for crawling through and the tip of a shoe sticking out of it. The shoe disappeared suddenly.

"I see you," said Wil. He laughed and ran to the tree. Scrambling onto to his hands and knees, he peered into the hole.

"Surprise!" shouted Sophie, Phinneas and Beatriz.

"Isn't this the best hiding place you've ever seen?" said Phinneas. "Come on in. It's really warm in here."

"Protected from the wind," said Beatriz. "And it's quiet too."

There was just enough room for the four of them inside the willow tree. "It's like being in another world in here," said Wil. "Maybe this is what one of the tombs that Meretseger guarded was like."

"Only we're not dead, are we?" said Sophie. She hesitated. "Well, are you going to show them?"

Wil gingerly pulled the gold chain from his neck and brought out the gold ring and black medallion.

"That ring looks like a signet ring our uncle has," said Beatriz, her eyes bright. "But isn't there usually something engraved on it—a letter or something? There's just scratches on this one. And what's on the medallion?"

"Look at that," said Phinneas, holding the medallion close. "There's a tiny gold serpent and a bee. Those must be the first two lessons your grandmother was talking about, right?"

"Yeah, I guess so," said Wil, wishing for the umpteenth time that his grandmother had never given him the black medallion nor the gold ring. It isn't fair, he thought. My life is in danger because of a couple of pieces of cheap jewellery. No sooner had he thought this, than he was overcome with guilt. Gran didn't ask to die, and now she was dead. And the ring and medallion were obviously not cheap; both of them were really beautiful.

"Have you seen another symbol, a third one?" asked Beatriz hopefully. "What's the next lesson going to be?"

"No. Dunno," said Wil, secretly thinking that he didn't really want to know what was coming next. "Why should I do these lessons anyway? I didn't ask for them."

"It doesn't matter, Wil," said Sophie matter-of-factly. "You don't have any choice. You're the keeper of the black medallion now, and you're the one who's got to do it."

Sophie must have sensed his desperation, for she said, "All right, all right, we're the ones who've got to do it." She turned to Beatriz and Phinneas. "And you can't tell anyone about this," she said.

"Why not?" asked Beatriz.

"Because they might try to take the medallion and the ring away from me," said Wil. "And it's supposed to be secret."

"And because we don't know exactly what the Serpent's Chain is and what it might do to Wil," said Sophie. "Aunt Violet had a fit after she touched the black medallion once, and then she said something in a very scary voice. *Beware the Serpent's Chain.*" Sophie imitated Aunt Violet's deep, rasping voice, and Wil felt the hairs on the back of his neck stand on end.

Beatriz and Phinneas must have felt the same way, because Phinneas suddenly looked very sombre, and Beatriz said, "Right," only her voice didn't sound as strong as it had a moment earlier.

"But I thought you were just talking about throwing the medallion and the ring into the river and forgetting about them completely," said Phinneas.

"That was different," said Wil. "Swear on serpent's blood that you won't tell anyone."

"We swear on serpent's blood that we won't tell anyone," said Beatriz and Phinneas together.

"That's done then," said Wil, his voice hard.

"We better get back," said Sophie. "Aunt Rue and Aunt Violet are expecting us home for supper. And your mum and dad are probably wondering where we are."

As they walked back along the path, Wil still had the uneasy sensation that something or someone was watching them, but he did not mention it to the other three.

IX Investing in Futures

It must be a good omen if we're close by those snakes.

LUDENTIA SOMNIA, NUMQUAM FUGETIS
A ET BE ET CE AEQUAT DE
FRAUDATE, PRAEDICITE, FINGITE ANIMIS
ECCE, CRUSTUM IN CAELO, IMPROBUS PORCUS VOLAT
MISCHIEF DREAMS, NEVER FLEE
A PLUS B PLUS C EQUALS D.
MYSTIFY PROPHESY FANTASTICIZE
HO, PIE IN THE SKY, THE RASCAL PIG DOTH FLY

"Oh, children, I'm so glad you're here," said Aunt Violet, when Wil and Sophie walked in the door. "I was about to come and get you. You did have a good time, didn't you? I hope you slept well. Did they feed you? Did you get any work done on your snake project?"

"We had a great time," said Sophie.

"Good," said Aunt Violet. "And I have a surprise for both of you."

"Surprise?" asked Sophie. "What is it?"

"I have finally found it!" said Aunt Violet.

"Found what?" asked Wil, wondering why Aunt Violet's cheeks were so pink.

"Found what?" repeated Aunt Violet. "The place, of course!"

"What place?" asked Sophie, looking as puzzled as Wil felt.

"The new shop…on Main Street," said Aunt Violet triumphantly. *Auntie Vi's Fortune-Telling*! We're looking at the place tonight. The landlord is meeting us at seven o'clock sharp and there's just time for supper and then we'll go. We have to make a decision tonight," she bubbled on, "because there's someone else very interested in it. On the one hand, we can't miss an opportunity like this—certainly it's very affordable. On the other hand, we don't want to make up our minds before we actually see the place, do we? What if we don't like it?"

She laid out the knives, forks and spoons on the table, but gave two forks and a knife to Wil, three spoons to Sophie and kept one fork and two knives for herself.

"There's no need to feel pressured, Violet," she muttered to herself, "just because someone else is interested." Then she pulled a piece of paper out of her pocket and handed it to Sophie. "Here you are, children. What do you think?"

It was a photograph of what looked like a storefront shop; but the photograph was too blurred and dark to really see what it was like, thought Wil. Aunt Violet, however, was so nervous, unsure and enthusiastic all at the same time, that he said, "It looks…it looks great, Aunt Violet. Doesn't it, Sophie?"

Sophie wrinkled her brow and nodded her head. "It's really exciting, Aunt Violet."

Aunt Violet had been plotting for more than a year to set up a new fortune-telling business. She had somehow kept it secret from everyone for the longest time—even Aunt Rue. If they had put all the bits and pieces together, though, Wil and Sophie might have guessed, for Aunt Violet had taken to snatching their cups of tea from them—before they had even finished drinking the contents—so that she could practice predicting the future.

Then there was the night the salesman from the Perfect Products company came to sell Aunt Violet a crystal ball. Will would never forget the sight of the colourful marbles growing larger and larger until the living room was filled with shining glass orbs suspended mid-air. But Wil and Sophie had not thought all that much about Aunt Violet buying the crystal ball, even though Sophie still had a copy of the Perfect Products *Official Chance Entry Form* for the annual Mystery Trip draw taped to her bedroom mirror.

Nor had they taken much notice of the fact that Aunt Violet had carried a copy of the *Burning Heart* magazine around with her for at least a month—the one with the picture of the crystal ball on the cover and the gushing, carnation pink headlines MAKE A FORTUNE SELLING FORTUNES!

And Sophie and Wil still hadn't caught on to Aunt Violet's scheme, even when they saw her avidly reading two books they had found thrown out—*First Principles of Managing a Business* and *Fortunes' Future.*

"Anyway, I didn't want to go alone," said Aunt Violet, smiling. "I need a second opinion—and a third," she exclaimed. "Rue is working late, and Mr. Bertram wanted to come, but he had a meeting of the members of the Library Board. So, it will be just the three of us."

"Where is Main Street, Aunt Violet?" asked Sophie. "Is it far from here?"

"Oh, it's not in MiddleGate, my dears. It's outside. There are much greater business opportunities in Winnipeg itself and a much greater audience."

Wil and Sophie looked at each other silently. Sophie was clearly thinking the very same thing that he was. The whole thing was suddenly sounding like a snake-bitten scheme, if ever there was one.

"Let's have our supper, shall we," said Aunt Violet happily. "I've baked trout for you and a fresh loaf of bread. And I even remembered to leave the butter out, so it wouldn't be too hard. Come, children, or we won't have time to eat."

Wil and Sophie quietly switched the knives, forks and spoons, for Aunt Violet still had not noticed the mix-up. Then they dutifully ate the trout that Aunt Violet served—Wil was relieved to see that the fish was already cut up in pieces, so he didn't have to eye a dead fish eyeing him while he was eating. Aunt Violet, herself, seemed far too excited to take more than a bite or two.

"Aunt Violet, are you sure we shouldn't wait until Aunt Rue or Mr. Bertram can come with us?" asked Wil.

"Whatever for?" said Aunt Violet brightly. "This is an adventure, isn't it?"

✣ ✣ ✣

It was a clear, cold night with a hint of frost in the air and the stars were already twinkling when Wil, Sophie and Aunt Violet alighted from the MiddleGate Bus.

"What happens if people who don't know about MiddleGate try to get on the MiddleGate Bus?" asked Wil, as they waited at the corner.

"But they don't, my dear," said Aunt Violet.

"Why not?" asked Wil.

"Well, for one thing, they'd have to see the bus first, wouldn't they?" replied Aunt Violet.

"You mean we can see the bus and they can't?" asked Wil.

"That's right," said Aunt Violet. "It's like those Blue Morpho butterflies whose wings flutter brown and iridescent blue so quickly that you're not sure you've even seen them."

"But when we go to Narcisse, we get off the bus and everyone can see us," said Wil.

"It just depends, whether the bus's invisibility charm is engaged or not," said Aunt Violet. "Oh, the light has finally changed. Come quickly!"

They crossed Main Street and walked past several tall buildings, past a large parking lot, past a tiny restaurant filled to the brim with people. The smell of something delicious and mouth-watering flooded over the sidewalk—it must have been pizza, thought Wil. He imagined a large, crusty pizza slathered with three different kinds of cheese. His mouth watered.

"I think it's just in the next block or two," said Aunt Violet. "Not far…I hope. That does smell good, doesn't it? I think we should have eaten more supper."

Main Street was filled with people, who all seemed to be hurrying somewhere, but for a man a couple of blocks away who had just put a wooden box down on the sidewalk and was now standing on top of it. The man began to gesticulate wildly, pointing to the sky, as if he were talking to someone. He was holding a black book in his right hand, and he kept throwing his head back and shaking a fist at the stars.

Even at this distance, Wil could hear the man clearly. He was shouting at the top of his lungs, "I, Euphemus, say swimmeth despise railroad penny from an instant difficulty swamped under serpent glass. Gemstone truth roast rot from keeper's gate!"

None of it makes any sense, thought Wil. "Is that man crazy, Aunt Violet?" he asked, as they drew nearer.

"I'm not sure," said Aunt Violet. "Did I hear him say his name was Euphemus? A strange name. His words are—" She paused, obviously trying to think of the right word. "They're elusive, aren't they?"

"What does elusive mean?" asked Sophie.

"Well, it can mean many things," said Aunt Violet. "His words hide, they're confused, obscure, mysterious…yes, that's it," she said.

"Mysterious is a good word. His words are mysterious. And look where he has stationed himself. Right in front of my favourite doorway in the whole city."

It was the ornate wrought iron door decorated with two green serpents staring at each other; they looked as if they were guarding the door. Wil recognized the snakes immediately, for he had seen them the very first day he arrived at the train station in Winnipeg.

By the time they reached the man on the wooden box, a crowd had started to gather. People were pointing at him and a few were giggling. Others seemed enthralled and were hanging on his every word.

"Wait, Aunt Violet," said Wil, "I want to hear what he's saying."

"Just for a moment," said Aunt Violet, "or we'll be late. I don't want to keep the landlord waiting. It certainly wouldn't make for a very good first impression."

The man on the wooden box was red in the face with the exertion of thunderous speech-making. "Wait never straw rain underneath falls ministerium," he roared. "Up the boiling nightmare spinach days lest mountains crumble. To dust, to mumble fogshuffle hoarfrost vox. Audacious blaze, hear gossip spell when wing'd fish rampart."

Wil glanced at the woman standing to his left. Her hands were clasped together under her chin, as if she were praying. She was obviously transfixed by the man's words and appeared deeply moved by his message.

"I don't understand anything he's saying, even though it's English, I think," whispered Wil to Sophie. "Do you understand?"

"No," replied Sophie. "But it sounds like it should mean something," she added doubtfully.

"Maybe it's all a riddle," said Wil, "and we have to guess what it means. I think I heard him say winged fish."

"Come, children," said Aunt Violet. "Time to go."

Reluctantly, Wil and Sophie followed Aunt Violet. Wil looked back at the man and was surprised to see that he was staring after them. Then the man turned back to the crowd, and holding up the black book high in the air, he took up his speech with renewed vigour. "For there is no good time to harness cloud gardens speckled." The man bowed his head, as did several people in the crowd, and his voice grew softer and softer until Wil could hear him no more. "Bend knees ankles neck all praise futurable high below under. Like fire under moss grows antimagistratickle freedom. Ground's grace spit to spirit farctate from fate to fate..."

Even though Wil had no idea what in snake's name the man was talking about, his curiosity was piqued by his words. Never had he heard anyone use words like this. The man was playing with the words—not only that, he was playing with words Wil had never heard before, if they even were *real* words. Words that crackled and sizzled.

Maybe each word didn't mean what it was supposed to mean, thought Wil, but really meant something else, and only those who knew the code would know what the real message was.

"Well, it must be a good omen if we're close by that doorway," said Aunt Violet. "And we're so close to the train station and the MiddleGate bus stop too. And remember Ursula von Scrum, the portrait artist we met at the Dragonfly Festival? Her studio is quite close by too," she said. "Another plus." She quickened her pace and pointed to the storefront up ahead at the corner. "I see it. And the landlord's not there yet—he said he'd wait outside for us—so we're not late, by serpent's grace."

The store had a torn, yellowed FOR RENT sign posted on one of the windows. A large crack lightninged across the window; it had been patched with frayed, grey tape. Dried leaves and stained, crumpled newspapers littered the doorway, which smelled of old, stale urine. Sophie and Wil peered into the shop, but it was hard to see anything.

Aunt Violet seemed undeterred by the rubble and the crack in the window. "I have a good feeling about this place," she said excitedly.

"So, I hope you didn't have any difficulty finding the place," said a deep male voice behind them.

Aunt Violet, Sophie and Wil turned. Standing there, hardly taller than Wil was a short, tubby man with a very round face.

"Mr. Gropple?" said Aunt Violet.

"Gropple, it is," said Mr. Gropple and he bowed first to Aunt Violet, then Sophie and finally to Wil. "Shall we look inside?" he asked. He smiled broadly at them and pulled out a big metal hoop from his pocket. The jangle of several dozen keys greeted their ears.

Wil wondered how Mr. Gropple could possibly know which key to choose. But the key he chose fit the lock perfectly and they stepped over the crumpled newspapers into the shop.

"Now, I forgot to mention I've turned the electricity off," said Mr. Gropple. "Doesn't make sense to keep the power on when no one's actually using the place—so I hope you don't mind if we use a flashlight."

Wil's eyes were blinded for a moment as Mr. Gropple turned on his flashlight.

There was a counter at the front, an odd assortment of shelves, an old clock hanging on the wall, a couple of wicker chairs with worn stuffed pillows, a round mirror and an overturned table. The whole place had the air of a building that hadn't been occupied in many years. The smell of cold neglect seeped through Wil's skin, making him feel glum. Thick layers of dust overlaid everything, and now that they were inside looking out, Wil could see that the windows were filthy.

"If you'd like any of this fine furniture, you're welcome to it," said Mr. Gropple. "It was all left by the previous tenant."

"That would be lovely," said Aunt Violet. "Now, as far as heating and all the other utilities are concerned, I believe you said these are included in the monthly rent?"

"That's right," said Mr. Gropple.

"And the repair of the glass in the front window?" asked Aunt Violet.

"Yes, yes, of course," said Mr. Gropple ingratiatingly. "I can make arrangements. Now, when we spoke, you hadn't told me what your plans for the establishment were."

"I'm starting a new business venture in ah…futures," said Aunt Violet.

"Ah, futures, eh? Trading in commodities and assets—lots of dollars in that," said Mr. Gropple, obviously impressed. "Competitive business, but then we're in the economic heart of the city here. The historic Bank of Montreal just down the street, one of the most impressive buildings in the city. The train station nearby, another architectural wonder. How long have you been in the business?"

What is Mr. Gropple talking about, thought Wil. What does Aunt Violet's fortune-telling have to do with money and banks and oddities?

"Oh, I've been dabbling for years," Aunt Violet exclaimed. "Years. In the family, you know."

"Yes, excellent," said Mr. Gropple, looking pleased at the prospect of having what he obviously thought was a reliable and rich tenant, thought Wil.

"Well, I think this will be just perfect for what we have in mind, Mr. Gropple," said Aunt Violet holding out her hand.

"Here's to futures, Madam Isidor," said Mr. Gropple, shaking her hand enthusiastically. "When would you like to take possession?"

X Heirs Apparent

“I think there’s something behind here,” said Sophie.”

MIRUM EST QUOD INTERDUM INVENIAS UBI DETERGIS
IAMDUDUM AMISSUM UDONEM ATRO ALBOQUE VIRGATUM
LIBRUM ILLUSTRATUM (QUEM NON EVOLVEBAS
EX QUO TEMPORE PUERULUS ERAS)
ANTIQUAM EPISTULAM AMATORIAM FRIANTEM IN PULVEREM
ATRAMENTO MUTATO IN FULVUM,
DILECTAM LIGULAM SUCCINO MANUBRIO RIMOSO,
PICTURAM MATRIS TE INFANTEM TENENTIS,
AVIAE AMPULLAM UNGUENTI ROSAE CAERULEAE
(UNA GUTTA MANET)
DILECTUM STILUM AUREUM (ADHUC AGIT)
ANTIQUOS LIBELLOS ET PROBATIONES
ANGULIS PAGINARUM PANNOSIS
MACROPODIDAE MASSAE PULVERIS, ATQUE UNUM
DURUM OBSOLETUM FRUSTUM CASEI.
EXTRAORDINARY WHAT YOU FIND SOMETIMES
WHEN YOU CLEAN, ISN’T IT?
LONG-LOST BLACK AND WHITE STRIPED SOCK
A PICTURE BOOK YOU HAVEN’T READ SINCE YOU
WERE A SMALL CHILD
AN OLD LOVE LETTER CRUMBLING TO DUST,
THE INK TURNED BROWN
YOUR FAVOURITE SPOON WITH THE CRACKED AMBER HANDLE

A PICTURE OF YOUR MOTHER HOLDING YOU
WHEN YOU WERE A BABY
A BOTTLE OF YOUR GRANDMOTHER'S BLUE ROSE PERFUME
(BUT ONLY A DROP REMAINS)
YOUR FAVOURITE GOLD PEN (IT STILL WORKS)
OLD SCHOOL NOTES AND TESTS, THE CORNERS
OF THE PAGES TATTERED
KANGAROO CLUMPS OF DUST AND A HARDENED,
STALE PIECE OF CHEESE...

It was several days after Aunt Violet, Wil and Sophie had visited the new shop—a stuck-in-the-house rainy afternoon. Aunt Violet was away buying supplies for Auntie Vi's Fortune-Telling, and Aunt Rue had come home from work much earlier than usual and had begun to clean the house furiously. She was just starting in on the kitchen and was taking every last dish out of the cupboards with a great clatter.

Wil and Sophie were sprawled on the living room floor trying to finish their homework for Mage Terpsy. They had been racking their brains to come up with English animal idioms, those common figures of speech that make absolutely no sense when translated word for word into another language.

"How many more are we supposed to have?" asked Sophie, nibbling on her pencil.

"Mage Terpsy told us to come up with twelve, I think," answered Wil.

"What's on your list?" asked Sophie, peering over at Wil's notebook.

"I've got *snake in the grass,* you know, someone who betrays you even though you trusted them—"

"Like Miss Heese," said Sophie grimly.

"Yeah, like Miss Heese," Wil replied. "Then there's *don't let the cat out of the bag.*"

"Right, don't reveal a secret by accident, I've got that one too," said Sophie, "and *between you and me and the cat's whiskers,* when you want someone to keep what you're telling them a secret."

"I haven't heard that one before," said Wil. "I just thought of another one. *Has the cat got your tongue?*" He scribbled it down in his notebook. "Why are there so many for cats anyway?"

"People adore cats," said Sophie, scratching Cadmus, who was sleeping on top of her school bag.

At the sound of a plate smashing to the floor, Wil and Sophie looked up from their papers. "Are you all right, Aunt Rue?" they asked.

"Just a dish, children, not me," said Aunt Rue. "It was old and cracked anyway. Are you two going to be finished your homework soon? It feels like it's been years since we've really given the house a good scrubbing."

"We're almost done," said Sophie.

"What's worse?" Wil whispered. "Doing homework or cleaning the house?"

"Good question," said Sophie, as she looked out the living window, which was streaked in rivulets of water. "We can't go out to play anyway, not unless you want to pretend to be a cold fish or something."

"Cold fish!" exclaimed Wil. "There's another one. *Don't be a cold fish.*"

"*Like a fish out of water* and *like a fish needs a bicycle,*" said Sophie excitedly.

"*What about drink like a fish*?" said Wil. "I've heard that one before. Don't know what it means exactly though."

"It means to drink far too much alcohol—more than is good for you," called Aunt Rue from the kitchen.

"But fish drink water," said Wil. "They'd die if they drank alcohol."

"Look, it's just an expression," said Sophie. "Write it down. Good, last one!" She shut her notebook and jumped up. "We're finished, Aunt Rue."

"Excellent. Why don't you start in on the living room? You can dust the books. And make sure you don't forget to take the cushions off the sofa—heaven knows what you'll find under those."

An hour later, Sophie and Wil stood back triumphantly and admired their work. The living room practically sparkled. The windows were clean, the books straightened, the dust and cat fur lurking under the grandfather's clock had been vanquished.

And an added bonus—they found a shiny doubler underneath the sofa—their very own doubler to buy treats at Lulu's Jolly Lollies, the new candy shop that had just opened up in MiddleGate.

"You never know what you're going to find when you clean up," Aunt Rue said. "It's amazing. I just found an old pitcher at the back of the top shelf. It came from my mother. Thought it had disappeared years ago."

"We forgot one thing," said Sophie.

"Who cares?" said Wil, looking as if he wanted to curl up and take a nap.

"We forgot to look behind the radiator," said Sophie.

"Do we have to?" said Wil, and he flopped down into a chair and closed his eyes. "Let's not and say we did. I've had it."

"There might be something interesting behind there," said Sophie stubbornly.

"Probably just spider webs," mumbled Wil and he yawned. "I'm too tired even to eat supper."

Undeterred, Sophie got down on her hands and knees to look under the radiator. "You're right. Lots of spider webs. But look, there's a ruby marble here too."

"Hey, that's not the marble that Phinneas gave me for my birthday, is it?" With a sudden burst of energy, Wil bounded out of his chair.

"You didn't even miss it," said Sophie accusingly, holding up the ruby marble to the light.

"I did," protested Wil. "Give it here. I hunted all over the house for it. I bet it was Cadmus's fault."

"*Please* would be nice," said Sophie. "And don't blame Cadmus." She tossed Wil the marble and turned back to the radiator. "I think there's something else," she said, peering behind the radiator. "It looks like a notebook."

She squeezed her arm behind the radiator and with difficulty pulled out an old, tattered black notebook covered in cobwebs.

"What's that?" asked Wil.

"I don't know," said Sophie. She wiped away the cobwebs and opened the notebook. "It's got sketches in it—pages and page of sketches. Look at them all. Why…these are beautiful." She showed Wil one of the drawings—ripples of water, rocks and polliwogs.

"That's good," said Wil admiringly. "There's a catfish in that one too. I didn't see it at first."

"Who do you think did all these?" said Sophie excitedly. "Aunt Rue, look what I found!"

"What have you got there, Sophie? A book?" said Aunt Rue, who was standing on a chair in the kitchen. She wiped her hand across her forehead, brushing a long strand of hair out of her eyes.

"It's a notebook with drawings in it," said Sophie.

At the sight of the notebook, Aunt Rue's face blanched. She swayed and looked as if she were going to fall from the chair.

"Aunt Rue, be careful," cried Wil and he ran into the kitchen.

Aunt Rue steadied herself against one of the cupboard shelves. "Where, by serpent's grace, did you find that, Sophie?" she asked in a shaken voice.

"Just...just behind the radiator," said Sophie, feeling scared. "It was covered in cobwebs. Probably been there for a very long time."

"At least ten years, if not more," said Aunt Rue in a dull voice. She climbed down from her chair, walked unsteadily over to Sophie and held out her hand.

Sophie passed over the notebook and Aunt Rue opened the cover with a shaking hand. A small faded photograph of a dark-haired woman was taped inside. The photo was so faded it was hard to see her face. She was wearing a long cloak. There was an inscription underneath, which Sophie read it out loud.

My dearest Bellabelle,
May we always be able to hear
the footfall of a caterpillar
bubbled breath of a fish
sound of a cat opening one eye
whisper of a snowflake falling
echo of the copper moon's eclipse.
Love you forever and always, Cyril

Sophie felt as if she could hardly breathe. "Snowflakes don't make a sound when they fall to the ground," she said. "That's like the chain holding the wolf monster Fenrir. You know, the chain that's made of things that don't exist, and it's the strongest chain in the entire world."

"Cyril—is that Sophie's father?" asked Wil, pointing to the signature at the bottom.

"It's his writing," said Aunt Rue.

"Who is Bellabelle then?" asked Sophie.

Aunt Rue hesitated, then said, "Bellabelle was Cyril's nickname for your mother. Her real name was Isabelle."

"I never knew her name," said Sophie. She felt if she were about to cry and took her glasses off. The frame was as grey-mottled as pigeon feathers. "You never told me her name."

"You never asked," said Aunt Rue, in a small, strangled voice.

Sophie took the sketchbook back from Aunt Rue and held it tightly. "My mother used to draw?" she asked. "She loved to draw?"

"Yes," said Aunt Rue. "Yes, she did. She was always drawing—just like you."

"And what happened to all her drawings?" asked Sophie, her eyes not leaving Aunt Rue's face.

"I don't know," said Aunt Rue, shaking her head. "I came home one day after Cyril disappeared and your mother was gone. There was a fire blazing in the fireplace, but no one was here. And every single last one of her sketchbooks and drawings was gone. There was nothing left. No note even."

"She burnt everything?" asked Wil.

"She must have," said Aunt Rue. "I thought there was nothing left...until now."

⁜ ⁜ ⁜

With her blanket draped over her shoulders like a cloak, Sophie pored over each page of the notebook, trying to understand the purpose behind each stroke, line, shading, dot. It was the only connection she had ever had with her mother, who had obviously loved to sketch outdoors. There were many drawings from down by the river.

Were they done before I was born? Sophie wondered. Did she take long walks by herself and sit by the river? Did my father sit there beside her, watching her draw? Perhaps she drew them when she was carrying me inside her. That meant that I—even if I wasn't born or even named yet—I was with her when these drawings were made. The drawings belonged to them both. This last thought gave Sophie much comfort.

Sophie turned back to the inscription to read over the poem written by her father again. "*The footfall of a caterpillar...the bubbled breath of a fish... the sound of a cat opening one eye...*"

Just at that moment Cadmus, who was sleeping at the end of her bed, lazily opened one eye. His whiskers twitched, as he looked at her, and he yawned a huge yawn, revealing sharp, pearly white incisors and rough, pink tongue. Without a sound...

Sophie thought again of the Norse wolf monster Fenrir. He was held by chains made of things that could not be found, could not be seen, could not be smelled, could not be heard, could not be tasted...could only be felt.

The great sadness of never hearing her parents tell her a bedtime story, never having picnics with them, never hearing them laugh, never watching them make supper together, left Sophie's heart aching. One fat tear rolled down her cheek and fell onto the sketch of the rippling water and the catfish. The pen ink darkened then spread. Stricken, Sophie stared at the catfish as it grew mottled and plump.

Jumping out of bed, she tiptoed down the hallway to Wil's room, with the sketchbook in her hand.

Wil's light was still on. He looked up from the book he was reading, startled. "What's the matter?" he asked.

"The drawing blotched," said Sophie, holding out the sketchbook so Wil could see, "and the catfish changed colour. Have you looked at the black medallion lately?"

"No," said Wil shortly. "I've been ignoring it," he said. "I don't want to have anything to do with the Serpent's Chain. I just want to forget the whole thing. I don't care. It's not fair. If the others are like Rufus Crookshank…"

He didn't finish his sentence, but Sophie understood exactly what he meant. She felt as if they were being asked to do something that was far beyond their years and knowledge.

"I think we better look at the medallion," she said.

"Fine," said Wil flatly. "You can look, if you want to, but I'm not going to…and you don't have to tell me if it's changed either, because I'm definitely not interested."

Wil closed his eyes, turned his head away and held out the black medallion in Sophie's direction.

"Hmm," said Sophie.

"Well?" Wil asked, his eyes still closed.

"Well, what?" asked Sophie.

"Well, what do you see?' said Wil. "Why aren't you saying anything?"

"But you said you weren't interested," said Sophie.

"Right," said Wil, "but that's not what I meant."

"Well, what did you mean?" asked Sophie. "Look for yourself then. Either you want to know or you don't."

"Oh, for snake's sake," exclaimed Wil. "This is stupid." He opened one eye and squinted at the black medallion.

There, beside the snake and the bee was the tiny shimmering outline of a fish—a fish with long whiskers.

"Great," he said, and he looked accusingly at Sophie.

"It's not my fault," she said. "I knew it was going to be there, as plain as the snout on a snake. You can't just ignore it and hope it will go away, because it won't."

"Now what are we supposed to do?" said Wil.

"Serpent's scale, I don't know," said Sophie, "but it's better that we know what we're up against."

Wil only frowned, stuffed the medallion under his shirt and turned back to his book.

XI The Gullet

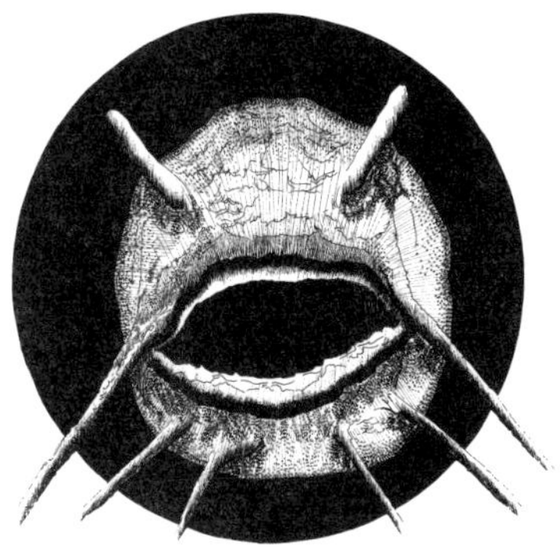

The fish was trying to say something to him.

HEU! OS, GURGULIO, GUTTUR, GULA,
HIATUS, RICTUS...ANIMUS MEUS PALPITAT.
YIKES! A MOUTH, A MAW, A GAPE, A GOB
A YAWN, A JAW...MY HEART'S ATHROB.

The following week, Wil and Sophie helped Aunt Violet every day after school to clean the shop. Wil had to admit that Aunt Violet had been right. With the windows cleaned and repaired, wooden floors scrubbed and polished, furniture oiled, purple tablecloth and gold stars, silver candlestick with two dragons (that he and Sophie had found), paintings of strange symbols, shining crystals, beeswax candles, new glass lamps, herbal sachets, teapots and tea cups...the shop was looking very good.

In fact, it was looking more than very good. It looked fantastic and magical, thought Wil, just the sort of place that people would want to come to have their fortunes told.

The floor was still creaky and the windows were crooked, but there was something special about the place. Everyone seemed to feel it as soon as they walked through the door, and there had been a steady stream of people stopping in to say hello and ask questions.

Aunt Violet was gracious to everyone, and no one left the shop without a small bundle of herbs—"to give you sweet dreams," she said.

The only hitch in renovations had been a slightly tense moment, when someone walked in just as Aunt Violet had bewitched five bushy brushes into painting the back wall a glorious cerulean blue, as brilliant as the winter sky. The door to the shop had opened and in stepped a portly woman wearing a fur hat, decorated with the head of whatever unfortunate animal—it looked like a ferret, Wil decided—had given up its life for the sake of fashion. The dead ferret's eyes, which must have been black glass, seemed to look around the shop with as much appreciation as its owner.

"I couldn't help but see your beautiful sign," the portly woman exclaimed. "How exciting that we're going to have our very own fortune teller in this neighbourhood! I've done a little dabbling in the divinatory arts myself...the most interesting prediction I ever did was the one about my Uncle Herbert..."

Aunt Violet, trying to look interested in Uncle Herbert's prediction, had glanced quickly back at the swishing paintbrushes, which thankfully were very near to the ceiling. She muttered a quick freezing charm under her breath and the brushes froze in place.

Wil watched the paint on the paintbrushes begin to dribble, according to the forces of gravity. The freezing charm had obviously not been strong enough. He watched, fascinated and horrified, as the blue drips of paint grew larger...and larger...and larger.

Sophie tried to get Aunt Violet's attention, but Aunt Violet was too busy edging the portly woman to the door.

And still the portly woman seemed not to notice the paintbrushes.

Finally, Aunt Violet took her by the elbow firmly and steered her to the door. "Thank you so much for dropping by—Mrs. Elkerhorn, you said your name was?—and I do look forward to seeing you again, and hearing more about your Uncle Herbert. Please take one of my herbal sachets. I promise you'll have a very good sleep if you put it under your pillow."

With the door firmly closed behind Mrs. Elkerhorn, Aunt Violet had scurried to the back of the shop and the paintbrushes were soon busy at work again.

"Sneaking snakes," exclaimed Aunt Violet. "I certainly didn't take into account that so many people would visit before the shop even opened!" She looked very pleased, nevertheless, that the shop had already attracted so much attention. "I really had no idea. I thought people would be a little suspicious, but everyone has been most welcoming. I'm beginning to think we should lock the door, though, if we're to get any work done."

"But then people will only peer in at you like you're a fish in a fishbowl," said Sophie.

"You're probably right, my dear," said Aunt Violet, and she pulled out a lacy handkerchief from her sleeve to mop her brow. "Have we cleaned all the cupboards behind the counter yet?" she asked, and she stooped down to look inside one of the cupboards. "Lot of good storage space here."

"They were all empty," said Wil.

"Empty? You couldn't have looked all that carefully, children. I'm surprised you missed this!" she said and she held up the sculpture of a hand.

Aunt Violet looked as if she had suddenly sprouted a third arm, thought Wil.

"Look how long the fingernails are," squealed Sophie.

The hand—or more properly half an arm, a wrist and a hand—had long, black, curved fingernails. The hand was closed in a tight fist.

"That's amazing," said Sophie. "How could we have missed that?"

"It was obviously biding its time," said Aunt Violet. She chuckled. "Perhaps it thinks the shop is clean enough now to present itself. I've got just the spot for you," she said, addressing the hand, and she placed it on top of the table covered in the purple cloth with the gold stars.

As if this was exactly what the hand had been waiting for, its fingers uncurled; the palm of the hand now faced upward

"It looks like it wants to hold something," said Wil.

"Look at that," said Aunt Violet. "I've read about these. They're called *manusmanus,* if I remember correctly. And anything that they hold cannot be stolen or damaged in any way. A circle of protection extends outwards in whatever place they live. "How lucky we are," she said. "These are very rare."

"Maybe it can hold the *BUZzz* ball," said Sophie, her eyes shining.

"What a good idea," said Aunt Violet and she unwrapped the crystal ball, which had been stored on a shelf, and carefully placed it onto the palm of the hand. At once the long fingers closed in around the ball.

"And I was worrying about how secure the shop would be," said Aunt Violet. "We won't have to worry about that now. But I will have to make enquiries, as I'm not sure exactly how to take care of a *manusmanus.*

"Who would have abandoned such a thing?" she mused. "Surely whoever it was didn't know that it was a *manusmanus,* because if they had, they would never have left it behind."

Cradled in the palm of the *manusmanus,* the *BUZzz* crystal ball was purring softly. Wil looked around to see if Aunt Violet was watching,

but she was now busy with yet another visitor, who had just stepped into the shop.

Wil turned back to the *BUZzz* ball, wondering if he would see anything in it. Without special training, you could only see your own reflection, but he remembered what had happened the last time he gazed into a crystal ball. He had seen a horrible, hairy face with five fierce eyes—two huge, bulging ones and three smaller ones in the middle of its head. Only later did he understand that it was the head of a bee.

This time, however, he only saw his own worried-looking reflection. Relieved, Wil picked up the cloth that was lying beside the ball and polished a smudge from the glass. The ball purred more loudly and a tiny gold spark flashed inside it. Entranced, Wil peered deeply into the ball a second time and almost fell backwards with fright.

The face of a whiskered, monstrous fish, its mouth black and gaping, glared back at him. It reminded him of that dead fish on Master Meninx's dissecting table the day he had visited the infirmary when one of Mage Radix's plants had bitten him. The strange thing was that the fish in the crystal ball had large lips, if you could call them lips, and they were moving. The fish was trying to say something to him, but there was no sound, only the soft purr of the *BUZzz*. With a jolt, Wil recognized the fish was mouthing the word *So-o-o-o-ph-e-e-e-e-e.*

"Sophie," whispered Wil.

As he whispered Sophie's name, the fish looked as if it were about to lunge suddenly right out of the crystal ball and swallow him whole. Wil jumped back in surprise. The crystal ball would have toppled from its stand, but for the fact that the *manusmanus* suddenly gripped the ball tightly. Aunt Violet was right about the hand, thought Wil. Nothing could happen to the *BUZzz* ball now.

Wil tiptoed over to Sophie, who was sweeping the last bit of dust from the corner by the counter. "Sophie, you've got to see this."

"What?" asked Sophie, looking at him curiously.

"Come take a look in the crystal ball," said Wil.

"Why?" asked Sophie. "Did you see something in it?"

Wil nodded. "It was going to jump right out at me!"

"I thought we weren't supposed to be able to see anything in the crystal ball, until we had special training," said Sophie, as she walked over to the crystal ball and peered into it.

"Nothing," she said, sounding miff. "Every time you look in it, you see something. It's not fair."

"It doesn't matter," said Wil impatiently. "What's important is that there was a *catfish* in there and it was calling *your* name."

"What do you mean it was calling *my* name?" asked Sophie, looking a little scared.

"Its lips were moving, only it wasn't making any sound."

"How many whiskers did it have?" asked Sophie.

"I...I didn't count them," said Wil

Sophie gave him a withering look.

"Well, at least I can see things in the crystal ball," said Wil. "That's got to be good for something."

"Yeah," said Sophie without any real enthusiasm. "It probably has something to do with the medallion or that gold ring of yours."

"You think so?" said Wil. "So, if I weren't wearing the medallion and the gold ring, you think I wouldn't be able to see anything in the crystal ball?"

"Not exactly," said Sophie. "It's just that the medallion seems to have a life of its own. It can send out a powerful beam of light, it tried to escape from Rufus Crookshank's clutches—"

"That's stretching things a bit, isn't it?" asked Wil. "It just rolled down into a crack in a rock."

"All I'm saying, if you'd listen to me, is that medallion protects you," she added.

"Fine protection the medallion offers," said Wil, "if both of us were kidnapped. You don't think it's a little fishy this whole thing?" he said mischievously. "It's just a plain old medallion after all, and the gold ring is heavily scratched. It's probably worthless."

"Not if your grandmother died in an attempt to keep them from falling into the wrong hands," retorted Sophie. "And not if Rufus Crookshank is back in prison for trying to steal the black medallion. If it's so worthless, why were they going to so much trouble to protect it?"

Sophie was right. His grandmother had died only one day after giving him the black medallion and gold ring. She must have had some premonition about what was going to happen.

"Children," scolded Aunt Violet. "How will we ever get the shop ready to open, if you're going to stand about jibbering and jabbering.

"I'm sorry, my dears," she said. "It's just that I'm so excited and there's so much to be done and—" At this, she suddenly hugged them both. "Thank you for all your help and encouragement. I couldn't do this without you.

"I just knew this was the right place," she said, surveying the shop proudly.

At that moment, the shop door opened again. "I saw your beautiful sign out front—"

XII Swish'ysh the Tail

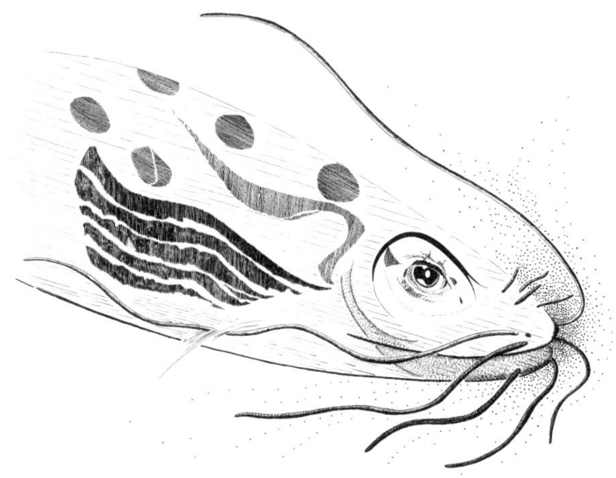

VERBA SIMILIA NIVI HIBERNAE—
DELIQUESCEBANT ANTEQUAM ALIQUIS AUDIRET.
WORDS LIKE WINTER SNOWFLAKES—
THEY MELTED BEFORE ANYONE HEARD THEM.

It was too cold, too grey, too wet for humans but perfect fish weather, as the old saying goes.

A woman wearing stone-grey robes crouched by the side of the river near the ancient willow tree whose branches stretched out over the river. She rocked back and forth slowly; the brown waters pulled at her bare, muddied feet, as if entreating her into the water. The spit of cold rain and autumn winds stung her face; she did not flinch.

"Time swish'ysh its tail," muttered the woman, her voice no louder than the creaking of the willow's branches above. She threw out her cloak and wraith tendrils of mist began to rise from the river as she whispered

Earth and shadow moon's pearly scales
Foul water, per'ysh Fyshes, foul water, we unw'ysh.
The promise, the hope and the belief
Return'ysh them, by my leave
Misty Fog, by your grace
Near this place, we meet'ysh face-to-face.

The impatient fingers of the wind tried to snatch the words away as they were spoken, but the words had already melted away, leaving nothing but swirling, foggy mist. The woman smiled to herself, but at the *kreee-ka-wi-eee* of a night bird, she started from her reverie and turned…

xiii To the Deep She Leaps

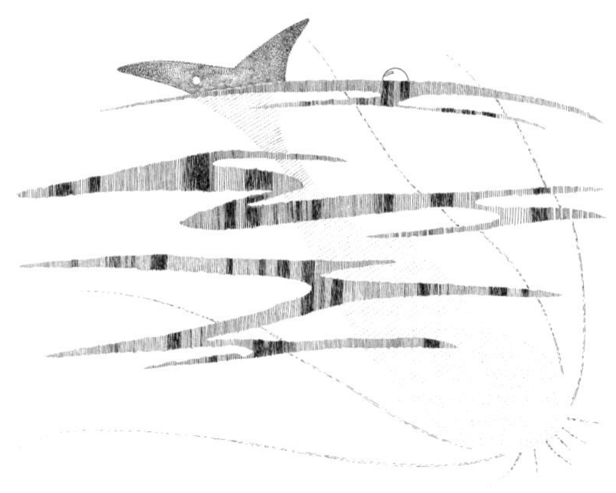

VETUS FLUVIUS
SALIT PISCIS
ASPERGO ACCIDIT
OLD RIVER
FISH LEAPS
SPLASH

XIV Fogmudfish

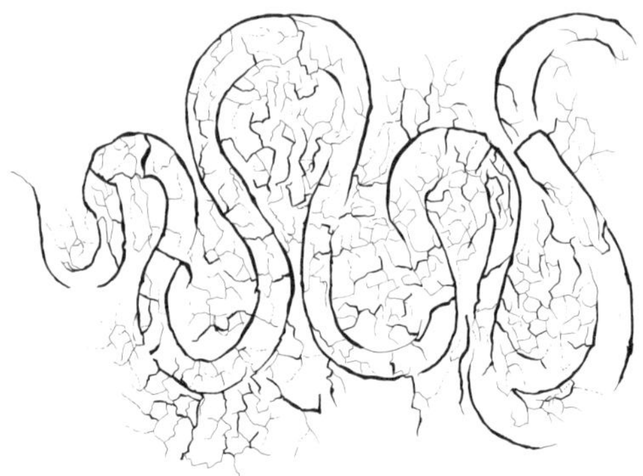

The crazed mud pulled at their shoes, while the fog played at their heels.

ODOR PRISCI PISCIS
AD NARES ADGRESSUS EST.
VETUSTI MICANTES OCULI
EUM CONTEMPLABANTUR.
AN ANCIENT, FISHY SMELL
ASSAILED HIS NOSTRILS.
AND ANCIENT, GLITTERING EYES
FIXED ON HIS.

Kicking at old, sodden leaves on the sidewalk, Wil and Sophie wandered morosely down Half Moon Lane. The air was foggy and moist. The Bain family was away for the weekend and Sunday afternoon was stretching unendingly, until Aunt Violet swept them both out of the house—*to air out the cobwebs in your heads,* as she put it.

"How are we supposed to air out our brains in this weather?" said Sophie. "We should have stayed home and practiced our parts for the Meretseger play. I'm getting so nervous, my stomach's just churning around thinking about it."

"There's no point in practicing without Phinneas and Beatriz," said Wil. "It wouldn't be nearly as much fun, and besides, we've already practiced it to death. If we practice it any more, I really will die."

"It's all very well for you," said Sophie. "All you have to do is lie there, with your eyes closed, not saying anything—I had to memorize all those words."

"*You* try to make it look as if you're not breathing, when you really are," said Wil. "Anyway, that headdress you made looks good. Everyone will be really impressed."

"You think so?" said Sophie doubtfully, but she sounded pleased, and Wil noticed that the frames of her glasses turned a slightly lighter shade of blue.

"Let's go down by the river," said Wil. "Maybe it won't be so foggy there."

"To that big, old tree," said Sophie, "the one we hid inside with Phinneas and Beatriz."

With a destination, their footsteps quickened.

✣ ✣ ✣

On the whir of a duck's wing, the fog gently swirled around the children and nudged them towards the river, hurrying their footsteps, caressing their hair. The river path tunnelled into misty white in the distance, all sound dampened, it seemed, by the heaviness of the air—but for the *rat-a-tat-tat* hammer of a woodpecker and the shrill cry of a seagull ripping the fog for an instant. The tree tops were cloaked in fog, and the dark tree trunks rooted to the earth looked like the legs of giant, unseen creatures guarding the river.

Sophie and Wil ran along the path to the ancient willow tree, the crazed mud pulling at their shoes, the fog nipping at their heels. Laughing and breathless, they crawled inside the tree and sat there catching their breath; the fog eddied in the branches above.

Sophie picked up a small branch and began to scrape the mud from her shoes. "I thought you said the fog wouldn't be so thick down by the river," she said.

"Guess I was wrong," said Wil.

"Did you bring anything to eat?" asked Sophie hopefully. "My pockets are empty."

"I don't think I have anything either," said Wil. He squirmed as he checked his pockets.

"Ouch!" exclaimed Sophie. "Watch your elbow."

"Sorry," said Wil. "Nope, nothing." He crawled out from the tree and stood up.

"Where are you going?" asked Sophie, her voice sounding muffled from inside the tree.

"I'm going to see how cold the water is," Wil answered, and he clambered down the bank to the river's edge.

The fog was dancing over the water and the trees on the other side of the river loomed up out of the mist. Wil felt as if he were in another world, far, far away from MiddleGate. Everything was so still; even the muddy water, silken smooth, was lapping gently at the rounded smooth stones by the river's edge. He stepped onto the stones and bent down to feel the water.

And as his fingers touched the water, he heard voices whispering in the air all around him—but no one was there.

"Sophie," Wil called, his voice catching in his throat. "Sophie, are you there?"

"You don't need to shout," said Sophie. "I'm right here."

Wil glanced around to see Sophie standing right behind him. "I didn't even hear you come down," he said. "Did you hear what I heard? The voices?"

"Voices?" said Sophie, sounding puzzled. "No."

"That's funny," said Wil. "I thought I heard voices. They were everywhere—whispers, but I couldn't understand what they were saying. Sshhh, listen, there they are again."

Sophie's glasses turned pale mauve and her eyes widened. "I hear them now...but there's no one else here, just us."

The fog swirled around the children, holding them close. A splash by the river startled them both and they turned to see what it was. There, standing before them, was a woman wearing long, silvery robes. Her hair was matted and whiskers trailed from her chin. But it was her eyes that were the most startling. Pale and wide-set, they glimmered like two moons.

The woman was surrounded by shimmering figures—a young girl wearing diaphanous clothing, her body covered in colourful tattoos, a woman wearing a long blue cloak, who gazed at Wil and Sophie with what seemed like great sadness, two young children about six and nine, one girl, one boy, both with blond hair almost white, several young men wearing rough denim jackets, an old man with grizzled beard and ragged clothes.

The figures seemed real enough, but their eyes were an unearthly, glowing green. They were whispering something, but Wil could not understand the words. Their hands reached out to Sophie and Wil, as if to pull them into the water, while the woman in the blue cloak bowed her head.

Even though he had not been touched by them, Wil felt their wet cold. He and Sophie drew back from them, frightened, but the figures only pressed forward.

The woman raised her hand. At her gesture, the figures joined hands and encircled Wil, Sophie, and the woman. They danced around them until Wil began to feel dizzy. An ancient, fishy smell filled the air, as the woman gazed at them both. But she said nothing; she seemed to be waiting for them to speak.

"Who…who…are you?" asked Wil finally.

"Wait'ysh for you," said the woman, her voice a mere whisper. "In your world, my name be'ysh Catfysh."

"You're…you're a fish?" asked Sophie incredulously.

"Human'ysh myself and walk'ysh heavy on the earth," said Catfysh. "I carry'ysh a message."

"Who is the message from? And who are they?" asked Wil, looking at the young children, who in turn were staring wide-eyed at him. Their glowing green eyes unnerved him.

Catfysh ignored his first question. "Those who give'ysh themselves to the river join'ysh the Fyshly Realm," she whispered. "Beware'ysh. The Serpent's Chain grow'ysh long; magical and non-magical worlds be'ysh in danger." She began to sing hoarsely.

Black Star, Twin Sphinxes divine
Fyshly Earthly Realms a sign
Lamp to learn'ysh
Linked chain unmasked
Medusa, Athena, the royal bulls' roar
Shirk'ysh not from the Task
For fear of more
For fear of more.

Wil turned to Sophie and whispered, "What's she talking about?"

"I don't know," Sophie whispered back.

Wil turned back to Catfysh. "But what are we supposed to do? Why can't you do it?"

"Will'ysh need will'ysh done, according to the ancient medallion," whispered Catfysh. "My place be'ysh with the River's Waters."

The Palace of the Blazing Star
Gaze'ysh upon it from afar and
Lest The Golden Boy be'ysh drowned
Great Sphinxean Guards be'ysh found.

With that, Catfysh's cloak whirled around her, and serpent tendrils of mist eddied above Wil's and Sophie's heads. Catfysh turned back to the river and stepped into the water with her followers.

"But…but…will…will we see you again?" asked Wil.

Catfysh only smiled. Her silver whiskers grew longer and her grey robes spread upon the water as she waded deep. One last time she spoke.

Break'ysh, shatter'ysh, rattle'ysh ice.
Look'ysh for me as winter flee'ysh.
Twist'ysh, coil'ysh, shake'ysh and toil'ysh
Slither'ysh hither mud, blood and flood
Cloud under thunder twist'ysh and turn'ysh
Bend'ysh the serpent, bend'ysh to me.
No human form, when next we meet'ysh.
Tell'ysh no one and when you look'ysh for me
Know'ysh that I be'ysh Fyshly free.

"But if you're a fish, how will we know it's you?" asked Sophie.

"*Ex barba ictalurum*—its whiskers tell'ysh a Catfysh," she replied.

With that, Catfysh's voice faded, as she and her sober companions slipped beneath the water's surface…and they were all…quite simply…gone.

Only the ripples on the river remained, and Wil and Sophie were left by themselves—save for a pair of geese who honked noisily, then took flight into the air, their wings whirring and long, graceful necks straining. As if pulled by the geese, the fog lifted from the river and dissolved; the sun pored through the clouds and warmed Wil and Sophie.

Wil watched the last, glistening ripple dwindle away. A single rainbow bubble bobbed on the surface of the water…and then, the bubble broke.

"I can hardly wait to tell Phinneas and Beatriz," said Wil excitedly.

"Didn't you hear her say, *Tell no one?"* said Sophie.

"Oh, right," said Wil. "Right," he repeated, his heart heavy.

"Do you think we'll ever see her—or them—again?" asked Sophie.

"I'm afraid so," said Wil. "But if all catfish have those whiskers, how will we know if it's really her? I wish I hadn't lost that book Peeping Peerslie gave me. He must have been really insulted because I never see…I mean, I never hear him in the library any more."

"Why don't you try asking Mr. Bertram again about the book?" said Sophie. "If you stop and think about it, how many fish actually come and want to talk with you? Besides, didn't you see how many whiskers she had?"

"No," said Wil, feeling irked. "I guess I'm not in the habit of staring at someone's face and counting how many whiskers they have."

"I bet you don't even know how many barbels a catfish usually has, do you?" asked Sophie.

Wil ventured a guess. "Six?"

Sophie laughed.

"Since you seem to know so much about it," said Wil, "why don't you tell me?"

Sophie laughed again, then relented. "Eight."

"So, how many did Catfysh have?"

"Ten."

"Are you sure?"

Sophie pulled off a large, sticky clot of mud from her jacket and threw it at Wil. "Of course, I'm sure," she said.

XV She-Who-Loves-Silence

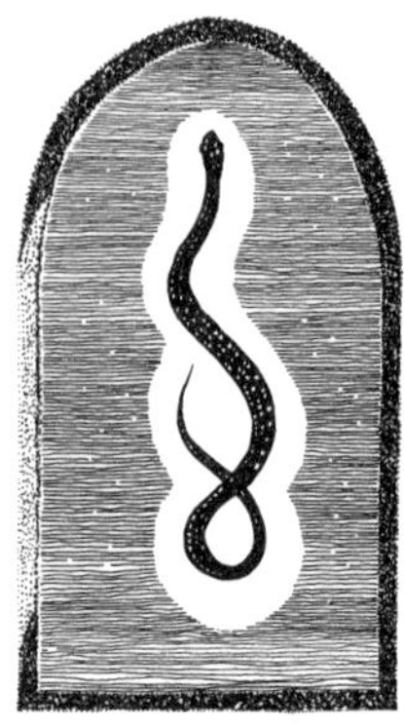

"Let My Serpent Tell the Truth."

FELES RAPUIT LINGUAM, TUA VERBA DESUNT?
GENUA HORRESCUNT, PEDES FRIGESCUNT?
TREMENS, TIMENS, PAULUM LANGUENS
MANUS SUDANT, TUSSIS, BALBUTIS,
ANIMUS PALPITAT, TIMOR OCCUPAT
STOMACHO TURBATO, PALPEBRIS VIBRATIS
SUBITO RIDES, TE FLETURUM SENTIS
INTENTIS OCULIS OMNES TE INTUENTUR
MAVIS IPSOS ABIRE
SED SICUT LEO FORTIS SIS, NEQUE CAPER PAVIDUS;
VIRTUS TE SERVABIT, QUOD NIHIL ALIUD QUAM FABULA EST.
TREMBLING AND SHAKING—FEELING A TRIFLE FAINT?
YOUR HANDS SURE ARE CLAMMY,
YOU STUTTER AND YOU COUGH.
YOUR HEART'S ALL A-FLUTTER, AS THE WILLIES TAKE YOU OVER.
WITH A CHURNING IN THE STOMACH, A TWITCH IN THE EYE,
A SUDDEN CASE OF GIGGLES, YOU THINK
YOU'RE GOING TO CRY!
EVERYONE IS STARING, YOU WISH THEY'D GO AWAY.
BUT BE BOLD AS A LION, NOT TIMID AS A GOAT.
DERRING-DO SHALL SAVE YOU, FOR
IT'S ONLY A PLAY!

The shadows cast by the glowworm lanterns loomed long against the classroom walls. Mage Terpsy hovered over the lanterns, making sure the light was steady. "Class, our fery virst *Serpent Tails* performance today by Sophie, Wil, Phinneas and Beatriz.

Sophie, standing outside the classroom door and waiting for the play to begin, giggled nervously to herself and wondered if Wil had noticed that Mage Terpsy was up to her old tricks—for it sounded as if she had just said *fairy worst* instead of *very first.* She adjusted Meretseger's headdress of five snakes, which she had made from the shiny, gold paper Aunt Violet had been saving for a special occasion.

Two thieves in ragged clothes—Phinneas and Beatriz—crouched by a corpse laid out on the floor and wrapped in a white sheet at the front of the room. The part of the corpse was ably played by Wil, who was trying not to breathe too loudly.

"This is a fine ring!" exclaimed one of the thieves, who attempted to pull the ring from the finger of the corpse. The ring seemed stuck, however, and would not come off—despite the thief's best efforts.

Meretseger strode into the room. "Who Dares Disobey Us?" she said in a deep voice—several people began to giggle, but Meretseger ignored them.

The two thieves threw down the arm of the corpse and quivered before the goddess.

"Thou Hast Dishonoured Us," said Meretseger. "Thou Hast Dishonoured the Dead. No One May Enter this Tomb with an Impure Heart." Meretseger pulled out a long snake from her robe and threw it down.

The snake hit the corpse—to Wil's credit, he only twitched once from his Eternal Sleep—and bounced onto the floor, where it stared balefully out at the class, its mouth open wide and yellow fangs exposed.

Merrily Klimchak screamed.

"It's just a rubber snake, Merrily," someone whispered. "What's the matter with you?"

"I know," whispered Merrily. "I was just surprised, that's all."

"Sssshhh," whispered Mage Terpsy. "Quiet, everyone!"

The two thieves scrambled to their feet, trembling before Meretseger's Majesty.

Meretseger's headdress wobbled slightly, but the effect only heightened the sense of mortal danger, for the gold foil caught the light of the glowworm lanterns, momentarily blinding everyone in the class.

"Kneel Before Us-s-s-s," said Meretseger. Her words were dangerously soft and quiet.

The two thieves fell to their knees and touched their heads to the floor three times.

"O, Meretseger, spare us, we beg you," said one of the thieves.

"O, Meretseger, we do not wish to dishonour—"

"Thou Shalt Die," Meretseger shouted in a thunderous voice and she took off her headdress and held it high in the air. The gold foil flashed angrily by the lantern light.

At this, both thieves prostrated themselves and trembling, they moaned, "O Greatest Serpent, She-Who-Loves-Silence, Guardian-of-the-City-of-the-Dead, forgive us, for we meant no harm."

One thief crawled forward and clutched the feet of Meretseger.

"O, She-Who-Forgives, my child shall surely die without the remedy I must buy. The corpse's ring will help the still living to live, who then may sing your praises.

"O, Meretseger, I only seek the graces of my beloved," cried the other thief. "Her father forbids us from marrying until such time as I bring him a ring set with a rare stone."

Meretseger stood silent and as still as a cold, marble statue; she seemed to be considering their stories.

In fact, Sophie could not remember what she was to say next. As the moment stretched into what felt like an aeon, Sophie felt like screaming and running out of the room. Her heart was pounding so hard, she was sure that everyone in the entire class could hear it.

Got it! she thought.

Meretseger held her right arm parallel to the floor and waved it in a sinuous serpent motion. "Our Heart is Moved by Your Sorry Stories. Therefore, Let My Serpent Tell the Truth. By the Sacred Sands of Egypt and the Waters of the Nile, by the Tears of the Crocodile, by the Breath of Anubis the Jackal God, If You Lie, My Serpent Shall Blind You with its Venom. If the Truth Falls from Your Mouth, Let My Serpent Leave you in Peace.

The two thieves fell to trembling on the floor again.

Everyone watching stared at the rubber snake lying on the floor, its mouth and fangs as vicious as ever, waiting to see what would happen next.

Suddenly the snake jerked backwards and appeared to bite the thief who had told Meretseger that he only wished to marry his true love. The thief howled in pain, clutched his eyes and cried piteously, "I am blinded. I cannot see. Help me, I cannot see."

⁜ ⁜ ⁜

Afterwards, everyone crowded around Phinneas and Beatriz to get a look at the ring (one of Aunt Violet's) and kept telling Sophie how scary she was, especially when it looked like her arm had actually become a snake.

Sophie was pleased to see that Sylvain and Sygnithia Sly, for once, looked jealous at all they attention they were getting.

The snake attracted great interest too.

"How did you get it to move like that?" asked Merrily Klimchak.

"It was magic," quipped Sophie, who had managed to snap the black thread from the snake after the play, without anyone noticing.

"All four of you have certainly set the standard for those to follow," Mage Terpsy said enthusiastically. "Note, class, that this group not only prepared a brief but excellent introduction to the Egyptian gods and goddesses with wonderful drawings, but they also had a very interesting assignment for everyone to learn more about hieroglyphics. And now this small dramatic play, which certainly did convey very well Meretseger's wrath and sense of justice.

"All of you, take inspiration for your own presentations. I look porward with *farticular* excitement to see what you'll come up with next!"

As his small notebook was in his locker, Will muttered *porward* and *farticular excitement* to himself several times so he could write them down later, along with *fairy virst.*

XVI Good News (Or Is It?)

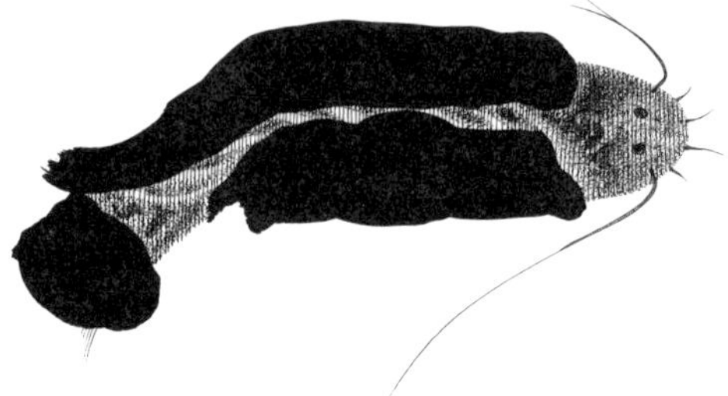

An old, rancid fish smell was coming from inside his book bag.

QUAERIS LIBELLUM, COMMUNEM CLAVEM,
QUAERIS COLLOQUIUM, VOCEM MEUM DUCAM.
CAVE QUOD PETIS, RES IPSA FIAT VERUM
EVENTUS IMPRUDENTES QUIS PROVIDERIT?
EVENTUS IMPRUDENTES MALUM COQUIVERINT
UBI AUDIERIS HOC MONITUM IPSIS IN CARMINIBUS,
MANUS ABLUAS UT ODOREM PISCARIUM PERDAS.
A QUEST FOR A BOOK, PASSE-PARTOUT
A QUEST FOR AN INTERVIEW, TU-WHIT, TU-WHOO
BE CAREFUL WHAT YOU ASK FOR, IT MAY COME TRUE.
UNINTENDED CONSEQUENCES, WHO FOREKNEW?
UNINTENDED CONSEQUENCES, THEY MAY BREW.
WHEN YOU HEAR THE CAUTION IN THIS DOGGEREL,
WASH HANDS TO VANQUISH FISHY SMELL.

Mage Tibor was dancing from foot to foot when they arrived for their afternoon class. “I have a surprise for you all, class. Such news… hmmm…I cannot keep it to myself for very long!”

Everyone looked questioningly at Mage Tibor, whose blue half-spectacles were all askew on his nose.

“My dear old friend Vitellus Albumen—we were about your age… hmmm…when we first met—Vitellus Albumen is coming to MiddleGate soon and has agreed to visit Gruffud’s Academy.”

"That name sounds familiar," Wil whispered to Sophie. "Do you know who it is?"

"I've seen his name somewhere too," said Sophie, "but I can't remember where."

In a flash, Wil remembered where they had seen the name. It had been on that card right by the blue egg in Mr. Egbertine's *Musée des Oeufs*—the blue egg that Wil had accidentally broken last year (with disastrous consequences).

"I know," whispered Wil. "He's the one who gave that blue egg to Mr. Egbertine."

"For those of you who don't know who Vitellus Albumen is," said Mage Tibor, "the man is one of the greatest Explorers…hmmm…our magical world has ever known."

He waxed on for practically the whole class about Vitellus Albumen's exploits. How he had hunted for the large and elusive ape-like yeti in the remote, mountainous regions of the Himalayan mountains in Nepal and Tibet. How he had almost been taken prisoner by a gigantic hairy *sasquatch* in Canada's northwestern forests—but had fortunately escaped. How he had proven beyond the shadow of a doubt the existence of the eight-toed *ogopogo* in Lake Okanagan of British Columbia. How he had pursued the mysterious, frightful, long-necked, bulbous-bodied water monster *mbilintu* of the Congo swamps. And how he had been one of the few who had ever actually seen a flaming *firebird* in the wilds of Iceland and lived to tell the tale. He had even managed to bring back several of the large blue eggs from an abandoned firebird nest.

Wil remembered all too well the oozing vapour that spilled from a blue egg when it was broken. Even the tiniest amount was enough to turn your mind to a pasty, porridge-like state.

"All these unexplained mysteries…hmmm…they prowl and howl, skulk and slink, lurk and leap, creep and shriek," said Mage Tibor solemnly to a wide-eyed class. "And Vitellus Albumen has been at the forefront of exploring these unknown frontiers…hmmm…where many others would fear to venture."

At the end of cartology, Wil's hand was cramped from trying to write down everything Mage Tibor had said. Vitellus Albumen must be one of the bravest men alive, he thought, as he shook out his cramped hand.

"How could one person do all that?" he said after class.

"His mother must have died from worry already," quipped Phinneas.

⁜ ⁜ ⁜

At the end of the day, Wil visited the library to look again for the fish book. Mr. Bertram was busy helping several other people, although he waved at Wil and smiled. Despondent, Wil wandered over to the shelves with all the fish books.

It sure wasn't like the old days, he thought, when he had worked at Pirsstle and Bertram's Antiquarian Booksellers in Toronto. Even though Mr. Bertram was now living in MiddleGate, it seemed as if he hardly ever saw him. His work at the Library seemed to keep him very, very busy; there was always someone who needed help or he had a meeting to go to. And whenever Mr. Bertram visited them, Aunt Rue seemed to go very quiet.

Aunt Violet had made cryptic comments about Mr. Bertram having felt as if he had to leave MiddleGate after his old friend Cyril Isidor had been accused of murder and then disappeared. Plus she had muttered about something having happened between Aunt Rue and Mr. Bertram—but according to Aunt Violet, it was all "ancient history," whatever that meant.

Half-heartedly, Wil took one or two fish books down and leafed through them, but did not see any pictures of fish with whiskers. As he was standing there disconsolately, he heard a voice in his ear.

"You wouldn't be looking for that fishy book, would you?" said the voice.

"Peerslie, where have you been?" exclaimed Wil. He looked up, as always, towards the place where Peerslie's voice was coming from—this time, it was directly above his head. "It's been weeks."

"Oh, I've been keeping my whiskers clean," said Peeping Peerslie, "and I know when I'm not wanted."

"All right, I'm sorry, but you've got to admit the fish on the cover of that book was a little too real and the book did smell like an old fish," said Wil. "How was I supposed to know the book was so important? And how did you know I would need it?"

"Ghostie secrets, cannot betray," said Peeping Peerslie. "So…," he said breezily, "you didn't want it when I gave it to you, but now you do?"

Wil had the distinct impression that Peerslie was swooping triumphantly through the air above his head, because the hanging lamp was swinging crazily back and forth.

"Peerslie, please," said Wil pleadingly. "What can I do to make it up to you?"

"Let me think," said Peeping Peerslie. "Extra homework, have you?"

Wil laughed, remembering the day he had discovered that Peeping Peerslie was always trying to do other people's homework only because he didn't have any himself. "Peerslie, you can have as much homework as you want!" said Wil.

"Whee-e-e-e-e-e!" whooped Peeping Peerslie.

"Peerslie, sshhhhhhh!" said Wil. "Do you want to get us both expelled from the library?"

"But the librarian is your old friend," said Peeping Peerslie in a more subdued voice.

"That doesn't matter," said Wil, even though he thought it probably would help, and even though it was Rufus Crookshank (disguised as the librarian Miss Heese)—and not Mr. Bertram—who had liked to badger everyone about the Library Rules, particularly Rule No. 1. *No Noissse.*

"Now that that's settled," said Peeping Peerslie in conversational tone, "have you visited Master Meninx?"

"Why?" asked Wil, wondering why in snake's name he should talk to Master Meninx.

"Perhaps you should...and don't forget the homework or—"

With that, there was a small bang, like a cork being popped, and Peeping Peerslie was gone. An old, rancid fish smell suddenly filled the air. It was coming from inside his book bag. Holding his nose, Wil looked in the bag. There, sandwiched between his numeristics notebook and the *Magical Grammar and Palaver* text, was the long-lost book. The fish on the cover had the same drooping whiskers and watery, unfocused eyes swivelling in their sockets. Wil gagged and quickly closed the bag.

⁜ ⁜ ⁜

By the time Wil got home from school, it was almost suppertime. As he came into the house, Cadmus sniffed at his book bag, spat and hissed, then ran out into the front yard and hid underneath the raspberry bushes.

"Where were you?" asked Sophie, who was sitting in the living room doing her homework. "I walked home with Beatriz and Phinneas, but that was at least an hour ago." Her nose wrinkled. "You stink! What's that horrible smell?"

"I was in the library, looking for that fish book," said Wil, holding his book bag behind his back. "Remember the one that Peeping Peerslie gave me at the beginning of the school year?"

"Did you find it?" asked Sophie eagerly.

"Can't you tell from the smell?" said Wil. "Peeping Peerslie finally gave it back to me, but only after I agreed to get more homework for him."

"Wil, where have you been?" exclaimed Aunt Violet, as she came into the kitchen carrying a large box of mismatched teacups up from the basement. "If you're going to be late, you've got to let me know. Sophie didn't even know where you were." Aunt Violet looked down sharply at Wil. "What in snake's name have you brought into the house? Something smells terrible."

"Sorry, Aunt Violet," said Wil. "I was in the library, and that smell... it's...it's a...it's a school project."

"Well, get it out of the kitchen and take it upstairs to your room, or we won't be able to enjoy our supper. And just because you were in the library doing homework doesn't excuse the fact that we didn't know where you were—and especially when I made a special dessert for tonight, since you had your presentation today." Aunt Violet waggled the dishcloth in front of his face. "You know I have half a mind to say no cake for you, young man." But her face softened and she gave him a quick hug. "We won't bother waiting for Aunt Rue; she said she was going to be late."

✣ ✣ ✣

Aunt Violet ladled the baked eggplant from the frying pan into a serving bowl along with soggy onions—they reminded Wil of limp, white seaweed. Eggplant juice squirted out and splat on the table. There were blotchy bits of red too, which he assumed were tomatoes. The eggplant skin was no longer a beautiful, glistening purple-black; it had turned brown and wrinkled. The mushy flesh of the eggplant and clusters of small seeds seemed alive, or rather, as if they had once been alive once, but now were quite dead. It looked like Aunt Violet had gutted a fish or something.

"This is a yummy dish. I don't think I've made eggplant for you before," said Aunt Violet enthusiastically. "Takes a while to prepare, but it's certainly well worth the effort."

Not wanting to hurt Aunt Violet's feelings, Wil tried to muster some enthusiasm, hoping that his face didn't look as pallid green as the frames of Sophie's glasses. "It looks really good, Aunt Violet," he said. But between the stench of the fish book and the sight of the eggplant, he wasn't feeling very hungry.

"You haven't told me how your presentation went today," said Aunt Violet, and she spooned the runny eggplant stew onto each of their plates.

"You should have seen it, Aunt Violet," said Sophie. "Merrily Klimchak practically hit the ceiling, when I threw down the snake onto the floor."

"Yeah, and it hit me," said Wil, "but I managed not to move…too much. It was so hard trying not to breathe, I mean I had to breathe, but I didn't want everyone to see my chest going up and down."

"Not very corpse-like," said Aunt Violet, with a laugh.

"I almost forgot my lines," said Sophie.

"The silence was really dramatic," said Wil, and he eyed the eggplant stew with trepidation, then slurped the tiniest mouthful. It actually didn't taste as bad as it looked. "And everyone was waiting to see if Meretseger was going to punish the thieves."

"Mage Terpsy said we did a *really* good presentation," said Sophie.

"All that practicing paid off!" said Aunt Violet, while she passed them a basket of warm bread. "By the way, do you remember that man we saw named Euphemus, and he was standing on top of the wooden box and shouting? He came into the shop today, and from what I can gather, he's from the Yukon originally; he's been travelling all over—delivering his message wherever he goes."

"You mean he actually talked with you," said Wil, "in real sentences?"

"He does have a rather unique way of speaking," said Aunt Violet, with a bemused smile.

They were halfway through their soup before Aunt Rue finally returned home. She bustled in the door and threw off her coat. This was a different Aunt Rue than Wil had ever seen, and if Sophie's and Aunt Violet's faces were anything to judge by, they had never seen Aunt Rue like this either. Aunt Rue was smiling and there was a lightness to her footstep. She actually looked happy.

Aunt Violet hurried to ladle out more eggplant stew. "Good news, Rue?" she said.

"Maybe," said Aunt Rue. She looked at all their expressions and laughed.

"What happened, Aunt Rue?" asked Sophie impatiently.

"Something at work?" asked Wil.

"I still can't believe it," said Aunt Rue, "but Minister Skelch himself called me into his office today."

"What did he say?" asked Sophie.

"Let her speak, Sophie," said Aunt Violet. "You're too impatient." She turned to Aunt Rue and said, "Rue, take us out of our misery."

"Well, the story is," said Aunt Rue, "that after Lucretia Daggar was relieved of her position—"

"Didn't they use the word *retired* in the official reports?" said Aunt Violet.

"Now, who's interrupting, Aunt Violet?" said Aunt Rue. "Anyway, after her position came open, they posted the job as they usually would, and there were a number of excellent applicants. One, in particular, a man by the name of Decimus Tizzard, was offered the job. He had outstanding qualifications—even had his Middlebury certification, had done extensive fieldwork in India and his references were superb. He was offered the position of Assistant Deputy Minister and accepted immediately.

"He got along very well with everyone—I really liked him—morale around the Secretariat was considerably buoyed, especially after the whole, sordid fiasco with Lucretia Daggar."

"What happened, Aunt Rue?" asked Wil.

"It turned out that Decimus Tizzard had faked all his credentials and even his references. Middlebury had never heard of him and the man had never even set foot on the Indian subcontinent."

Aunt Rue looked triumphantly at the three of them. Wil had no idea what it all meant and looked over at Aunt Violet. She looked equally mystified.

"Well, Minister Skelch called me into his office today," said Aunt Rue, "and encouraged me to apply for the position!"

"You mean, you'd be the Assistant Deputy Minister?" asked Aunt Violet, her hand at her throat.

"That's exactly what it means," said Aunt Rue.

"Nothing's for sure in this world, children," Aunt Violet hastened to say, "but it does sound very promising. If Minister Skelch himself—"

In his mind's eye, Wil could see the Minister as clearly as if he were standing right there in the kitchen. He didn't trust the man. There was something about him that bothered Wil, and it wasn't just that he always seemed to be late, always hurrying off to another meeting, always pompous and self-important. And even if he had not, as Wil had at first believed, been the real villain behind the murder of hundreds, if not thousands, of the snakes of Narcisse, the Minister seemed to be hiding something—Wil could not quite put his finger on it. Or it was as if the Minister were avoiding something, as if he didn't really enjoy his job as Minister of the Secretariat on the Status of Magical Creatures. It was odd how the Minister had not even been interested in meeting Esme that day when Wil, Sophie and Mr. Bertram had gone to the Secretariat to register Esme as a magical creature—even though Esme had helped to save the snakes of Narcisse from destruction.

Maybe the fact that the Minister had called Aunt Rue into his office was actually not a good sign. Maybe I should say something to Aunt Rue, thought Wil, but then, she'll think I'm being snaky.

"Wil, aren't you going to try dessert?" asked Aunt Rue. "Are you feeling all right?"

With a start, Wil looked down at the plate and small silver fork set before him. There…reposing in all its glory, a large, beautiful, gleaming slice of luscious lemon cheesecake, drizzled in golden yellow glaze, dusted with sugar powder.

Wil's mouth watered. But he knew he had to say something. "Do you think you can trust Minister Skelch, Aunt Rue," he asked.

"Trust, Wil?'" asked Aunt Rue, looking puzzled. "He's the Minister."

"I know," said Wil, "but just because he's Minister doesn't mean…I mean, that Tizzard man turned out to be a rotten egg, didn't he?"

"Oh, Wil," said Aunt Rue. "That's really sweet of you. You're trying to protect us, so we aren't disappointed, if it doesn't come through." She ruffled Wil's hair. "That's very thoughtful of you."

Sophie took the very last bite of her cake and smacked her lips. The frames of her glasses matched the cake perfectly. "Yum!" she said with a dreamy smile on her face. "Can I have another piece, Aunt Violet?"

"May I," replied Aunt Violet sternly, but her eyes twinkled as she spoke.

⁜ ⁜ ⁜

Cadmus was crouched outside Wil's bedroom, his nose practically glued to the crack under the door.

"Cadmus, you know you're not allowed in my room," said Wil, leaning down to scratch Cadmus's ears. "Esme doesn't really like your company, I'm sorry."

Cadmus meowed then scampered down the hall to Sophie's room.

As Wil opened the door to his bedroom, the smell of fish filled his nose. He groaned. He had completely forgotten about the fish book, which he had stuffed into the bottom drawer of his dresser. No wonder Cadmus had been glued to the other side of his door.

What am I supposed to do with that book? he thought. I could read it and give it right back to Peeping Peerslie, get it over with quickly.

"Esme, are you up for some reading tonight?" asked Wil.

Esme didn't answer, of course.

"Even if you could answer me, I wouldn't blame you if you didn't," he said. "I can't even think properly with that fish smell in here."

He strode over to the dresser and yanked open the bottom drawer. The smell of the book practically pushed him over. "Ugh," he said. "I can't read you, not tonight," he said. "No way." He took a towel and tied the book inside, then he opened his window and hung the towel on a branch of the tree just outside the window.

He shut the window firmly and climbed into bed.

He could still see the pale shape of the towel dangling from the branch, but already the smell in the room was getting weaker—that, or else, his nose had given up, tried to make the best of a bad situation and was telling his brain that the smell wasn't really that horrible after all.

XVII Why?

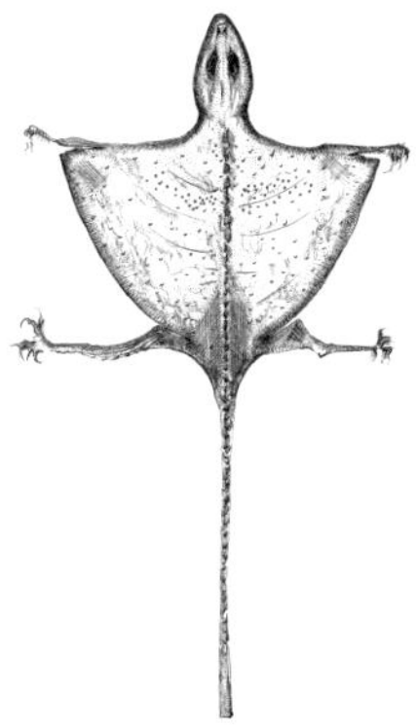

Above the door hung a dried, dessicated creature.

UNUS, DUO, TRES, QUINQUE, OCTO
SPIRA HELIANTHI, SQUAMAE ANANATIS
VEL CORPUS HUMANUM SI TIBI PLACET.
DUO MANUS, DUO PEDES, CINQUE DIGITI, TRES PARTES
CERTO NON VULGARES, CONVERSATIONES
FIGURAE LATENTES MANIFESTO IN LUMINE
NOBIS GAUDIUM DENT.
ONE, TWO AND THREE, FIVE, EIGHT
SUNFLOWER SPIRAL, PINEAPPLE SCALES
SEASHELL WHORL, HIVE OF BEES
EVEN CORPUS HUMANUM PLEASE.
TWO HANDS, TWO FEET, FIVE DIGITS, THREE PARTS
SURELY NOT HUMDRUM, HEART-TO-HEARTS
PATTERNS HIDDEN IN BROAD DAYLIGHT,
THESE SHOULD BRING US MUCH DELIGHT.

The next day was bright and sunny, but very cold, with clear blue skies. Wil decided to visit Master Meninx during the lunch hour. After telling everyone he had to get something from his locker, Wil left the West Hall early, leaving Sophie, Phinneas and Beatriz still munching tuna fish sandwiches from a large platter on their table.

Master Meninx was the school physician; and the infirmary was near the main office, just down the hall from Stone Hall. The first, last, and only time Wil had visited the infirmary was for a good case of *carbunculosus*—an itchy and painful rash—contracted when he had mistakenly brushed against one of Mage Radix's prickly cactuses his very first day at Gruffud's.

Wil stood staring at the small sign on the large, white infirmary door: *Master E. Meninx*. He took a breath and knocked on the door.

"Come in," said a voice.

The infirmary was exactly how Wil remembered it—a long, white room lined in shelves with hundreds of glass flasks, filled with coloured powders and clotted liquids or strange bits of plants and animals. And it had the same unmistakable, sharp, sour smell—like ammonia and apple cider vinegar.

The only thing missing was the gigantic fish—Wil now knew it must have been a catfish—that Master Meninx had been dissecting the day of Wil's visit.

Master Meninx was sitting at his desk reading. He was a small man with a circlet of brown hair on a marbled head. He looked up and his eyes slowly focused on Wil.

"May I help you?" he asked.

"I'm looking for information," Wil said.

Master Meninx looked at Wil from over his glasses. "Ah, information," he said. "And what sort of information are you looking for?"

"Do you remember last year I had a rash from one of the cactuses?" Wil asked.

"Yes, *carbuncolusus*, as I recall," said Master Meninx.

"When I came here, you had a fish on your table, it was dead and you were cutting it open," said Wil, thinking that Master Meninx must be wondering why in snake's name he wanted to know about a dead fish.

"*Ictalurus punctatus*," said Master Meninx. "Channel catfish."

"It had lots of whiskers," said Wil.

"Eight, to be precise," said Master Meninx. He looked at Wil shrewdly. "What would you like to know about the channel catfish…Mr. Wychwood, isn't it?"

Wil gulped. Actually, he didn't know exactly what he wanted to know. He had the almost irresistible urge to tell Master Meninx everything all at once. I've been seeing fish everywhere I go and Peeping Peerslie gave me a library book about fish (but I haven't been able to read it yet because it smells terrible, like an old, rotting fish). And my cousin Sophie and I were down by the river, and we were surrounded by fog and then there was this strange, old woman and she had long whiskers and there were ghosts with weird, green, glowing eyes floating all around her. The woman called herself Catfysh and she said the balance between the magical and non-magical worlds had been disturbed and that Sophie and I would have do what needed to be done, but she didn't tell us what it was we had to do…

All this was racing through Wil's mind, and he stopped himself from speaking, when he remembered Catfysh's instructions. *Tell no one.*

"I…I…I…don't know," said Wil lamely.

"What do they eat, how long do they live, where do they like to hide?" suggested Master Meninx.

"No," said Wil. He took a breath and then blurted out, "Is it possible for a fish to become a human?"

Master Meninx looked very surprised. "Why do you need to know?" he asked finally.

"I had a dream," said Wil, "that I met an old woman; she was wearing a silver cloak. She waved her cloak and slipped underneath the water—I think she turned into a fish."

"Did she say anything to you in this dream?" asked Master Meninx.

"Um…no," said Wil. "No, it was a very short dream."

"That sounds like an interesting dream, Mr. Wychwood," said Master Meninx. "It's not often that such things come to us. I would take it as a gift if I were you. There are many stories of humans being transformed into fish and fish taking human form. They are part of the mythologies of people all around the world.

"I have a particular interest in fish. Would you like to see my collection?"

"Sure," said Wil, thinking that Master Meninx must have different kinds of gold fish and snails and things. He had had a teacher in grade two, who kept a Siamese fighting fish in the classroom. It was a brilliant, rich blue colour with a veil tail. He remembered vividly how the fish used to puff up and flare its fins whenever a mirror was held up to the fishbowl and it saw The Enemy.

Wil followed Master Meninx to a metal door at the end of the office—a door he not noticed before. Above the door hung a dried, dessicated lizard, which had been mounted on wooden sticks. Its arms and legs were unnaturally stiff and outstretched. Wil felt queasy as he looked at the lizard.

That queasy feeling exploded when Master Meninx opened the door.

Shelves and shelves and jars and jars of fish—pickled fish, their bodies twisted and warped, skin mottled and wrinkled, eyes clouded and unseeing. Pale corpses floating in their glass sarcophagi. Shining row after shining row of them. And not only fish. Other jars had pickled snakes in them…frogs, salamanders, and giant toads—their pale limbs were splayed and motionless, suspended in green liquid. Each and every jar was carefully labelled with the name of the creature, a date and the place where it had been captured.

Wil had never seen so many dead things in one place. It was overwhelming. He hardly knew what to say, but Master Meninx was obviously so proud of the collection, that Wil had to say something.

"It's…it's…it's amazing," Wil stammered. "What…ah…ah…what do you do with all these…things?"

"I study them to understand how they live," said Master Meninx.

"But they're all dead," exclaimed Wil.

"Oh, these creatures aren't dead, Mr. Wychwood—*pisces immortales facti sunt,*" said Master Meninx. They're immortalized. *Fatum ignominiosum effugerunt atque numquam ipsi se patientur mandi et devorari. Neque putescent neque in pulverem decrescent.* They shall never suffer the ignominious fate of being chewed and digested. They shall never rot, nor shall they dwindle to dust."

Wil felt woozy, as if he were about to faint. If Catfysh really were a fish, he wondered, and Master Meninx caught her, would he try to pickle her too?

Somehow, he didn't think that would go over very well with Catfysh.

✣ ✣ ✣

His mind still filled with all the jars of dead fish and reptiles, Wil slid into his seat in numeristics just as the class was about to begin.

"Where were you?" asked Phinneas.

"I…I was…I was looking at fish," whispered Wil.

"Are we quite ready to begin, Mr. Wychwood," said Mage Adderson, her eyes gimlet sharp, "or shall the class wait for your little conversation to end?"

Wil felt his face redden. Sygnithia Sly and Regina Piehard were snickering behind him. He ducked his head and busied himself with pulling out his notebook and pencils.

"As all of you know," said Mage Adderson, "one of the basic principles in numeristics is that numbers, whether we appreciate it or not, rule our lives. Even if you are entirely ignorant of numerical relationships, they underlie everything that we do, including the design of our buildings. In large, public, monumental buildings, however, numerals can play an even more ambitious role than mere functional ratios.

"According to the principles inherent in numeristics, the dance of numbers actually has the capacity to inspire ordinary humans to look beyond their own small, petty lives. A building becomes a blueprint for living perfection, exhorting all those who live and work within its walls, indeed within the city-at-large, to strive for that state of perfection.

"It is for this reason that I have made arrangements for a special field trip in a couple of weeks to Manitoba's Legislative Building. Within our world it is known, of course, as the *Palace of the Blazing Star*, a historic building that draws upon ancient Greek, Roman and Egyptian traditions. The school tour is offered by the staff at the Legislative Building, and so it is geared primarily to a non-mage audience. But I did not want to refuse the tour, as that might have appeared odd. So keep in mind, as we take our tour, that there are many layers of knowledge embedded in the building. And I need not remind you that you are not to betray the existence of our community on this tour. If those outside MiddleGate were to suspect its existence, history may repeat itself.

"What is of most interest to us in this class, is how many aspects of the Palace of the Blazing Star appear to be designed according to the

Fibonacci sequence, an important concept for our magical studies. A very important concept," repeated Mage Adderson.

Mage Adderson paused while the piece of chalk rose from her desk and wrote FIBONACCI SEQUENCE on the board in large letters. "Please note the spelling. There is one *B*, one *N* and two C's in Fibonacci. Anyone spelling this word incorrectly on your homework assignments or tests will have marks deducted.

"Does anyone know what the Fibonacci sequence is?" Mage Adderson looked around the class much as an eagle would scan the landscape for prey.

No one lifted a hand.

"No?" said Mage Adderson. "When I was your age, I was already reading Gottridge's famous treatise on the Fibonacci sequence. I can tell that there are none so enthusiastic in this classroom. A pity…certainly a pity."

The chalk began to write a series of numbers of the board.

0, 1, 1, 2, 3, 5, 8, 13, 21…

"Notice that each number represents the sum of the two numbers previous. 1 plus 0 equals 1. 1 plus 2 equals 3, 2 plus 3 equals 5, 3 plus 5 equals 8, and so on. These numbers are part of the famous mathematical sequence discovered by Leonardo Fibonacci, a 12th century mathematician. This pattern—considered by many to be a divine blueprint for life—underlies many of nature's projects, from how a seashell grows, the growth pattern of seeds in a sunflower, and even the measurements of human fingers, hands and arms.

"We will be exploring the Fibonacci sequence over the next couple of weeks in class, and I have placed several books on reserve in the Library for your use.

"I will be asking you to analyze the building in terms of these numbers, particularly the first six—1, 2, 3, 5, 8 and 13. Think of it as a scavenger hunt. When we visit the building next week, I want you to search out every instance of the sequence that you can find.

"And your homework for this week is to calculate the first twenty-five numbers of the Fibonacci sequence."

✣ ✣ ✣

"I can't believe how much homework we've got," groaned Beatriz after numeristics. "And having to calculate the first 25 numbers of the Fibonacci sequence is a bit much, isn't it? They get big awfully fast."

"At least Adderson didn't ask us to do the first one hundred," said Sophie. "It could have been worse."

"Right," said Phinneas.

"I really don't get the point," said Wil. "Why does it matter, anyway, how many Fibonacci numbers are part of the Palace of the Blazing Star? It's just an old building."

"If Dad heard you say that," said Beatriz, "we'd all get a long lecture about—"

"Fortunately, he's not here," said Phinneas, "and we've already had one lecture...and we don't need another!"

⁜ ⁜ ⁜

After supper, when the dishes had been cleared, Wil and Sophie started in on their homework. Wil was leafing through a book that Sophie had taken out of the library—*Magical Numbers and Symbols in Stone*. "Would you look at that!" he exclaimed.

"What did you find?" asked Sophie, without looking up from her numeristics notebook, in which she had written long columns of calculations. "I haven't had a chance to look at it yet."

"There's a picture of the Manitoba Legislative Building. That's the Palace of the Blazing Star, right?—and there's a gold statue on top. Have you ever been inside?"

"No," said Sophie impatiently, and she erased what she had just written. "I've only seen the outside of it. You can see the big dome way in the distance when you're walking by the river behind Phinneas's and Beatriz's house."

"Maybe Adderson's assignment will be interesting after all," said Wil. "There's a picture here of two huge bison right inside the building. They're massive—they must weigh tons and tons."

"I hate these Fibonacci numbers," said Sophie, ignoring Wil and erasing another series of numbers from her notebook. "I keep adding them up wrong. It's like the numbers are wriggling, writhing and sliming all over my page."

Wil laughed and handed his numeristics notebook to Sophie. "Here, I've done those already."

"That's cheating," said Sophie, but she grabbed the notebook from Wil.

"It does look like a real palace in there," said Wil, "with all those stone steps going up. I wonder if we count the stairs...maybe that'll be a Fibonacci number. But the picture's too small to see."

Sophie frowned down at her notebook. "Can you believe it? I made a mistake back at 144. I've got to erase practically everything."

"I wonder what's on top of the roof there," Wil said, squinting at another picture of the building from the outside. "It's hard to tell, but it looks to me like...it looks like those are two sphinxes."

"What?" asked Sophie, looking up from her notebook. "Did you say *sphinxes*?"

"What do they look like to you?" asked Wil, and he passed the book to her.

Sophie peered at the pictures. "What are they doing there? Why would there be two Egyptian sphinxes on top of the Palace of the Blazing Star?" she asked. "Catfysh, didn't she say something about a black star and sphinxes—"

"—and bulls," said Wil excitedly. "Do you think she was talking about the bison statues?"

XVIII The Palace of the Blazing Star

"The Golden Boy was untouched. It was a miracle, they said—like a phoenix rising from the ashes."

CREDE VERBIS, SUIS MAGICIS ARTIBUS ANTIQUIS
ULTRA FINIS LIMINIS TEMPORIS
AUXILIUM AB EA PETAS, ET CONSORTES PETAS PLURES
UT TERRAE PISCIUM ET HOMINUM ET RELIQUORUM,
PALUDES ET SILVAE, HARENAE ET LUTUM
NON PATIANTUR TRISTEM ET TERRIBILEM MORTEM.
TRUST HER WORDS, HER MAGYK ANCIENT-OLD
BEYOND THE CATCH OF TIME'S THRESHOLD.
SEEK HER HELP AND SEEK MORE ALLIES—
LEST FISHLY, HUMAN AND OTHER LANDS,
SWAMP AND FOREST, MUD AND SANDS,
SUFFER A SAD AND DREADFUL DEMISE.

By the time of the field trip to the Palace of the Blazing Star, it was the second week in November and very cold. A sharp-toothed north wind and prickly snow scratched at Wil's face as he stepped down from the MiddleGate Bus. Shielding his eyes from the snow, he looked up at the roof of the Palace of the Blazing Star and saw the twin stone sphinxes there, one staring east and the other staring west. They looked very far away and small, hardly magical, and Wil was disappointed.

Mage Adderson quickly herded everyone up the stone steps—so quickly that Wil had barely enough time to count the steps. "One, two, three, four…"

"Hurry up, Wil," said Sophie. "The others are already inside."

"Five, six, seven..."

"Why are you muttering to yourself?" asked Sophie, looking at Wil as if he were crazy.

Wil didn't answer Sophie. He frowned as they reached the top. There were only twenty steps, not twenty-one.

A security guard sitting behind the counter at the front entrance was squinting at a list of names as Wil and Sophie squeezed in through the doors, and everyone was chattering excitedly and shaking snow from their jackets.

"—expecting you. Class of grade sixes, ten o'clock, right?" said the guard. "Ms Adderson, would you mind signing your name in our registry? The tour guide will be with you in just a moment. Could everyone please leave their jackets and bags in the large white bins? You're welcome to take your notebooks with you, but no bags are allowed in the building for security reasons. No jostling there, kids."

The guard laughed. "This is a big place! Lots of room for everyone," he joked, as he handed out red-and-white striped badges with the words *Guided Tour* on them.

Mage Adderson turned to the class, her expression grim. "I expect everyone to be on their best behaviour here. Failure to do so may result in your being prohibited from attending field trips in the future. And remember, everyone, that there are several layers of knowledge embedded in this building. I expect that you will find many interesting numerical relationships among its elements."

A woman wearing a white shirt and tie and black skirt hurried into the foyer, her sharp heels clicking with self-importance. "Welcome, welcome to the Manitoba Legislative Building, the seat of the provincial government of Manitoba," she said. "My name is Athena. I'll be your tour guide today, and I'll certainly be happy to answer any questions you may have."

"Why don't you all come this way," said the guide, and the click of her heels herded everyone along. "We'll start here in the Great Hall."

The sounds in the Great Hall were muted. No words could be distinguished, but all the sounds of human activity—cleaners polishing brass railings, a small group of tourists photographing the stairs, several suited men striding along on one of the upper floors—all the sounds swirled like eddies of smoke from a candle just extinguished.

"The building was designed by architects Frank Worthington Simon and Henry Boddington III," said the guide and she cleared her throat. "Can everyone hear me? You may want to move in a little closer. The acoustics in the hall tend to swallow voices up. Now, this building is practically in the very centre of North America—only 18 miles or 29 kilometres from the longitudinal centre of North America actually. Construction on the Legislative Building began in 1913 and continued until 1920. The original cost of the building was to have been $2.3 million and it actually ended up costing $19 million.

"Did you hear that?" whispered Wil to Sophie. "Nineteen million. I wonder how much it would cost to build now."

"You may be interested to know that the replacement value of the Building is now estimated to be over one billion dollars," said the guide.

Whispers buzzed at the guide's words and Wil grinned at Sophie, who grinned back. There was the answer.

"The crowning glory of the Legislative Building is, of course, the statue on top of the dome flanked beneath by twin sphinxes. The Golden Boy, as everyone calls him, is probably the best known symbol of Manitoba. The statue was designed by the sculptor Georges Gardet of Paris and cast in 1918 at the Barbidienne Foundry in France.

"The statue was modeled after the Greek god Hermes, messenger from the gods to humans, god of boundaries, god of poets, the god of trade and business. Hermes was also a psychopomp. Anyone know what that means?"

No one volunteered an answer, although someone muttered, "You'd have to be psycho to remember everything she's saying. Hope Adderson's not going to test us on this stuff."

The guide looked around brightly at everyone. "No takers?" she said. "Well, then…as a psychopomp, Hermes guides human souls, brings dreams, is the inventor of fire and a watchman of the night, but some say he is also a cunning thief at the gates. And from Hermes, we have, of course, the word "hermeneutics," meaning the *art of interpreting hidden meanings*. This building, as you will no doubt find, holds many, many secrets."

Wil's mind began to spin from all this information and then he heard whispering behind him. A language he didn't know…

"*—Der Golden Boy ist der griechische Gott Hermes. Der Gott der Grenzen und für diejenigen die sie übertreten, der Gott der Literatur und ausdrucksreichen Dichter, der Gott des Handels. Der Bote von Göttern* *zu Menschen, Psychopomp—der Leiter der Seelen, Bote von Träumen, Schöpfer des Feuers, der Wacht durch die Nacht über den listigen Dieb an der Pforte.*"

There was laughter—but not the kind of laughter that happens when something funny has been said, thought Wil. It had a nervous edge to it.

Wil didn't understand what the words meant—although he thought he had caught the word Hermes in there somewhere. He turned around to see who was speaking.

Three more people had joined the class tour. Two of them, a man and a woman, were both older and tanned, with startling white hair. They carried cameras and guidebooks, and were pointing to a picture of The Golden Boy in one of the books.

They must be tourists, thought Wil, and the younger man, who had a shaved head and several earrings in each ear, is translating for...his friends—or maybe they're his parents.

"—how The Golden Boy travelled to Winnipeg," continued the tour guide. "The Barbidienne Foundry was bombed during World War I and partially destroyed. But, miraculously, The Golden Boy was untouched, like a phoenix rising from the ashes."

"*Die Barbidienne Giesserei war zerbombt im Ersten Welt Krieg und vernichtet,*" whispered the young man with the shaved head. "*Aber Der Golden Boy war unberührt. Es war ein Wunder, sagten Sie—wie ein Phönix emporsteigt aus die Asche.*"

Wil turned again and watched the tourists. The older man and woman were nodding their heads at the young man's words.

"*Ein Phönix aus die Asche,*" repeated the woman, and she looked at Wil and smiled. The woman really had the most piercing, blue eyes he had ever seen—it was quite unnerving.

The three tourists left the tour after that and strolled off to examine the stone lions' heads lining the Great Hall.

Wil turned back to listen to the tour guide, wondering what the woman with the blue eyes had said, and what the younger man had been telling them.

"The Golden Boy was rushed to the seaport," continued the tour guide, "and stowed aboard a French ship carrying wheat. But the ship was commandeered for the transportation of troops before it had a chance to set out on its voyage. And The Boy lay deep in the hold of the ship. He travelled many miles across the Atlantic Ocean and back again. The ship was in constant danger. When the war ended, the Boy finally arrived in Halifax and was shipped to Winnipeg, where he was hoisted to the top of Manitoba's then new Legislative Building. And his torch was lit in 1970 as part of Manitoba's Centennial Celebration.

"The same sculptor who made the Golden Boy also designed the two North American bison flanking the Grand Staircase here. Each bison is hollow and weighs 2,268 kilograms or 5,000 pounds. Story has it that the bison sculptures were slid in on rafts of ice during construction so as not to scratch the exquisite marble floors."

"I think it's a male," whispered Phinneas, as he peered underneath one of the sculptures.

Wil leaned down to take a look himself and grinned. "I think you're right," he said.

"As we ascend the Grand Staircase," said the tour guide, "you may notice that the staircase is arranged in three flights of thirteen steps made of Carrara marble. The number thirteen figures prominently throughout the building. There are also thirteen light bulbs in the lamps that light the rotunda at the top of the stairs.

Wil quickly scribbled in his notebook...*2 bulls, 3 flights of stairs (grand stairs) with 13 steps, 13 light bulbs (rotunda).* Four Fibonacci's so far, he thought.

"There are Egyptian, Greek and Roman motifs throughout the building. Above our heads here, the head of Athena, the armed warrior goddess, goddess of civilization and wisdom, protector of the city and my namesake," said the tour guide with a tinkling laugh. "And at the top of the stairs, you can see a stone carving of the head of Medusa, covered in snakes. Her name comes directly from the Greek, meaning guardian or protecteress. Gazing upon her could turn onlookers to stone, according to some of the myths. Both Athena and Medusa watch over the entrance to the building, as do the bison and, of course, the lions' heads. The building is filled with many such decorative and stylistic elements.

"The stone from which the Legislative Building was built is Tyndall limestone from the town of Garson and is 500 million years old, dating to the time when this area was a tropical sea. The cream-coloured stone is filled with fossils; you will find them throughout the building. The fossils are easy to locate because they've been darkened by the touch of many people over the years. And when we get to the second floor, you'll see one of the fossils that some of us say is the ghost of the man who built the Legislative Building." The tour guide laughed again as she said this. "It really does look like a skull."

The guide led them down a set of stairs to a large, circular, low-ceilinged chamber—the Pool of the Black Star. In the very middle of the room was a black eight-pointed star.

"The acoustics in this room are quite special," said the tour guide. "If you stand here in the middle of the star and sing, you can hear the sound throughout the whole building. It echoes and reverberates in quite a special way. Would you like to try?" she asked, looking at Beatriz.

Beatriz's face turned beet red, but she stepped into the middle of the black star.

"Try saying something," said the tour guide encouragingly. "Why don't you say the word echo?"

Beatriz threw back her head and shouted *ECH-O-O-O!*

The word funneled up through the circular opening in the ceiling to the great dome above, rebounded back down and echoed in the chamber of the Pool of the Black Star.

A flurry of *Can-I-try's?'s* broke out, and the tour guide smiled. "You see what I mean? The designers must have known exactly what they were doing when they designed the building. They knew this room would function as an echo chamber. It's proportioned that perfectly."

As they were standing in the room of the Pool of the Black Star, Wil had the strangest sensation that someone or something was watching him. He looked behind him. There was only a tall lamp by the wall of the chamber, but when he glanced down at the foot of the lamp, he saw a whiskered fish-like creature with two outstretched wing-like fins staring up at him.

It winked.

Wil closed his eyes and opened them again. The creature was now nothing but a hard, metal decoration at the bottom of the lamp. He must have imagined that it was alive.

An hour later, by the time the tour had ended, Wil's list of Fibonacci's had grown, including five different kinds of columns in the building, eight triangles and points in the Black Star, eight lamps between the columns in the Pool of the Black Star, eight columns circling the perimeter of the round room on the second floor, thirteen lamps in the rotunda above the Pool of the Black Star, thirteen circular circles around the chamber door to the Legislature, thirteen lights lining the corridors…

Mage Adderson had been right. The Fibonacci sequence seemed to be everywhere. Mage Adderson, for her part, looked as if she were really enjoying herself. Being surrounded by a building that so adored the order of numbers could not help but make her very happy, thought Wil.

✣ ✣ ✣

That night, at supper, Wil and Sophie could not stop talking about their visit to the Palace of the Blazing Star, in between bites of delicious roast chicken, rice and corn. Aunt Rue and Aunt Violet listened with great interest to their adventures.

"I haven't visited the Palace of the Blazing Star in years," said Aunt Rue. "And I'd forgotten the heads of Athena and Medusa were there. I do remember that echo chamber though. You really feel like you're at the centre of the world when you're standing in the middle of that black star, looking up at the dome high above."

"The last time I went was…actually I can't remember the last time I went," said Aunt Violet, "it's been that long. Just shameful.

"It's odd that you both were there today, because I heard something interesting from one of the visitors to the shop. Word about the shop has really been spreading, you know. I think I'm going to have to start taking people by appointment only soon."

"I can't tell who it was, of course, because I have to protect the identity of anyone who comes to visit. Whatever details they tell me about their personal lives must remain mostly confidential, but I don't think I'd be contravening anything by telling you what I learned. It was after our session anyway.

"They said that they'd heard there was a political plot afoot, something to do with the Manitoba Legislative Building, our Palace of the Blazing Star. They're hiring more people for security apparently. No one's quite sure what the threat is, but everyone is taking it very seriously. I wonder if they will keep giving tours to the general public."

"That's terrible," said Sophie. "We can't let anything happen to that building. It's the most…the most beautiful building I've ever been in," she declared. "It does make you feel as if you're at the centre of the world."

✣ ✣ ✣

As Wil sat on his bed and stroked Esme's cool, smooth scales and thought back over the day, he wondered again about that fish creature or whatever it was at the base of the lamp in the echo chamber.

"It really did wink, Esme," he said.

Esme coiled around his wrist, her tongue flicking at the air.

"Do you think I imagined it?" he asked.

Esme turned away from Wil and slithered down his arm onto the bed. She slid across the covers towards the window.

Wil's eyes followed her and his gaze fell on the towel, which was still hanging from the branch of the tree outside his window. He had completely forgotten that it was there.

"You want me to look at that stinky book?" he said. "Do I have to?"

Esme looked back at Wil, as if to say, "If you don't want to know what I think, don't ask me."

"All right, all right," he said. "I'll look at it—but not for long. You really want this whole room to smell like rotten fish?"

Wil picked up Esme and dropped her back into her cage. She burrowed into the soil immediately, and Wil had to laugh. "You think the smell won't get you under there?"

He walked over to the window and opened it, then reached for the towel. He could feel the book still nestled inside.

He closed the window, and holding his nose, he opened the bundle.

Being outside in the fresh air seemed to have taken the edge off the book's fishiness. Wil sniffed the cover. As a matter of fact, the book didn't seem to smell very much of fish at all, and the cover of the book seemed like a perfectly ordinary cover. The catfish on it did not look at him, waggle its whiskers, twitch its tail, or do anything at all out of the ordinary. Wil heaved a sigh of relief.

"Esme, it's safe to come out. The book won't bite you! It doesn't smell any more."

But Esme must have decided to retire for the night; she didn't even poke her snout out.

Wil opened the book at random to page 59 and began reading about ancient Egyptian headache remedies—anti-headache incantations, spells and conjurations that were recorded in the magical texts of the New Kingdom. What did all this have to do with catfish? He continued to read on. The chapter began with the observation, *Magic is Useful with Medicine and Medicine is Useful with Magic.*

> *Interestingly, King Narmer, one of the Egyptian Kings, was represented in part by the sign of the catfish. The catfish is also a symbol of a night demon that tortured the god Horus with headaches of such severity that he was forced to live in the dark. A recipe for pains on one side of*

the head calls for the skulls of catfish to be heated until they turn to ashes. The ashes are then boiled in oil and the afflicted head is rubbed with the mixture for four days.

That's really gross, thought Wil. Who'd want to rub dead catfish ashes on their head? You'd have to be really desperate.

Another strategy was to recite a special spell several times over a snake coiling in the hand, and then the head should be rubbed with the coil.

"Did you hear that Esme?" Wil whispered. "You can help cure my headache, if I ever get one."

He continued reading down a list of other substances reputed to cure headaches: various kinds of fishbones, stag's horn, ass's grease, cow fat and goose fat, honey, coriander seeds, cumin, dill seed, the fruit of carob trees and others more obscure.

Wil began to feel as if he might get a headache soon if he kept on reading about headaches, and so he flipped to the back of the book, where there were recipes. On page 193, there was one for *Soured Catfish Heads.* That sounded interesting.

Save those catfish head for this succulent treat. Remove the insides and the eyes from the catfish heads.

At the bit about the eyes, Wil almost closed the book, but his curiosity got the better of him.

Boil the heads in well-salted water for 30 minutes. Cover the boiled catfish heads with three gallons of buttermilk in a large stone crock pot. Ensure the heads are completely covered with the buttermilk. Soak them for eleven days. Serve cold.

Hoping fervently that he would never be faced with a plate of soured catfish heads, he turned to the table of contents. As he skimmed it, he saw a chapter entitled *Catfish, Sovereign Ruler of the River.* That's the one I should read! he thought and turned to page 47.

The page, though, was completely blank but for a few stains that looked like water ripples.

Wil turned the page to 48, 49, 50, 51—all the pages were blank, but for the page number.

"What?" he exclaimed.

He flipped back to page 193, but now it too was blank.

"What happened to that *Soured Catfish Heads* recipe?"

He turned the book over to look at the front cover. And the fish was gone!

"What kind of a book disappears its own pages—and even its own cover?" he whispered, and he opened the book again to page 47. This time the ripples shimmered and the whole page turned to water; a bubble floated along its surface, then popped.

A voice spoke. It seemed to come from inside the book… from underneath the water. The voice was soft, so soft he could barely hear the words. He bent his head down and his nose wrinkled, for the water smelled very fishy.

Glorious where she doth dwell
far below 'neath water's swell,
Catfysh, Protecteress the Immortelle.
For once thou see'st her, shalt thou ever forget
whiskered visage, eyes moonset?
Trust her words, her magyk ancient-old
beyond the catch of time's threshold.
Seek her help and others besides
lest fishly, human and other lands,
swamp and forest, mud and sands,
suffer sad and dreadful tides.

With that, the book gently (and firmly) closed of its own accord.

How long Wil stared at the cover of the book, replaying what the voice had told him—*her magyk ancient-old.* A splinter of doubt—

"But how can I trust what this book says?" he said. "Catfysh herself might have bewitched it somehow."

As he spoke the words, he felt a sudden warmth from the black medallion hanging beneath his shirt. He pulled it out. The figure of the golden fish was so bright that the symbols of the snake and the bee beside it were quite dim in comparison. The medallion grew heavy as a stone in his hand.

XIX Remember

"No one can catch Catfysh!"

AD MERIDIEM
ALNITAK, ALNILAM ET MINTAKA
TRES ASTRA IN ZONA ORIONIS MICABANT
TO THE SOUTH TWINKLED
ALNITAK, ALNILAM AND MINTAKA,
THE THREE STARS ON ORION'S BELT.

It was already the middle of winter, the term well behind, and Winterlude Festival was in full swing. Bundled in their winter coats, wool scarves, hats, mitts and heavy boots, Wil, Sophie, Phinneas and Beatriz hurried over to the snowcandy stand and bought four striped and towering swirls of purple and yellow snowcandy with the special blue Winterlude coins. Fairy floss, dragon's beard candy, cotton candy—snowcandy by any other name—soft and as fluffy as a cloud, a heavenly sweet that melted in your mouth. The Winterlude Festival wouldn't be the same without it.

Squealing and laughing, they clambered to the top of the icy ditchball hill. It was nearing sunset and the crowds were assembling on top of the hill for the start of the ditchball games, which always began at sundown.

Wil lagged behind the others, remembering all too vividly everything that had happened last year, when he had been injured in the game. He had been playing on the silver and black Nox team against the gold and blue Lux team. He could still hear the crowd's chanting in his mind. "*Ditch, ditch! Bewitch the ditch! A stitch, a snitch, a switch, the ditch! A quitch, a scritch, the ditch, the ditch!*" And then the large rainbow-coloured ditchball had fallen right on top of him.

"Let's go," Wil said abruptly, thinking that he never wanted to play a game of ditchball again in his entire life. When Mage Quartz had asked him if he wanted to play again this year, Wil had politely declined.

"What's wrong?" said Phinneas , looking down into the long icy ditch, which had been cut right through the middle of the hill. "We just got here. Aren't we going to stay and watch the game?"

"You can if you want to," said Wil. "But it wasn't very much fun when I got hit by the ditchball last year and then ended up getting dragged off by Rufus Crookshank."

⁜ ⁜ ⁜

Cradling cups of hot chocolate, the four children wandered down to the river to watch the skaters. They could hearing chanting in the distance, "*Ditch, ditch! Bewitch the ditch! A stitch, a snitch, a switch, the ditch!*

The ditchball game must have started, thought Wil.

The first stars were just beginning to fill the cold, clear sky, which was darkening to that wonderful, deepest of blues that only a winter sky enjoys. It was a blue to rival the velvet folds of royal robes encrusted with pearls and diamonds. A blue to rival the promise of fresh wild blueberries in a snatch of thick cream. A blue to rival the dangerous sheen of a firebird egg, the shout of a larkspur bloom, the proud feathers of a quarrelsome blue jay.

Ice dancers wearing tall icicle crowns were gliding hand-in-hand in a long sinuous line on the frozen river. People lined up along the riverbank to watch them and clapped and whistled as the line of dancers swooped past.

Sophie pointed to a couple of small, wooden ice shanties where a circle of people were standing. They were all looking down at something. "What's going on over there?" she asked.

The four children tromped down the side of the riverbank to get a closer look. Someone had chopped a large hole in the ice, a hole at least a foot wide and half a foot deep. Dark, shadowed water sloshed at the icy edges of the hole and glinted by the light of three large candles in storm lanterns.

A man dressed in a heavy jacket with a fur hood, which obscured his face, was holding a fishing line—it had a small fish dangling from it. The man removed the fish from the hook and gently slipped it back into the icy water.

"Better luck next time," quipped someone in the crowd.

"Fishing in winter?" said Wil. "Who would go fishing in winter? Are there fish?" he asked.

"Of course there are fish," said Phinneas. "Didn't we just see one? They don't care if it's cold and snowy."

The man with the fur hood stuck another bit of bait on the end of his fish-hook and lowered the hook into the water just below the surface, then fished it down slowly and jigged the line so that it quivered slightly.

"What if he catches something?" asked Wil. "He's not going to kill it, is he?"

"What's the matter?" asked Beatriz. "They're just fish. We eat them all the time."

The man with the fur hood tugged at the line a couple of times, but nothing else, for the moment, seemed interested in biting.

"I know," said Wil, "but this is…this is different. It's hard enough on a fish just to get through the winter until spring, let alone having someone go after you with a hook like that. How would you feel?"

A great groan from the ice answered Wil's question. Wil imagined the groan was asking, *Who's Wil?* Or perhaps it was *Whose will?*

"Did you hear the ice groan?" asked Wil.

"The voice from the icy deep," said Beatriz with a laugh.

"No, really," protested Wil. "I didn't know ice could groan. I heard it…it…it sounded like it said, *Whose will?*—or something."

But Beatriz and Phinneas had already pushed to the front of the crowd to watch the line in the water, and didn't hear what Wil had said.

"Maybe it was Catſysh," whispered Sophie. "Or the ice was carrying a message from her."

"Do you think…she's here…underneath us?" whispered Wil.

The ice groaned again. This time, Wil thought he heard, "Wils-s-s-so, r'm'mb'r." But whether it was the ice or merely the wind in the branches above their heads, Wil wasn't sure. "I hope that man doesn't catch Catfysh," he said.

"No one can catch Catfysh!" said Sophie.

A chill gust of wind swirled snow powder around their faces, and Wil fancied that Catfysh was laughing at them. High above their heads, the northern lights streaked across the sky like a great, glimmering, jade fish. And like a school of silver minnows, the ice dancers darted along the surface of the river's ice and turned as one, their skates flashing.

XX A Lady's Malady

A large, pink envelope—as pink as bubblegum—
with a fancy letter V on it.

DELUDENS, ILLUDENS, PERTURBANS,
CAUTUM IUDICIUM, INCERTUS PROGNOSIS.
OPERAM DEMUS UT SPEREMUS OPTIMA.
OMNES QUOS ROGAVIMUS NOBIS IMPERAVERUNT
UT REQUIESCEREMUS.
MORBI HUIC SIMILES NON PEREUNT
UNA NOCTE, UNA HEBDOMADE, UNO MENSE, DECEM ANNIS.
DELUSION, ILLUSION...OR IS IT CONFUSION?
CAUTIOUS DIAGNOSIS, DOUBTFUL PROGNOSIS.
THE BEST WE CAN DO IS HOPE FOR THE BEST.
ALL THOSE WE CONSULT SAY PLENTY OF REST.
SUCH MALADIES AS THIS DO NOT DISAPPEAR
OVERNIGHT, IN A WEEK, IN A MONTH...OR TEN YEARS.

Winter's grip on MiddleGate had not lessened by the middle of February. Sophie was beginning to feel as if snow and ice and sleet would never give way to spring's fog and puddles and mud. Every time she looked in a mirror, the colour of her eyeglass frames seemed to have settled into a permanent beige, the colour of old potato skin.

And Aunt Rue seemed to have gone into a permanent slump after her interview at the beginning of the year for the position of Assistant Deputy Minister. It was almost six weeks since the interview, which had gone very well. Minister Skelch continued to utter encouraging words and mutter about "committee decisions, administrative delays, the usual bureaucratic inertia, you know"—but Sophie could tell that Aunt Rue had lost hope of ever being offered the job.

When Sophie cast about for something to say to bolster Aunt Rue's spirits, her mind felt empty with nothing but dry crumbs, a broken quill pen and a crumpled ball of paper rattling around in it.

Mr. Bertram had not visited them in weeks, even though he always greeted Sophie and Wil enthusiastically whenever he saw them in the library and often had several books set aside for them. Wil kept talking about missing the days of Pirsstle and Bertram's Antiquarian Booksellers when he and Mr. Bertram had had all the time in the world to unpack and examine the latest shipment of books from Australia and New Zealand or elsewhere overseas.

Cadmus had taken to sleeping long hours; and when he wasn't sleeping, he meowed to be fed. His moulted fur gathered in clumps in the corners of her bedroom, on the stairs, underneath the chairs. Sophie had even found a tuft stuck to her toothbrush one morning.

Nothing was happening and nothing ever would happen, thought Sophie. Each day was a slow-motion round of the same old classes, the same old people, homework done and homework not done. Even though the days were slowly getting longer and it was no longer dark at four-thirty in the afternoon, Sophie felt some days as if she could barely put one foot in front of the other. It wasn't a question of sleep; instead a sense of dull fuzziness coated everything, from walking up the stairs, to reading a book, to eating lunch with everyone—as if she were waiting for something to happen.

Even Esme seemed affected by what everyone kept referring to as the *February scalies* and had taken to hiding under the soil in her cage; she had moulted twice since the autumn.

But Aunt Violet was full of schemes as always. She and Ursula von Scrum, the artist they had met at the Dragonfly Festival last summer, had been meeting regularly for tea, and von Scrum had agreed to paint a portrait of Aunt Violet for her shop. The idea was that those visiting Aunt Violet would see the portrait and want to have a portrait painted of themselves. Aunt Violet had gone through practically every dress in her closet and tried them all on, but none had been quite right *to be immortalized*, as she put it.

Extra security measures at the Palace of the Blazing Star had quelled trouble, it seemed—if indeed there had been trouble brewing. Nothing had been reported in the *Daily Magazine*, as far as Sophie knew, and Aunt Violet said it was probably all rumour and gossip anyway. Instead, the upcoming elections—and the countdown race among Barry Burrymore, Stan Ruddler, Eliza Raizen and J.J. Rosie (and several others whose names Sophie couldn't remember) were dominating the local news.

Memories of Catfysh, her strange followers and her mysterious words had faded like an old photograph in Sophie's mind. She and Wil barely mentioned the name Catfysh any more. It was just plain easier not to think about Catfysh, especially since they had not been able to tell Phinneas and Beatriz about her. And there did not seem to be any particular urgency to her message, as the uneventful weeks and months slugged by.

It was mid-morning on a Saturday when Phinneas and Beatriz knocked at their door. Their cheeks were red, their noses dripping, and as they stamped snow from their boots, a whoosh of frigid north wind swept into the house.

Beatriz was holding a large, pink envelope—as pink as chewed bubblegum—with a fancy letter *V* on it.

"What's that?" asked Sophie.

And for the first time in days, the frames of her eyeglasses changed colour from boring beige to white tinged with rosy pink and gold flecks.

"Guess!" said Beatriz, holding the envelope behind her back.

"If it's got a *V* on it, it must be for Aunt Violet," said Sophie.

"Good guess, but…NO!" said Phinneas, who was dancing from foot to foot with excitement.

"Try again," said Beatriz, holding the envelope high above her head and twirling around.

"Give us a hint," said Wil.

"It has something to do with a holiday," said Phinneas with a grin.

"Holiday," said Sophie, thinking hard. "Is there a holiday soon?"

"Valentines!" said Wil. "February 14—it's got something to do with Valentine's Day, right?"

"We're having our very first party in our new house," said Beatriz. "Mum thought it would be a lot of fun, seeing as the winter is dragging everyone down."

"Aunt Rue and Aunt Violet are invited too," said Phinneas. "And everyone has to wear something very red or—"

"Or we won't let you in the door," said Beatriz, and she made an ugly face.

✣ ✣ ✣

Aunt Violet was thrown into a complete tizz-wozz by the pink envelope and its contents.

"We haven't had an invitation to a party in years, Rue! What in snake's name shall I wear? Something red, and all I have is purple, purple and purple."

"Purple is kind of like red," said Wil, obviously trying to be helpful.

"That's like saying that orange is the new pink!" exclaimed Sophie, looking at Wil as if he had just said the stupidest thing in the world. She leaned forward and whispered. "Didn't you learn anything from the bees?"

"Children, I think we've got two red cloaks in the closet," said Aunt Rue, whose voice was very flat these days. "Those would probably work very well for you." Not even the news of a Valentine's Day party had brought any spark to her eyes.

✣ ✣ ✣

Late in the afternoon, February 14th, only four hours before the Bain's Valentine's Day party, Aunt Violet disappeared into the bathroom and didn't come out for more than two hours, even though Sophie and Wil knocked on the bathroom door innumerable times.

"Aunt Violet," Sophie said, "why are you taking so long? Are you all right?"

"Of course, I'm all right," came the muffled reply. "I'm just making myself look beautiful." Aunt Violet began to sing an old ditty off-key. Her quavering voice sparked a volley of giggles from Wil and Sophie.

Won't you be my Valentine
Oh don't make me pine
For time's a-wastin'... time's a-wastin'...

"Can we see?" Sophie asked.

"Not yet...not yet," Aunt Violet replied, sounding a little edgy, and they could hear the sounds of running water.

When she finally opened the door, Sophie and Wil—who had been sitting outside the bathroom door for the last half hour, waiting for Aunt Violet to emerge—squealed.

Aunt Violet's hair was no longer purple. Instead, it was a dizzy, vivid, brilliant, shining, fiery, unapologetically gaudy, gushing, juicy red!

"You like it?" Aunt Violet said, patting her hair nervously.

"It's…it's…red," said Wil, stating the obvious. "You look really different."

"Can we still call you Aunt Violet?" asked Sophie.

"Aunt Cherry," whispered Wil. "We have to call her Aunt Cherry."

Aunt Violet laughed. "Aunt Cherry is a very nice name, but the red is temporary, just for tonight—the box says you can wash it out. I bought it specially at that new shop on the corner—the one that sells beauty supplies. The woman there—I think she said her name was Sharaminda—assured me that this was the top hair colouring they had. It's called *Roaring Red Rascal.* And I got a lovely dress to go with it. Wait until you see!"

Aunt Violet bustled down the hallway to her room and emerged an hour later, dressed in a fit of red ruffles from head to toe, topped with a large, round, white collar. She had painted her fingernails red and her lips were glazed with shiny red lipstick. Aunt Violet looked like a formidable three-dimensional Valentine's Day card. Either that or she was a giant, walking strawberry with whipped cream on top.

She could have shamed a tomato into thinking it was merely sunburnt, thought Wil. It was pretty impressive. "You look beautiful," he said, thinking that sometimes you don't really know a person, even when you think you do.

Aunt Violet was crazy. Not scaly crazy—the kind of crazy that's scary and hurts someone, and they'll send you to the MiddleGate Sanatorium for. But special crazy—the kind of crazy that makes you laugh and you're happy that you have an aunt like Aunt Violet.

Aunt Violet gave both Sophie and Wil huge hugs, and they were crushed by red ruffles and frothy lace.

✣ ✣ ✣

The Bain house was ablaze with light. Red streamers hung from the chandelier in the living room and red paper hearts were strung from window to window. The dining room table was filled with delicious foods. In the middle of it all was a bubbling, gurgling chocolate fountain surrounded by dishes of little cakes, chunks of pineapple, plump strawberries, juicy wedges of orange, slivers of banana slices.

The house was filled with guests, only a few of whom Wil recognized. Mrs. Bain looked radiant in a long white gown with a single, large red rose fastened at her shoulder. Her hair was gathered high on her head. And Mr. Bain was wearing a velvet red dinner jacket; brilliant red socks peeped out from underneath his trousers. Phinneas was sporting a pair of pants with wide red and white stripes and a white tie with a large red heart on it; and Beatriz had a puffy white crinoline skirt with huge red polka dots the size of grapefruits. She looked like a prancing tea cozy.

Every guest had taken to heart the instruction to wear something red. Ribbons and flowers in hair, jewels, belts, long gloves up to elbows, striped socks, fancy lace dresses, velvet robes, sequinned jackets all shouted red—but no one else had gone all out and dyed their hair red, not like Aunt Violet.

And even though Aunt Rue was wearing a long black velvet dress, she had tucked a brilliant red carnation in her braided hair. For the moment, she seemed to have shed her disappointment about not being offered the Assistant Deputy Minister job. Wil thought that she actually looked quite beautiful, even elegant.

A large bowl of fruit punch with juicy strawberries floating in it was set by the front door. Beatriz's and Phinneas's older sister Elenie was busy ladling out punch for the guests as they arrived, while their brother Olly took everyone's coats. Both of them had painted a large red heart on their face, a single black arrow from one cheek to the other, and Elenie was wearing the shortest skirt Wil had ever seen with black fishnet stockings and thigh high black leather boots. Their brother Luther, wearing a brilliant red top hat, was tending the fire.

"That fruit punch looks really bloody," said Wil, peering into the large glass punch bowl.

"Ziggy won't even look at it," said Elenie with a grin. "He thinks it'll kill him. We told him it was dragon's blood that we'd ordered in specially for the occasion."

Aunt Rue and Aunt Violet began chatting with several other guests, and Wil and Sophie scampered after Phinneas and Beatriz to dip strawberries in the fountain of chocolate. As he was about to dip his fifth strawberry, or was it his sixth—he had already lost count—Wil thought he heard the word *fish* fly through the air. Someone was talking about fish...that woman standing over by the living room window nearest the river. She was wearing a long, silvery blue sequinned dress, which reminded Wil of glistening fish scales, and a feather hat with an enormous crimson feather that swayed and dipped every time she spoke. The man standing beside her—he was wearing a small red bow tie around his neck—was leaning forward, obviously listening carefully to what the woman was telling him.

Wil hurriedly dipped the strawberry into the chocolate and moved quietly towards the window, trying not to draw any attention to himself. He pretended to be looking at the shelf of books behind a large wing-backed chair. He was listening so hard, his ears hurt; he scarcely noticed that Mr. Bertram had just arrived.

"It's a puzzling case of entrancement," the woman was saying. "She truly seems to believe that she's a fish and refuses to recognize her family as her own. She wants to return to the water. She actually escaped one day from our locked ward and we found her down by the river, just in time. We had to pull her out; she can't swim—not even a snake slither—she just flails about, not even realizing she's about to drown. Unfortunately, we've had to restrain her for her own safety. And the peculiar thing is she keeps babbling about a woman she calls Catfysh, spelled with a y—she was quite specific about that. And get this, the fish told her that the Palace of the Blazing Star was going to be invaded by terrorists. The ravings of an absolute lunatic—very sad really. You can imagine how distraught the poor woman's family is—they want their mother back."

At the words *babbling about a woman she calls Catfysh,* Wil's heart began to beat wildly. So the woman-who-thought-she-was-a-fish had met Catfysh too. And his next thought was, but the woman-who-thought-she-was-a-fish had to be locked up because everyone thought she was crazy.

"This kind of morbid magical malady is very difficult to deal with," said the man. "It will take time. There is no benefit to denying her convictions, for that will only alienate and anger her—but for her own protection, unfortunately, you will have to keep her in the locked ward. You also have to consider the effects of her ravings on the other patients.

"I have a colleague in France, a Professeur Jean Abeille, who may be able to advise you. He has taken on a few of the more difficult crossed-identity cases; he's had some success with cases of delusion originally thought to be quite hopeless."

"Master Snodley, Professor Venkataramaiah, I hope you're not talking shop tonight, as you? This is not the time for business," admonished Mrs. Bain. She smiled and held out a tray of goodies, decorated with red gum drops. "I won't take no for an answer. And I'm so pleased that both of you could be with us tonight."

"Mrs. Bain, our apologies. You're quite right to chastise us," said the woman in the long silvery blue dress. "It's a sad commentary if we're unable to converse on any other subject than work, isn't it—especially on such a festive occasion!"

Mesmerized by the shimmering fish scale dress, Wil suddenly remembered reading an old picture book in Pirsstle and Bertram's about a backwards, upside-down fish, whose fins and scales were turned back-to-front; it was a small, dark, dusky grey-blue fish, ordinary enough, but for the fact that it swam upside down and backwards. Terrible misfortune beset anyone who touched the fish or even looked at it, and that unlucky person invariably went crazy, so the story went.

What if…what if Sophie and I are crazy, because we saw Catfysh? he thought. And what if people find out, and they think we're raving mad and want to put us in locked wards? He tried to imagine what a locked ward would be like. Would it have a large padlock on the door or some other invisible means of not letting people out? Maybe there would be chains on the wall and they wouldn't let him go to the bathroom alone ever.

Wil returned to the chocolate fountain, his insides feeling queasy. Sophie, Beatriz and Phinneas were still there, dipping small pieces of white cake in the melted chocolate and Ziggy, wearing red flannel pyjamas covered in splatters of chocolate, was hiding underneath the table licking his sticky, chocolate-covered fingers.

⁜ ⁜ ⁜

It was well past midnight by the time they all returned home. The night air snapped and crackled with icy stars, taking Wil's breath away. A large, pale pink halo surrounded the full moon, as if the moon too had costumed itself for the Valentine's festivities.

"What a wonderful party," declared Aunt Violet. "I haven't had such fun in a long time—well, if you don't count all the fun we've had with Auntie Vi's Fortune-Telling Shop."

Aunt Rue looked radiant, her cheeks flushed pink with the cold. Wil had seen her give the red carnation to Mr. Bertram part way through the evening; and Mr. Bertram had tucked it into the lapel of his black jacket, which had a shiny red lining.

It was only when Sophie and Wil were brushing their teeth together in the upstairs bathroom and finally had a moment alone, that Wil finally broached the subject that had haunted him all evening.

"Do you think we're suffering from delusion?" he asked, as he squeezed toothpaste onto his brush. He looked at himself in the mirror and bared his teeth.

"What are you talking about?" mumbled Sophie, with her toothbrush still in her mouth.

"I overhead two people talking," said Wil. "Did you see that woman in the long, silvery blue dress and the hat with the red feather, and there was a man talking with her—he had that red bow tie that looked like it was choking his neck?

"Yeah," said Sophie. "What about them?"

"They were talking about a crazy woman, who thought she was a fish and she'd seen an old woman with silver whiskers. And the woman with the whiskers had told her the Palace of the Blazing Star was going to be taken over."

Sophie lowered her toothbrush. "Catfysh?" she said.

"They said the crazy woman almost drowned because she threw herself into the river. They said she keeps insisting she's a fish but she can't swim at all, not even a snake slither."

"We're not the ones trying to jump in the river," said Sophie, spitting toothpaste out into the sink. "We saw Catfysh and we saw all those ghosts or spirits around her, or whatever they were. Remember that woman in the blue cloak—she looked so sad—and the one with tattoos, and those two small children? No, we didn't imagine them. They must be all the people who have drowned in the river. We're not crazy." She paused and grinned. "At least, I'm not crazy anyway."

Ignoring Sophie's joke, Wil looked in the mirror, as if he were speaking to himself. "Well, I definitely think we shouldn't tell *anyone* about Catfysh. We don't want people thinking we're psycho or incurable or something. They might try to put us in the MiddleGate Sanatorium, if they find out. If you'd heard that man talking at the party, you would have gotten the heebie-jeebies too—he was talking about *morbid magical maladies, hopeless cases and locked wards.*" Wil began to brush his teeth furiously.

XXI White Night and Black Sand

The map, stained by time, was coloured with rich crimson, yellow and blue inks.

VOLCANO FREMIT VOLCANO MUGIT
FUROR ORBEM TERRARUM TURBET.
ACCIDIT ANTE, ETIAM ACCIDET;
TALIA HOMO NUMQUAM COGNOSCIT.
A VOLCANO MAY SNORT, A VOLCANO MAY RUMBLE,
ITS FURY CAN SEND THE WORLD ALL A-TUMBLE
IT'S HAPPENED BEFORE, IT WILL HAPPEN AGAIN,
BUT SUCH THINGS ARE BEYOND MERE MORTAL KEN.

Still tired from the Valentine's Day party two nights before, Sophie edged her way slowly to her stool in cartology. This was her favourite class, the only one in which she could draw as much as she wanted.

Although Gruffud's Academy was known as an academy for the magical arts, the art studio was closed. The last teacher, who was very elderly, had keeled over right in the middle of a class. The studio had been shut down ever since; no one was allowed entry to the dusty room, which was still filled with brushes and paints and canvases. Sophie had peered in the window of the door wistfully many times. When they would be hiring a new teacher was a great question mark. So cartology was really the only class for people like Sophie who loved to draw.

Mage Tibor rubbed his hands with glee after everyone was seated. "I am very, very pleased to say that we have…hmmm…a wonderful surprise today for you, class." Mage Tibor grandly threw out one arm and pointed to the back of the classroom. "As I promised you several weeks ago, we are honoured with the presence of our guest speaker, an old friend of mine from school days...Vitellus Albumen!"

Everyone swivelled around on their stools to look towards the back of the classroom.

Sophie was not sure what she was expecting a Real Explorer to look like. But she knew it was nothing like Vitellus Albumen.

Vitellus Albumen was extremely tall and thin—so tall and so thin, that Sophie thought he would surely blow away at the first hint of a storm or high winds. Even his face was long and narrow, his eyes were close-set and his hair was so wispy it looked as if it were about to fly off his head.

"I am so pleased to meet you all," said Vitellus Albumen in a voice as wispy as his hair. "Young people such as yourselves are so full of boundless energy that I can now only dream of!"

But his words belied the fire in his eyes when he began to speak about his travels. "I'm sure you have questions about many of my adventures, but today, I'm going to tell you about my most recent explorations in Iceland—or as they pronounce it there, EES-land."

"I have just returned from a place that can be as bleak and wild, uninhabited and desolate as anywhere on earth could possibly be. Where you meet no man, no woman, no child, no bird, no living creature for miles around. Where the line between the sea and the sky is invisible. Where hot belches from the belly of the earth make you think that you have entered Thor's own fiery forge. Where there is a deep crevasse in which men accused of witchcraft and sorcery were thrown to die—and to this day, it is said that restless spirits circle around unwary travellers and try to pull them down into the chasm.

"The hot springs in this land bubble and the scorched volcanoes live. Let no one take for granted that a volcano sleeps, for a volcano may snort, a volcano may rumble and its fury can send the world a-tumble.

"This is a land of hot and a land of cold. A land so barren in parts that you would think you took a wrong turn on the way to the village store to buy a bottle of milk and you've just found yourself on the moon. The sulphurous smell of eggs wherever you go. And the sand is black, black as the ashes of bones. In fact, Titus—I mean, Mage Tibor—I brought back a sample of it for your sand collection." Vitellus Albumen held up a glass vial of black sand to show the class.

Mage Tibor grinned from ear to ear as he took the vial of black stuff. "Marvelous," he said. "This will make a very special addition to my collection."

"And the food, wonderful food. Fish, fish, fish and lamb, lamb, lamb. Everything revolves around fish and lamb. But there seem to be more tourists than fish and sheep nowadays!" said Vitellus Albumen with a laugh.

"I couldn't resist buying a reproduction of one of the old maps for you as well, Titus—one rendered by Guthbrandur Thorlaksson…predates the very famous one published in 1590, although they share some similarities. I thought it would make a fine addition to your classroom—that's if you've got room for it." Vitellus Albumen scanned the classroom, obviously looking for a spot for the map.

Mage Tibor had papered the classroom so enthusiastically with maps, however, that there was scarcely room to put up anything more, at least not without having to take down or cover something else. Even the ceiling was filled with beautiful star charts and images of the planets.

"Well," said Vitellus Albumen and he cleared his throat, "I'm sure you'll find a good spot for this one. These old maps are so beautifully rendered with sea creatures guarding the waters unknown. Coastlines may be distorted, entire islands missing, fjords and bays elongated, highlands randomly recorded, but the beauty of the map, the excitement of the explorer mapping the unknown, these shine through. You should certainly take the map's notations with a grain of salt—for instance, I'm not sure that there are horses that can run twenty miles in one burst!"

Sophie had never seen such a beautiful map—it was stained by time and coloured with rich crimson, yellow and blue inks. The sea creatures jumping the waves seemed alive; Sophie could almost smell the salt air. Mage Tibor took the map from Vitellus Albumen reverently. He appeared so overcome at the gift that words failed him.

"Note the great, round, beaming sun shining to the north, there," said Vitellus Albumen, pointing to the map. "*White Night,* children," he whispered, "when the sun barely sets before it rises again. A sight to behold! The time when the elusive firebirds hatch in the Land of the Midnight Sun.

But we shouldn't forget this is also the land of ten million puffins (*fratercula arctica*)—or as they call them there *lundi* (LOON-dih)…and the little pufflings, dark grey down fluffballs, known as *lundi pysja (LOON-dih PEESH-yar).*

Vitellus Albumen's words were hypnotic. As he spoke, Sophie drew pictures—a stone with ancient runes carved into it, a puffin with a colourful, heavy beak and white face, a goblet inscribed with magical symbols…

⁜ ⁜ ⁜

"That was an amazing class, wasn't it?" said Wil, as he walked with Phinneas, Beatriz and Sophie along the stone corridors to the next class—verbology with Mage Terpsy. "But I thought we'd get to ask more questions. I wanted to hear more about those firebirds—they sounded scary."

"Yeah," said Phinneas. "He never did tell us where he saw them—but come to think of it, it wasn't clear if he actually did see them."

"I don't think I'd want to visit EES-land," said Wil. "Even the name is enough to put you off—who'd want to go where there's so many stones and rocks and live volcanoes?"

"And ice and deep crevasses with restless spirits," said Sophie, shivering. "But that map really was beautiful. The fish and whales looked like they were alive…and the black sand, the way it glinted—who would have come up with the idea of collecting sand in the first place?"

"I always thought sand was just…well, plain old brown sand," said Beatriz.

"That black sand must get really hot in the sun," said Phinneas.

"Do you think Mage Tibor would show us his sand collection?" said Wil.

"White Night and black sand," muttered Sophie, wondering how people could live in Iceland if there were so many volcanoes. She had written down some of the names of the volcanoes—*beautiful* names for *dangerous* things: Hekla, Askja, Katla, Krafla, Eldfell ("fire mountain"), Strokkur, Surtsey, Laki.

And how could people sleep if it wasn't dark? Why go to bed at all if night were day?

XXII Two Twigs

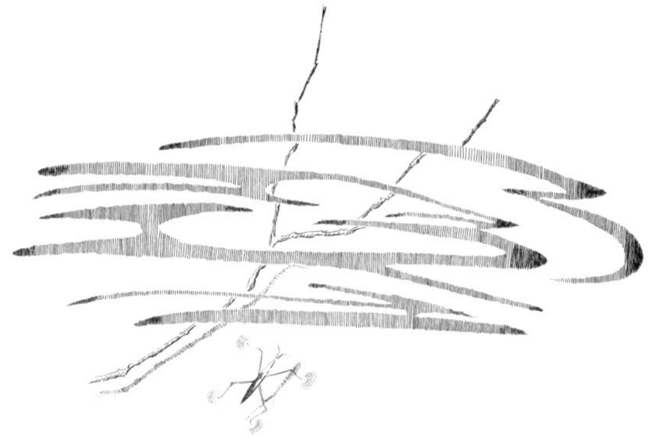

A slight haze was beginning to drift over the river,
blunting what the eye could see and the ear could hear.

FURO, FREMO, SPUO, CREPITO.
NUBES MATER
FULGUR PATER
FLUMEN ET RIVULUS LIBERI MEI
ARCUS CURRUS MEUS AD TERRAM LECTUM MEUM
PRECES SUNT MIHI SUB CUMULATIS NIMBIS.
QUID, QUO, QUANDO, QUOMODO, QUIS?
I RAGE, I ROAR, I SPIT, I PATTER.
CLOUD, MY MOTHER
LIGHTNING, MY FATHER
RIVER AND BROOK, MY CHILDREN TRUE
RAINBOW MY CHARIOT TO EARTH MY BED
ANSWER TO A PRAYER UNDER THUNDER-HEAD.
WHAT, WHERE, WHEN, AND HOW AND WHO?

Only one month later, the river's ice cracked. Almost overnight, a thin strip of rippling water slashed the river's white carpet of ice and snow; thirsty pigeons gathered at the icy edge of the water and egged each other on to dip beaks and sip. Then the snows started to retreat from the river, leaving behind large, dirty mounds that reminded Wil of miniature mountain ranges. One crack became two, became three, and open waters burst free; but still the river remained imprisoned, jammed, wedged by great logs and monstrous shelves of thick ice.

Lakish puddles formed by day and froze by night on the streets and sidewalks; and Sophie and Wil smashed the lacy icescapes gleefully each morning.

And every day—if they had finished their homework or weren't playing with Beatriz and Phinneas—Wil and Sophie ventured down to the riverbank quietly and stealthily, telling no one why—at least, not the *real* why.

"We're just going to see if the ice on the river is gone yet," they said, whenever they were asked what they were doing.

"Well, make sure you don't fall in or you'll catch your death of cold, and stay away from the mud by the river," Aunt Violet would exclaim. "I don't want *any* muck tracked into the house."

Tall grasses, thorny thistles and burrs did not stop Sophie and Wil from venturing down the riverbank. Even the crazed mudflats that threatened to pull their boots from their very feet did not deter them. Hoping against hope, Sophie and Wil hunted for signs of Catfysh—for spring was finally in the air.

But to no avail.

By the last week in March, the cracks had thickened, the ice was moaning and pieces of ice, like small icebergs, were breaking away and floating downstream. Then, one day, at the end of the first week in April, with a sudden cacophony of crashing and crunching, clinking and chinking, the ice broke free of its jam. The break was quick and irrevocable—as quick and irrevocable as a flock of swirling, white seagulls lifting suddenly into the air from the water, their wings churning the blue sky. Thousands and thousands and thousands of pieces of ice jostled and thudded and jolted, speeding the current in some great race.

Smooth ice glistening and glinting, as clear and translucent as the finest crystal jewels. Ice charred like igneous rocks thousands of years old, clotted with bits of grass and driftwood. Ice so encrusted and riddled with holes, there was more hole than ice.

The great rush of ice streamed past Wil and Sophie as they stood watching from the riverbank; it was all over in half an hour. Faint tinkles of ice kissing ice dwindled; and a groan broke for the last time as a great shelf of ice held by a fallen willow tree spun round and lurched off.

Sophie felt as if she could almost hear the last chunk of ice shout, *Wait for me!*

✢ ✢ ✢

The word *flood* was on everyone's lips. It filled the newspaper and dominated the local news, supplanting all coverage of the upcoming elections. There were hourly reports on the radio about how high the crest of the headwaters was and how far it was from MiddleGate. And as the waters rose, so did the sense of general unease. So much snow had fallen over the winter that the water levels were now dangerously high. And to add to everyone's worries, there had been thunderstorms and rain every day for the past week.

As Sophie and Wil scrambled down the sodden riverbank just before suppertime, both of them slipped in the mud.

"Just great," said Sophie ruefully. "Aunt Violet's going to have a snake when she sees our boots."

It had been a particularly bad day. Mage Terpsy had been in a very foul mood and shouted at everyone for being too noisy in verbology. Mage Adderson gave them twice the amount of homework they usually had in numeristics. In cartology, there was a surprise pop quiz on the earth's longitudes and latitudes and meridians. And Mage Radix was so grumpy that he accidentally cut off the wrong leaf from one of his favourite plants and blamed the mistake on the class.

To top it off, Mage Quartz had forced everyone to practice shadow-cutting, although there was hardly enough sunlight to make one gold coin, as the old expression goes. And even though Wil (with the help of Esme) had defeated Rufus Crookshank in a deadly shadow game last spring, he found himself reluctant to learn more about shadow-cutting—as if he didn't want to relive the fight with Crookshank. Mage Quartz, generally known for his enthusiasm and patience with his students, had pulled his two-braid beard in apparent frustration and cautioned him, "You can't just count on good luck to aid you in this game, Mr. Wychwood."

And then, after school, Beatriz and Phinneas had had an argument with each other about who had the most freckles. Wil had sided with Phinneas and Sophie had sided with Beatriz—and then the whole thing had blown up. Mr. Bain said it didn't matter how many freckles either one of them had, and that should be the end of the discussion. When Beatriz and Phinneas had continued bickering, Mr. Bain suggested that it would be better if Wil and Sophie visit another time.

"If she doesn't come today," said Wil, squinting at the river, "that's it—okay? I'd really like to just throw the medallion and the ring into the river and forget about the whole thing."

"We talked about this before," said Sophie. "You know you can't do that."

"Oh no?" said Wil. "Watch me!"

Wil and Sophie crept right to the water's edge. The river's treacherous eddies coiled while rain drizzle splattered the slate-grey surface of the river. Haze drifted over the river, blunting what eye could see and ear could hear. The water levels were the highest they had ever been, as if the river was testing everyone. *See how high I can go, just try to stop me.*

"What's that over there?" asked Wil, pointing to two twigs sticking up above the water.

"Just twigs," said Sophie.

"Are you sure?" asked Wil. "You don't think it looks a little like her whiskers?"

Sophie gazed at the spot. She squinted, then frowned and shook her head.

"I thought I saw it move," said Wil. "Did you see the one on the left? I swear, I saw it move. Didn't you see it?"

"It must just be a branch poking out of the water," said Sophie. "It hasn't moved, not a smidge."

"I guess that's it then," said Wil, and they both turned away from the river, disappointed. "We'll probably never see her again," he said. "Maybe she's…maybe she's—"

"Dead?" asked Sophie.

"I hate that word," said Wil. "I looked it up in one of the dictionaries at Pirsstle and Bertram's one day, and it's stuck in my head ever since."

"What did it say?" asked Sophie.

"*Vital and living functions and powers have come to an end, and are incapable of being restored,*" said Wil dully.

"Your head must be really heavy," said Sophie.

"What do you mean?" asked Wil.

"How many words do you think a human brain can hold?" asked Sophie.

"It's not like the brain's a box and the words are all going to fall out," said Wil irritably.

"Forget'ysh so quickly?" whispered a hoarse voice behind them.

Sophie and Wil both turned quicker than a snake's tongue snap…

XXIII An Offering

His questions only fell on ripples in the water.

DONUM, DONATUM, MUNUSCULUM—
QUOMODO VOLEBAT UT SCIREMUS?
HOC AUT ILLUD DILIGEMUS?
POSSIT PARVUM IN LEGATUM COMMUTARI?
QUOD SI NON ACCIPIATUR
EA MENTE UT VELLEMUS?
SPERAMUS, ORAMUS, ROGAMUS, IMPLORAMUS,
OPUS TAMEN IMPERFECTUM SIT SI NUNC DEFICIAMUS.
A GIFT, A PRESENT, UN PETIT CADEAU—
BUT HOW DOES SHE EXPECT US TO KNOW?
WHAT ABOUT THIS…WHAT ABOUT THAT?
WILL SOMETHING SO SMALL PLAY DIPLOMAT?
WHAT IF OUR GIFT IS NOT RECEIVED
IN THE GENEROUS SPIRIT WE CONCEIVED?
WE HOPE, WE BEG, WE ASK, WE ENTREAT
AND IF WE FAIL, OUR TASK'S INCOMPLETE.

Her moonset eyes gleaming, Catfysh stood half way out of the water; fingers of fog swirled around her head. She glided out of the water and pulled her glistening silver-grey cloak around her. An overwhelming, pungent smell of fish and the sound of voices murmuring all around them filled the air…and slowly, the ghostly figures materialized. The same two small children with white hair, the sad woman with the blue cloak and the woman with the tattoos stood near Catfysh and gazed at Wil and Sophie. And there were many, many others—too many to count—all with the same unearthly green eyes.

"Those twigs—that *was* you!" exclaimed Wil.

Catfysh only smiled, and one of her whiskers twitched.

"We have'ysh not much time," she said. "The floodwaters rise'ysh and the Serpent's Chain take'ysh advantage of the imbalance in energies. Seek'ysh the help of the Sphinxes—but bring'ysh an offering. Sphinxes expect'ysh such.

"But first, return'ysh here with the offering and call'ysh. Call'ysh Catfysh. As long as the Fysh love'ysh their oceans, lakes and rivers, the bees their fields, the bears their forests, upon these vow'ysh my return."

Catfysh smiled once more and turned back to the river, drawing all the river spirits with her.

"But how do we know what sphinxes like?" asked Wil. "And how are we supposed to call you?"

His questions only fell on ripples in the water, and when even those ripples vanished, Wil and Sophie were left staring at the caked and crazed mudflats.

Though Catfysh had been standing right before them, she had left no footprints in the mud.

XXIV Four Lies

And if he didn't answer the question...

UNUS BRADYPUS SCIT QUOD ALTER
UNUS PENAEUS SCIT QUOD ALTER
UNUS LIMAX SCIT QUOD ALTER
SED RARO UNUS HOMO SCIT QUOD ALTER VULT.
A SLOTH KNOWS WHAT ANOTHER SLOTH WANTS,
A SHRIMP KNOWS WHAT ANOTHER SHRIMP WANTS,
AND A SLUG KNOWS WHAT ANOTHER SLUG WANTS;
BUT RARELY DOES A HUMAN KNOW
WHAT ANOTHER HUMAN WANTS.

"If you were a Sphinx, what would you want? asked Wil, as they walked home from the river.

"Well, a Sphinx is big and it's made of stone and it's Egyptian," said Sophie.

"Big and stone and Egyptian," repeated Wil. "That narrows things down, doesn't it?"

"For starters, we know a few Egyptian hieroglyphics," said Sophie, "and we know a little bit about their ancient gods."

"This is worse than being invited to a birthday party and you have to get a present for someone you don't really know," said Wil, "or even if you do know them, you can't think of anything anyway."

"Maybe we can paint the sphinxes' claws so they shine in the sun," suggested Sophie, looking at her own fingernails. "I've still got lots of that fingernail polish that Beatriz gave me for my birthday, you know, the one that keeps changing colour every few minutes. I bet a sphinx would like that."

"That's the stupidest idea I've ever heard," said Wil irritably. "A small bottle wouldn't hold enough polish to do even one claw."

"Fine…you come up with something then," said Sophie. "I'm just trying to make a suggestion. You don't need to bite my head off."

"Why are we talking about the sphinxes as if they were alive anyway?" said Wil suddenly. "And how could it possibly help us, when we don't even know yet exactly what we're supposed to be doing?"

"Portia and Portius are alive, and they're made of stone," said Sophie. "They've helped us before."

"Maybe we should go and ask them then," said Wil. "I remember Mr. Bertram telling me once—after a really nasty customer came into the store, wanting to return a book he'd bought the day before…I can't even remember what book it was, something to do with how to lose weight, I think. The man was really angry and said, 'You sold me a book I don't want or need.' The man was so huge, he would take up at least three seats on the MiddleGate Bus. And after the man finally left, Mr. Bertram said, *A sloth knows what another sloth wants, a shrimp knows what another shrimp wants, a slug knows what another slug wants, but rarely does a human know what another human wants.*

"But, maybe, just maybe, a stone will know what another stone wants," said Sophie.

⁜ ⁜ ⁜

Wil tossed and turned all night. He dreamt that the Great Sphinx of Giza was leering down at him and demanding the answer to a question. And if he didn't answer the question, then he would be crushed by the Sphinx's paw. He tried to offer the Sphinx a beautiful, juicy orange, but the Sphinx only spat on it. And when he awoke in the morning, Wil felt so tired that he could hardly put one foot in front of the other.

Aunt Violet took one look at him and said, "You don't look very well."

"I'm going to school!" said Wil.

"There's no need to shout at me," said Aunt Violet calmly.

"Sorry," said Wil, trying to lower his voice. "It's just…it's just that—"

"We're having a test today...in...in...verbology. We can't miss it," said Sophie earnestly. "And we're going to be home this afternoon anyway, because the teachers are having a big meeting."

Wil looked gratefully at Sophie.

"But I'm at the shop today," said Aunt Violet, frowning. "I don't want to leave you alone all afternoon."

"We'll be fine, Aunt Violet," said Sophie. "We're not babies. We can take care of ourselves."

"Well, I suppose so," said Aunt Violet, sounding unconvinced. She placed her hand on Wil's forehead. "I really think you're a little feverish," she said. "And I've got the Herbal Society holding their meeting here tonight. I was hoping you'd both be able to help serve the refreshments."

"I'm fine," said Wil. He took a huge spoonful of cold porridge and gulped it down. "See? I'm eating all my porridge," he mumbled, and porridge dribbled down his shirt.

⁜ ⁜ ⁜

It was well after noon before Wil and Sophie were able to visit Portia and Portius. They had told Phinneas and Beatriz they couldn't walk home with them and Sophie had muttered something about their having to find books in the library for Aunt Violet, which was a big lie. Wil and Sophie were both relieved when Beatriz had simply said, "Okay, see you two later."

"That makes two lies so far, as if snakes could walk!" said Wil. "A test and now this!"

"We're not hurting anyone," said Sophie. "We're just not telling the whole truth, that's all. Besides, Mage Terpsy did give us a surprise pop quiz. She must have been talking to Mage Tibor and they were sharing ideas about how to torture us. So, telling Aunt Violet this morning that we had a test in verbology wasn't a lie. When she asks about the test, we'll be able to tell her truthfully *it was awful and we definitely should have studied more.*"

"When you put it that way," said Wil with a grin, as they rounded the corner of the hallway and reached Stone Hall.

Portia and Portius were in the middle of one of their interminable arguments—about when the whole world would be destroyed, according to the Sun Stone calendar, which was a massive 25-ton 12-foot round

Aztec calendar. Wil and Sophie had actually learned about it one day in Mage Tibor's class.

"—periodic destruction and re-creation of the world, which so many of the ancient cultures believed in and believe in to this very day," said Portius.

"As I recall, it was on 4 Ollin (the Month of Movement) that they anticipated their current world would be destroyed," said Portia.

"Are you sure?" asked Portius. The stone serpent braids in his beard swayed as he spoke, which Wil always found very distracting.

"I'm as sure as that crack under your chin!" snapped Portia. "And the previous disasters occurred on 4 Tiger, 4 Wind, 4 Rain, and 4 Water, according to that calendar."

"I do *not* have a crack under my chin," said Portius, lifting up his chin. "Do I?" he asked in a worried tone.

Sophie peered under Portius's chin but with all the serpents waving about, it was hard to see anything, let alone a crack.

"No, of course, you don't," said Portia, her voice relenting slightly.

As if they had been arguing for the sake of arguing merely to pass the time and they were not really interested in the subject, Portia and Portius both turned suddenly to Sophie and Wil.

"What news, Mr. Wychwood and Ms Isidor?" asked Portia. "Any adventures to report?"

"Portia, how many times do I have to remind you that it's not wise to pry into human affairs," said Portius.

"I'm not prying," said Portia, with a look of annoyance, "merely gently inquiring. We old stones need our gossip, do we not?"

Portius leaned forward. "Well, do tell," he said. "What's up?" He turned to Portia and said, "So strange, isn't it, that one would say *What's up?* rather than *What's down?*"

Then both Portia and Portius stared at Wil and Sophie with keen interest, obviously waiting for a small chip of news.

"Nothing we can tell anyone—," Wil started to say, until Sophie nudged him.

"What Wil means is that we're not supposed to tell anyone what plans we have for Aunt Violet's and Aunt Rue's birthday party," said Sophie, trying to think quickly. "We're going to have a surprise birthday for them, because...even though we don't even know when their real birthdays are," she finished lamely.

"Children, this is a wonderful idea," said Portia. "It can be an Unbirthday Party. Why don't you have a Treasure Hunt for them?"

"One of the clues could be something like, *If you were going to give a sphinx an offering or a gift, what would it be?"* said Wil, obviously not understanding why Sophie was glaring at him. "They'd have to guess the answer and find whatever it was in the house."

"What would a sphinx like?" murmured Portius. "What *would* a sphinx like?"

"Not to have tourists taking its picture all the time," suggested Portia.

"Good try, dear Portia," said Portius. "I'm sure the noble Sphinx at Giza would like to have its nose back, no doubt. And you're probably just jealous that no one's taking your picture all the time, Portia—you, with your glorious serpentine braids, my dearest."

It was obvious they weren't going to get much help from Portius and Portia, thought Sophie, not this time.

Sophie and Wil left the two stone heads arguing about whether it would be a good idea to restore the nose of the Sphinx at Giza or whether the Sphinx was already so famous—being noseless, or half-nosed really, to be technically correct—that everyone would wish the nose hadn't been restored after all.

"Lie number three," said Wil. "By the way, are we really going to have an Unbirthday Party for Aunt Rue and Aunt Violet?"

"Why are you keeping tracking of my lies?" asked Sophie testily. "You were just about to ruin everything. I had to do something."

⁜ ⁜ ⁜

Portia and Portius stopped their arguing and gazed after the children.

"That was a very strange question, wasn't it," said Portia.

"They are embarked on another mission, I fear—and it must involve sphinxes," said Portius. "Perhaps they're doing another project about Egypt for Mage Terpsy. Now, back to the question. What do you think a sphinx would like?"

⁜ ⁜ ⁜

"Wait a moment," said Sophie, as she and Wil left Gruffud's and began to walk home. "I've just had an idea. If you were far, far away from home, wouldn't you get homesick?"

"Of course, I'd get homesick," said Wil.

"Well, the sphinxes originally come from Egypt. And even if they were carved here on this side of the world, they'd want to return back to their home place, their dynasty, right?"

"Sure. No problem. We'll just take the sphinxes to Egypt," said Wil, his voice scathing.

"Obviously not," said Sophie, laughing at Wil and shaking her head. "But we can bring Egypt to the sphinxes."

"What in snake's name are you talking about?" said Wil.

"I'm talking about sand," said Sophie, as if she were stating the most obvious thing in the world.

"Sure, we're going to go all the way to Egypt to get some sand," said Wil.

"We don't have to go to Egypt," said Sophie, speaking slowly, as if she were speaking with a very young child. "Mage Tibor must have sand from Egypt in his collection. Maybe he's still in his office," she said, and without waiting for Wil to say anything, she turned back to Gruffud's.

✢ ✢ ✢

Mage Tibor's office was down a long hallway in the east wing of Stone Hall, along with many of the other teachers' offices. Sophie and Wil both arrived at Mage Tibor's door panting; they knocked on the door timidly and were relieved to hear feet shuffling towards the door.

Mage Tibor opened the door and peered at them over his blue half-moon glasses. "Why, children, you're very lucky to…hmmm…catch me. I was just about to leave for the teachers' meeting."

"Mage Tibor," said Sophie, still trying to catch her breath. "We were…we were wondering if we could see your sand collection." She glanced at Wil, who was looking at her with an expression that seemed to be part admiration, part exasperation.

"My sand collection?" asked Mage Tibor, looking surprised. "I was going to bring in a few samples…hmmm…to class next week, but you're welcome to take a sneak peek, I suppose. No harm in that…hmmm?"

Mage Tibor's office was stuffed to the gills. There were maps folded, maps rolled up and tied with ribbons, maps framed and hanging on the wall…maps, maps, maps everywhere.

Several round magnifying glasses dangled from the ceiling light fixture. An hourglass filled with fine white sand sat beside a globe of the world on his desk, which was piled high with a stash of more maps.

Stockpiled in the four corners of the office were boxes of rocks and pieces of misshapen driftwood along with a lobster trap and fishing nets strung with glass balls, a large frayed basket of shells, empty bird cages, an open trunk with brown fungi the size of large frying pans stashed inside. Three antique brass telescopes rested against the windowpanes and a line of clear glass bottles, with pieces of paper folded up inside them, lined his windows. Several stuffed ducks and a stuffed great horned owl plus a large taxidermied raven sat on top of cabinets crammed with books in no particular order—at least, none that Sophie could discern. And suspended from the ceiling like the trailing tail of a kite, was the longest snakeskin that Sophie had ever seen—the skin, mottled and striped, must have been at least ten feet long. It was so long that Sophie hoped she would never, never, ever in her entire life meet the original owner of such a skin.

Yet, despite all these marvelous things, Sophie did not forget why they had come to see Mage Tibor. She looked around the office for jars of sand, but there didn't seem to be any. Where Mage Tibor could have hidden them was a mystery.

"Mind you don't trip," said Mage Tibor. "I'm in the midst of… hmmm…cleaning up my office, as you can see."

But even as Mage Tibor said this, Sophie had the sneaking suspicion that the office was as clean and as orderly as it ever would be.

Mage Tibor stepped over a tall pile of books sitting on the floor, reached into his desk and pulled out a small brass key.

"What's that for?" asked Sophie.

"It's the key to the collection," said Mage Tibor. "We'll have to go to an office down the hall. No room in here…hmmm…for even one piece of sand!" he said, and he chuckled.

Mage Tibor led them back down the corridor, through a small, unmarked white door and on to a hallway that Sophie had never seen before. They stopped in front of a door that had SPECIAL COLLECTIONS NO ENTRY written in large black letters, and Mage Tibor fitted the key into the lock.

Sophie and Wil stepped into a room as large as the office they had just come from, lined in small, narrow shelves storing hundreds of shiny vials of sand, all of them carefully labeled and numbered. There must have been millions, maybe even billions or trillions of grains of sand. Each vial contained a different texture and hue: chestnut browns, pigeon feather greys, sunset reds, whites tinged pink, pale yellows, greens and blacks. Grains of sand, large and small, rounded and shiny, coarse and sharp-edged, translucent and dense.

Sophie spotted a vial filled with dark black sand just like the kind that Vitellus Albumen had brought for Mage Tibor. And sure enough, the label on the vial cited the great explorer's name and the word Iceland, among other sundry details.

The whole room was so clean and organized that there would have been no home for even one unwanted, misplaced speck of dust—or sand. The whole effect was completely at odds with Mage Tibor's other office.

"There must be over a thousand vials in here," exclaimed Sophie.

"Two thousand, one hundred and forty-nine, to be precise, from over one hundred countries!" said Mage Tibor proudly. "I've collected some of them myself, but of course, friends…hmmm…know of my collection; they're always sending me little presents from…hmmm…the far reaches of the world. And I'm a member of the International Sand Collectors Society; we psammophiles—hmmm…we do like to trade sand and stories. Some day, I hope to have specimens from every country of the world."

"Do you have any from Egypt?" Sophie blurted out, hoping Mage Tibor wouldn't think she was being too abrupt.

"Egypt, Egypt," said Mage Tibor, "You did that very fine presentation about Meretseger for Mage Terpsy—she told me about it. Yes, yes I believe I do…Egypt—now where are you?" He closed his eyes and thought for a moment. "Yes, I remember!" He strode to the other end of the room and pulled down a vial with sand the colour of reddish-yellow ochre.

"Egypt," he said, holding out the small vial of reddish sand. "The Egyptians call the desert *deshret*—meaning the *red land*."

"Mage Tibor, do…um...do you think we could have a very, very, very small bit?" asked Sophie, trying desperately not to sound too greedy.

Mage Tibor looked taken aback. "I don't…I don't normally…"

"We want to give Aunt Violet something from Egypt for a birthday present, because she's always wanted to go to Egypt," Sophie blurted out.

"In honour of Aunt Violet, I suppose I could spare a few grains out of the gazillions in this room," said Mage Tibor, with a smile. "No one else quite like Aunt Violet. I hear Auntie Vi's Fortune Telling Shop is doing very well for itself."

Mage Tibor selected an empty vial from a box on the floor and then poured a few grains of Egyptian sand into it and corked it. "There you go," he said, handing the vial to Sophie.

"Thank you, Mage Tibor," said Sophie. She glanced at Wil and grinned.

"That will make a very fine present for your Aunt Violet," said Mage Tibor, not noticing that Sophie had started edging towards the door and was pulling Wil with her. "Gathered from the foot of the Sphinx of Giza itself! Everyone should have the opportunity to visit Egypt to touch the Sphinx in the very flesh...hmmmm....in the very stone. The Sphinx of Giza—a true wonder of the world. A face so mysterious that it seems it shall hold it secrets forever...hmmm...even without its nose."

Mage Tibor closed his eyes, as if he were standing at the base of the Sphinx and gazing upwards. "Made from sand, destroyed by sand," he murmured. "Did you know that the great Sphinx of Giza is one of the largest statues made from a single stone on Earth?" he asked. "And it was buried by the desert sands up to its shoulders until 1925."

⁜ ⁜ ⁜

"Lie number four," said Sophie happily, as she and Wil walked down the hallway and left the school for home.

"Lie number four," said Wil. His voice sounded grim. "You don't think you were a little pushy?"

"Catfysh said there wasn't much time, didn't she?" replied Sophie, walking more quickly. "We have to get back to the river."

Their plans to return to the river were dashed by Aunt Violet, however.

"But you were going to help me with the Herbal Society meeting tonight," she said, looking very hurt. "You didn't forget, did you?"

XXV Double Trouble Boil and Bubble

The crow cocked its head and croaked...
thinking nothing more about the matter.

ARBITRARE OMNIA QUAE CORNIX AUDIT ET VIDET
INSIDENS IBI SUMMA IN ALTA ARBORE.
DESUPER AUDIT HERBAS CRESCENTES
ATQUE LIBEROS ADOLESCENTES SPECTAT.
RIDET AMPLEXUM ROSCIDI VERMIS.
ACRI OCULO IN VENATU,
CIRCUMAGIT NIGRAS PENNAS.
NON NIHIL CORNIX AUDIT ET VIDET.
IMAGINE ALL THAT THE CROW HEARS AND SEES
PERCHED HIGH ABOVE THERE IN A TREE.
HEAR THE GRASS GROWING FAR BELOW,
AND WATCH THE CHILDREN AS THEY GROW.
CHUCKLE AT DEW-STRAPPED WORMS' EMBRACE,
BEADY EYE UPON THE CHASE.
BLACK FEATHERS DO A SLICK ABOUT-FACE
THERE'S NOTHING A CROW DOESN'T HEAR AND SEE.

Saturday morning, Wil and Sophie woke very early, got dressed as quickly as they could and tiptoed quietly down the stairs.

Sophie scrawled a note to Aunt Rue and Aunt Violet:

Going down to the river
back before lunch

Sophie XXXXOO

Then she drew a fish with bulbous eyes and two long whiskers, plus two small bubbles and one big bubble coming out of its mouth.

Wil looked over her shoulder. “I like it,” he said. “Only shouldn’t there be more bubbles?”

“Three’s enough,” said Sophie, and she put the note on the kitchen table, then went to get her jacket. She did not notice Wil scribble something inside the big bubble.

DOUBLE TROUBLE BOIL AND BUBBLE

They hurried out of the house, munching on crunchy ginger snap cookies Aunt Violet had made. A sudden burst of morning sun broke through the clouds as they trotted towards the river; at the same time, silvered drops of rain fell here and there.

And although Wil and Sophie didn’t see it high above their heads—at that moment, they were too busy talking about whether or not the sphinxes would be pleased with the sand from Egypt—the faint outline of a rainbow appeared.

It dimmed, then appeared again; this time, a *double* rainbow arched across the whole clouded blue. The seven colours of the second bow echoed those in the first, albeit paler and reversed.

Still, Wil and Sophie did not notice the rainbow, and if they had, they might not have hurried so quickly to the river, for in many stories one rainbow—let alone a double one—is thought to be a bridge between the real and the imaginary, a gate to the heavens, a messenger for the gods, a guardian of the Earth…and even a sky-wise trickster serpent.

“So what’s going to happen when we call Catfysh?” asked Sophie.

“I don’t know,” said Wil. “She probably wants to see what we’ve got for the sphinxes.”

“Then what?” asked Sophie.

“Then maybe she’ll tell us what it is that we’re supposed to do. I hope she doesn’t think we forgot about her. And since she seems to know about the Serpent’s Chain, I think we should ask her about the black medallion and how it always seems to know what’s happening before us. Because that fish on the medallion is shining pretty brightly, see?” Wil pulled out the medallion to show Sophie.

"It's brighter than the snake and the bee are," said Sophie. "What if the black medallion is like a compass, and it points you in the direction you're supposed to go like the North Star does. When you flick the circle and it spins, that's when the star appears."

"So the snake and the bee, and now the fish, are the steps we're taking along the path to reach the star," said Wil slowly, turning the black medallion over to look at the empty silver triangle on the other side. "But I wonder how many more steps there are."

"Too bad we can't ask the medallion," said Sophie. "Everything about the Serpent's Chain seems to be so secret."

"Only those who are supposed to know get to know, I guess," said Wil. "But if we've done two tasks already, and there are more tasks, and we do those, then what? Do we get a reward? Does a door magically open to a room with lots of treasure? Maybe we'll get three fishes, I mean, three wishes."

"Three wishes, that would be amazing, wouldn't it?" said Sophie eagerly, and she slid down the riverbank.

Wil pocketed the medallion and gold ring, then slithered down the riverbank after her.

The waters of the river looked cold and angry, the current was swift and a sudden breeze riffled the surface of the water. Wil shivered as he squatted down and touched the water. It was icy cold.

"How can she possibly swim in this?" he said. "How does anything live in water this cold?"

"That's why we're here, dressed in jackets and hats and gloves, and they're there," said Sophie.

"So how are we supposed to call Catfysh?" asked Wil. "She always just appeared before."

"I guess it would be stupid to yell *CATFYSH!* since she's in the water and wouldn't hear us," said Sophie.

"Besides, what if someone else hears us?" said Wil. "Maybe we should just put our hands in the water, and she'll taste us. I read in that library book Peerslie gave me that catfish have really sensitive skin; they're like a big swimming tongue. That's how they can hunt for food at night. If you were a catfish, you'd be able to taste chocolate cake just by sitting on it, that's what it said in the book."

"What a stupid idea. Who'd want to sit on a chocolate cake?" said Sophie, and she knelt down and sloshed her hands in the water.

Wil was startled to see the frames of her glasses suddenly turn from silvered pink to mottled blue-grey.

"It's freezing!" squealed Sophie.

"It's not that bad," said Wil, and he knelt down to feel the water again.

✣ ✣ ✣

Gossamer mist swelled up from the river's eddies, forming a misty cloud. The cloud glided silently—it was a great ghost fish—and swallowed the two children whole.

Only eerie voices and an ancient, fishy smell lingered in the air.

✣ ✣ ✣

One lone crow bobbing at the very top of an elm tree saw the mist, saw the children disappear. The crow cocked its head and croaked, then wings flapping, it flew off downstream in search of a tasty morsel…thinking nothing more about the matter.

XXVI Muddy Waters

NONNE INTERDUM VIDISTI NUBEM SIMILEM SERPENTI?
VEL AQUILAE? VEL ETIAM PISCI?
NESCIVERUNT UTRUM LIBERI FUERINT SOMNIANTES
SE FUISSE PISCES AN PISCES LIBEROS.
NONNE PISCES LIBERIS SIMILES
RIDENT LUNA, LUDUNT UNDA, CANUNT PLUVIA?
HAVEN'T YOU SOMETIMES SEEN A CLOUD
THAT LOOKED LIKE A SNAKE?
OR AN EAGLE? OR A FISH PERHAPS?
THEY DID NOT KNOW IF THEY WERE
CHILDREN DREAMING THEY WERE FISH,
OR FISH DREAMING THEY WERE CHILDREN.
FOR DO NOT FISH LAUGH WITH THE MOON
FROLIC WITH THE WAVES
AND SING WITH THE RAIN?

XXVII Tit for Tat, and Fin for Fat

The water welcomed them to its liquid embrace.

ANGUIS ANGUI PISCIS PISCI PULCHER
SI HABEAT CENTUM LINGUAS, CENTUM ORA
NON POSSIT DESCRIBERE HUNC MUNDUM.
A SNAKE LOOKS GOOD TO A SNAKE, AND A FISH TO A FISH.
IF ONE HAD A HUNDRED TONGUES, A HUNDRED MOUTHS,
ONE COULD NOT DESCRIBE THIS WORLD.

Two small fish dove into the water, leaving behind a misty haze. The water welcomed them to its liquid embrace, as a large catfish dipped below the surface.

✣ ✣ ✣

Bubbles...bubbles...bubbles blurred Wil's wits. The bubbles tickled him and made him laugh, but when he laughed, there were more bubbles. A taste of fish flooded his brain, a taste of fish so close that Wil almost thought that he had turned inside out and become a fish himself.

He kicked his feet...only he didn't have any feet.

He turned around to look for his ten, round, warm toes.

Gone.

In their place—a slick, grey fin. His toes, all of them...snatched!

Wil panicked and whipped his head around. Surely his feet were there, on the other side. He thrashed so quickly that he rolled three times and ended upside down staring at the sky, but the sky wasn't blue—it was shining, shimmering, bubblish silver.

The bubbles tickled him once again, and he hiccupped with fright. Where was Sophie? Wil gurgurgled air…no, it was water.

Cool water sloshed over, around, through him.

A single, large bubble escaped from his mouth and swirled lazily upwards, round and glistening. There was a very, very tiny image of a fish in it…but it did not occur to Wil—not yet—that the fish was himself.

From the corner of his eye, he felt a long, wormy thing trailing along beside him. It so startled him that he darted forward. The thing, whatever it was, followed him. He darted forward again and veered sharply to the right, but the thing ripped after him. And this time, there was not just one thing, there were three. He turned to the left and there were three more. They had surrounded him. Belly heaving, he steadied himself and prepared to make a dash for it.

But when he felt a swill of current tug the whiskers on his chin, he suddenly realized, I'm a fish. And not just any old fish. Not a goldfish. Not a sunfish. Not a wolffish. I'm a catfish—and if he had been precise about the matter, he would have told himself that he was, strictly speaking, a *channel catfish.*

Six bubbly inches of *ictalurus punctatus* (spotted fish cat)—otherwise known as silver cat, willow cat, forked-tail cat, fiddler, river fish, blue channel cat—with more than a quarter-million taste buds all over his smooth, silvery, blue-grey, scaleless body, eight sturdy barbels (whiskers), two nares (nasal openings), two fringed gills, two swivelly eyes, two invisible inner ears, fins with three sharp spines in his dorsal and pectoral fins (needle-sharp and able to inflict a painful wound), electro-receptors on his head to detect the presence of other living creatures, a long lateral line of small pores running the length of his body (to pick up sounds undetectable by his inner ears), and, of course, a forked tailfin.

Wil did not know that these unerring senses were the very reason catfish have been used for centuries in China to warn of earthquakes. But he also had one other thing no catfish usually has—a large, round, black spot on his underbelly.

Something brushed by Wil's tail and he looked around to see another small fish swimming right alongside him. It too had long whiskers dangling from its chin. And around each of its eyes was a large, muddy green circle touched by gold glints.

Sophie? he bubbled happily—but in fish-tongue, his words would have sounded to you something like *bub-bub-bub-ble-opal-po-p-p-p-p-pople-s-o-o-o.*

The longest whisker on the other fish's chin twisted into the shape of an S-shaped worm, and then the catfish with green circles around its eyes jumped, if jumped were quite the right word—a forward two-loop swoop-dart-dart.

Not to be outdone, Wil flipped over two times (actually, he flopped), rolled onto his back, and shimmied upside down. But he began to choke as a great belch of water slopped down his gulgullet. He wobbled, lurched and fell into a large rusty can ensnared in the weeds.

A squish of curious minnows darted closer to take a good look at the monster captured by the can.

looksee, bubbled the smallest minnow, *it's stucksied.*

Another ventured, *pipsysqueaksies, it's playing trixies!*

One of the larger minnows burped, *it'll bite our headsies off.*

not just our headsies, you foolyfishes, bubbled the largest minnow. *it'll skeasily chomp you scale to tail!*

A collective gasp from the minnows sent them darting in all directions. But the bravest among them ventured nearer and pinched Wil's tail. Two more darted forward, and when it appeared the monster was truly stuck, others joined in. The tickle of pinches felt nice at first…until one of the minnows nibbled and nipped.

Ou-ou-sh-sh-sh! bubbled Wil. His tail thrashed from side to side and he tried to swim backwards out of the can, but to his horror, his fins only propelled him forwards.

Through the can, he heard a squeal of bubbles, and then something pushed the can and rolled it over. He flopped out onto the mud. Dizzy, he gazed up at Sophie, whose large, round eyes were peering at him. Bubbles of laughter gurgled from her mawmaw (*fishmouth* in human-tongue).

Not funny! bubbled Wil. *You think you're such a Big Fish!* He flared his fins and his eyes bulged.

Follow'ysh! burbled a deep, echoing fishvoice behind them.

Wil and Sophie turned in unison. There loomed Catfysh, huge, gleaming and ferocious, her ten long whiskers trailing behind her. She turned tail and, without a backward glance at them both, scudded away through the river's muddy waters.

Wil and Sophie zipped after her.

The cool water combed Wil's whiskers, but his skin shishivered at the shadow of some large creature that emerged from the reeds and then retreated behind a mountain of rubber tires, bicycle wheels and boxes of old bottles littering the river bottom.

Wil tried to keep up with Sophie and Catfysh, but he was fintracked by all the messages he was tasting and hearing and smelling. Urgent messages bombarded him: *Keep away. Poisonous. Dangerous.* Other messages seemed to be merely *F.F.Y.I. (Fiskforwarded For Your Information)*—the sound of a worm burrburrowing deeper into the mudmuck, the scuttle of a crazyfish (*crayfish* in human-tongue) under a stone, the smell of something gillgobbered (*dead* in human-tongue) under a rock, the snackflopping of a stricken moth on water's surface. And still others... *Beware, something stalks close by. Beware stone falling.*

How he knew all these things, he did not know. Nor could he ask, for Catfysh was swimming so quickly, he could barely keep up.

What could possibly be so urgenturgent? Had the floodwaters reached MiddleGate? Why had Catfysh turned them both into fish? How would they become humhuman again? All these questions and more darted around in Wil's fishy head, while he swam as quickly as his fins would let him.

He was soon startled from his thoughts, however, by a deep, pulsing, rumrumbling sound, at first far away...and then it drew closer and closer. Now the rumrumble filled the water, filled Wil's brain.

He could not think.

A mammoth dark shadow passed overhead, then slowed and the rumrumbling sound stopped. Spooked by the enormous, elongated shadow, Wil nipped underneath a rotting log and cowered.

Catfysh and Sophie slipped out of sight.

When his whiskers finally gathered courage enough, Wil peered out cautiously. Something dangled down from the shadow, dancing in the water.

His whiskers fissfissled. Something delicious, irresistible—something he wanted to snatch.

There could be no harm in stopping to snabble a snack. Catfysh and Sophie would wait for him. *Hmmm-bub-bub-bubble-dee-lishishishous...* he could almost taste it.

But suddenly a large fish gallunged from nowhere—olive and gold scales with five darker saddles, and white along tail's lower edge. It was a walleye (Wil recognized it from pictures he had seen).

The walleye opened its monstrous mawmaw, and Wil cringed from the sight of its battalion of prickly, vicious, sharply teeth.

The walleye guzguzzled the delishishishous before Wil could even flip a fin.

But not a whisker twitch later, both the delishishishous and the walleye vanished.

It was as if they had never existed.

But a single bubble remained and it rose slowly skyward, jostled the boundary between water and air, and then it too burst, leaving no trace of delishishishous, no trace of walleye.

Only the mammoth dark shadow still lingered above, amidst dapdappled light.

Wil thought he must have imagined the whole thing.

Without warning, the walleye slapped back down into the water; its mawmaw was wreckripped.

Wil flung himself back under the rotting log and watched as the walleye juddered from side to side several times, like a dog shaking itself. It opened its mawmaw and gaped several times, revealing its sharply teeth again. The ragged flesh from the corner of its mouth wibbled and its glazy aluminium foil eyes glared.

The walleye turned...swam slowly...but surely...right towards the log where Wil was hiding. Wil shrank back deep inside the log. The walleye could smell him—he was sure of it.

Why don't you come out, come out wherever you are, burbled the walleye in a friendly fashion, *so that I may eat...er, meet you. I don't think I've tasted—I mean, I don't think I've smelled you before.*

No, th-th-thank you, bubbled Wil politely from the protection of the log, for he did not want to offend such a large fish.

The walleye's gleaming, aluminum foil eyes swivelled and eyed the exact spot where Wil was hiding.

That was a nice, little snabblesnack, burbled the walleye. Nonne hac die bonum est vivere vel mori? it said genially. It's a good day to live and die, isn't it? Natator hodie adsit, cras absit. Vita brevis est, vir qui festinat facit detrimentum—quae bona bonum est concoquere. Swimly today, gonely tomorrow. Life short, haste waste, and all that tedium-yum. We should have known there was a howhook, but that's what happens when we let whim dictate our actions.

The walleye was swaying back and forth as it spoke (reminding Wil of the swaying of a cobra). Despite his fear, Wil felt his mind becoming numb. He began to sway in time.

How do we look? asked the walleye abruptly. It turned so that Wil could see the side of its mawmaw.

Wil shook his whiskers to clear his head. He peered at the walleye's mawmaw and was very glad that he had not gone after the delishishishous. He wanted to findangle (*thank* in human-tongue) the walleye; but didn't think it appropriate to say he was glad that it had been walleye caught… and not him.

Wil edged forward to get a better view. *It looks nasty,* he bubbled at length.

Non est aliquid grave. No big deal, burbled the walleye carelessly. *Accidit ante, etiam accidet. It's happened before, it'll happen again,* and he turned to the other side. The aluminium pearlescent eye on the other side gleamed at Wil speculatively.

Would you like to see our special trophy? the walleye burbled.

I can see quite well from here, thank you, Wil bubbled timidly.

Several scars coursed along the walleye's jaw-line. And there, buried deep and firmly in the walleye's flesh hung an old piece of fishing line, like a black, frayed and tattered ribbon; the howhook was still attached—the old veteran's metal medal. The walleye wore the medal as if it were a proud war piercing—a prize it had won and now kept on display for everyone to see, with a brass plaque beneath it inscribed thus—

I HAVE LIVED TO TELL YOU MY TAIL.
TREMBLE, ALL YE WHO MEET ME!
VIXI CAUDICEM SCRIBERE.
TREMITE, OMNIA QUAE AD ME ACCEDUNT!

Wil shrank back as far as he possibly could underneath the log, pulling in his whiskers very tight.

I can tell you're impressed, burbled the walleye. *Smart fishie to hidiehidie. Multum est ad comedendum et multa sunt quae te comesse velint. There's lots to guzzle and there's lots what wants to guzzle you. Take my advice. Magna edunt parva sed tamen aeque parva edunt magna. The big devours the small, but to be fair, the small also devours the big. Take catfish, for instance,* and the walleye looked directly at Wil's hiding place and swam ever closer, as he said this. *Catfish do so enjoy walleye eggs for breakfast, and walleye, sander vitreus vitreus, such as I…well, don't these teeth enjoy crunching shadflybyes, crisp miniminnows, succulent crazyfish, tender snallywaggle snails, luscious leeches, juicy yellow perchlings and even…fresh off-the-bone catfiskie fillets—but only upon occasion, of course. Quid pro quo ac pinna pro pingui.Tit for tat, and fin for fat. It is a great pity we didn't have a chance to meet piscis pisci, fish to fish, you and I, isn't it? But you are just as well to keep to yourself; my fishbelly grows hungry and tires of this tête-à-tête."*

Inexplicably, the walleye spun about, and so brusquely that Wil was shocked. This was no wounded, dying fish, listing feebly in the water, but a true fishwarrior, ready to spring should fancy—or opportunity—strike.

At this, the walleye swam off, seemingly none the worsely for wear. And thankfully, it appeared to have lost any interest in Wil.

Not a moment later, a great roar exploded through the water; thousands and thousands of bubbles bombarded Wil. Bruised and battered and terrified, he finstumbled away. He was a Lostling—in a great river filled with dangdangersome things. Dangdangersome things that wanted to eat him all up.

Panicking, he shot out from the log, hoping to taste a hint of trail from Sophie and Catfysh.

Then he heard or felt something—something small. It was pesterstalking him. He turned towards the sound and almost jumped out of his fiskskin at what he saw.

XXVIII Black Hole

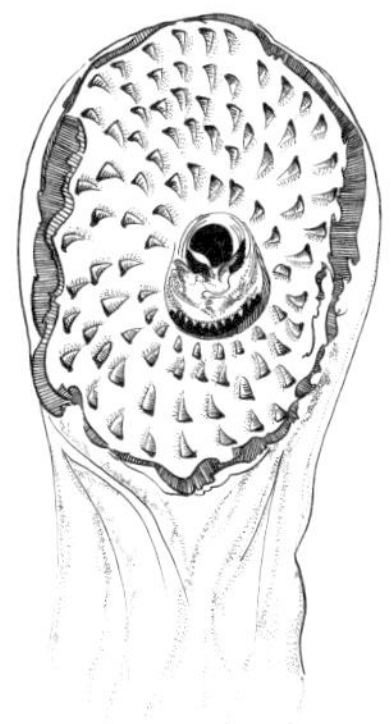

A gaping, flared mouth snaked through the water towards Wil.

SINE CORPORE SINE AURIBUS AUDIO
SINE ORE LOQUOR
CARENS OCULIS NUMQUAM VIDEO
NEQUE ME HUMANUM FATEOR
SED ME IUVAT VERBA ITERARE.
WITHOUT A BODY, I HEAR WITHOUT EARS
AND SPEAK WITH NO MOUTH.
HAVING NO EYES, I CANNOT SEE,
FOR I AM NOT PART OF THE HUMAN RACE,
AND YET I SO LOVE TO REPEAT WHAT YOU SAY.

A long, brown mottled creature—with ribboned, eel-like body, seven clefts along each side, and gaping, flared mouth—was snaking through the water right towards Wil. A gruesome, horrifying, sucking funnel, lined with rows of sharp, pesky teeth. (It was not until much, much later, that Wil realized this toothed, jawless, sucking mouth was a chestnut lamprey.)

Wil darted to one side to escape it, but the voracious mouth only pursued him more closely.

Wil dashed to the bottom of the river and skittered behind a large, sunken pine tree, which still had shiny Christmas balls hanging from its branches.

As he watched the creature, his gills a-quiver, a golden fish glided past. It did not seem to notice the sucking mouth and continued to snuffle along the bottom of the river, obviously scouting for worms or snails or crayfish or—

The creature zeroed in and locked onto the golden fish.

The golden fish lashed from side to side, trying to rid itself of the parasite, but it was too late. The mouth had already latched itself securely; its eel body trailed along the side of the golden fish like the tail of a kite.

There he is, bubbled a voice that was unmistakably Sophie's. *Hiding there, in those logs.*

Look'ysh for you everywhere, burbled another deeper fishvoice, which Wil recognized immediately as Catfysh's.

Wil scooted out from his hiding place and findanced around Catfysh and Sophie.

I am so gillgulpy to smell you! he bubbled excitedly. (*I am so happy to see you!* in human-tongue). *I got lost and there was a huge wall...wall... walleye, and it had so many teeth and I know it wanted to eat me even though it said it didn't,* he blubbered on. *And then there was this big mouth, it had thousands and thousands of teeth, and every single one of them wanted to crawcrunch me.*

Catfysh quickly flicked her whiskers over him (including his tail), as if to assure herself that Wil was still all in one piece, and Sophie did a triple loop in the water—making him feel quite dizzy.

Then, together, the three of them (Wil meekly following them both) continued on their expedition—or whatever it was that they were supposed to be doing...although it was still something of a mystery, at least to Wil. Catfysh did not seem to give a straightforward answer to anything. Wil, though, was beginning to understand that fishthinking was different than his own.

> The world is wide, the world is dangerous.
> Give too much information, it may be used against you.
> Eat or be eaten.
> Hiding is important if you are small and don't want to get eaten.
> Big fish were once little fish.
> *Bon appetit!*

They swam for what seemed like an extremely, exceedingly, very, very, very long time—but perhaps that is only because fish live mostly in the present. Yesterday and tomorrow are but dim bubbles that burst too easily.

Today is real, today stares you in the face… *Today bites,* thought Wil. He was so pleased at having caught such a thought as *Today bites,* that he had taken no notice of what lay ahead.

Catfysh had lead them directly into a churning black hole.

✣ ✣ ✣

They were thrown gill by fin, head by tail, gasp by gulp into a spinning vortex of black water.

XXIX No Unauthorized Personnel

"Give'ysh your gift to the Sphinxes."

AUDI NULLAM MAGICAM
VIDE NULLAM MAGICAM
DIC NULLAM MAGICAM
HEAR NO MAGIC
SEE NO MAGIC
SPEAK NO MAGIC

Coughing and spluttering, Wil and Sophie pulled themselves out of the black water.

Wil's limbs felt heavy and sluggish. He wanted nothing more than to slide gratefully back down into the water, but Catfysh pulled his arm.

"Hurry'ysh," she said.

"But why?" asked Wil, panting from the effort of breathing air. It took him a moment to notice that he was splayed out on a hard, shiny marble floor, a marble floor with a black star.

"We're in the Pool of the Black Star!" he exclaimed.

"How did we do that?" asked Sophie, who was looking as dazed as Wil felt. "Weren't we just in the river?"

Catfysh smiled her secret smile and her longest whisker twitched. "Much to learn'ysh, my young Catfyshes. The Black Star carry'ysh all to the river, all who know'ysh the secrets of this Chamber of Echoes, the Pool of the Black Star. *Fysh, fire, fog, and star*, she sang. *Piscis ignis nebula stella. Piscis ignis nebula stella.Piscis ignis….* Her voice grew softer and softer until the words could no longer be distinguished.

Wil pulled himself to his knees and then stood up with great difficulty and swayed.

That familiar, ancient, fishy smell assailed his nostrils.

Sophie stumbled up the stairs to the landing, where the lamps with the Janus heads facing in two directions stood guard.

"Look at the fishes here," said Sophie, pointing to the metal base of one of the lamps. "They're staring right at me."

"The custodians of the Pool of the Black Star," whispered Catfysh. "Come'ysh, hurry'ysh. The Chain," she whispered. "Quickly."

"The chain?" repeated Wil. Then he whispered to Sophie, "Do you think she means the Serpent's Chain?"

"What other chain is there?" said Sophie and she lurched after Catfysh, who was mounting the stairs to the Great Hall.

Catfysh's silvery, glimmering cloak swept behind her, and a slight trail of mist followed them. They passed several people carrying files and papers; but it was as if Catfysh, Wil and Sophie were invisible, for no one spoke to them, no one even looked at them—even though Catfysh with her whiskers and long cloak was hardly a common sight, thought Wil. They passed the security desk, where the guards were busy chatting about the weather and how high the floodwaters were.

"The river overflowed its banks late last night," said one of the guards, "they've issued a thousand sandbags to homeowners."

"It's nowhere near as bad as the Flood of the Century though," said the other guard. "It wasn't the Red River then, it was the Red Sea."

"They can't see us, can they?" whispered Wil.

"They only see what they want to see," said Catfysh. "Hear'ysh no magyk, see'ysh no magyk, speak'ysh no magyk."

Catfysh stepped out through the entrance door into the vestibule, then stopped suddenly and turned. She pointed to a stone carving above the door.

It was a stone lamp with a flame coming out of its spout. And beneath the lamp…right beneath the lamp, Wil saw it. It was a chain, a chain with squared links.

"That wasn't there before," he exclaimed, feeling puzzled. "I'm sure we didn't see that when we were here before. We would have seen it first thing. We would have seen it right away," he repeated, as if trying to convince himself. "We saw everything there was to see on the tour…all the Fibonacci numbers in the building, the horned bison—"

"Yeah, " said Sophie excitedly. "We had to do a big school assignment about how you bump into Fibonacci numbers everywhere you go in the building. And we saw the heads of Medusa and Athena, the stone lions, the statue of The Golden Boy, alias Hermes," said Sophie.

"And there are two stone sphinxes on the roof," Wil chimed in. "We haven't seen them up close—but we know they're up there underneath Hermes. Are you going to take us to see the sphinxes?" he asked. "You said we had to bring the sphinxes a present. Sophie's got one in her pocket."

"Good. See'ysh everything," said Catfysh, and for the first time, she smiled. "Remember'ysh, never look'ysh deeply into the Medusa's eyes." Her moonset eyes gleamed like stained aluminium foil, just like the eyes of the walleye. Then their gleam faded. "All who pass'ysh through the great door pass'ysh beneath the Chain, but they do not see'ysh it."

"You said the Palace of the Blazing Star is in danger," said Sophie. "From the flood?"

"From the Serpent's Chain," whispered Catfysh.

"The Serpent's Chain?" said Wil. "But everything looks normal. People are working, the guards look happy."

"But how would we know if the Serpent's Chain were here or not?" asked Sophie. "There must be more than Rufus Crookshank and Lucretia Daggar."

"So, the guards are members? Or maybe that person we walked by, the one who was carrying a stack of five or six books—how do we know she's not a member? You don't think this is carrying things a little far?"

At the expression on Sophie's face, Wil relented. "All right, sorry. You've got to admit, though, we don't have very much to go on."

Catfysh muttered, "They be'ysh here."

"How do you know?" asked Wil.

"The waters be'ysh calm. But what lurk'ysh beneath? Ancient knowledge be'ysh embedded in this building. But the time come'ysh not yet—unless hearts be'ysh pure and seek'ysh not private gain.

"The Serpent's Chain infiltrate'ysh the ranks of government. Hurry'ysh to the Sphinxes."

Still protected by the mist of Catfysh's cloak, they scaled the stairs to the second floor—past the wall with the stone fossil that did look suspiciously like a human skull—then hurried to the west corridor on the third floor. Catfysh stopped suddenly in front of a very ordinary dark wooden door with a brass handle, a door that looked like all the other doors. The door was locked, but Catfysh passed her hand over the lock and the door opened easily, leading them to another door that stood ajar. They mounted a set of narrow, worn wooden stairs, and past grey-green plaster walls—they reminded Wil of the colour of Catfysh's pale moonset eyes. Then more stairs, which wound up and around and led to a long hallway with large air ducts running its length. The air was stale and the ceiling so low that they had to stoop. Stepping around electrical cords that snaked along the hallway, striding past stacks of pipes and boxes, they came to yet another door, this one a creamy yellow, paint-chipped and stained with large letters across it.

NO UNAUTHORIZED PERSONNEL MAY ENTER

And scrawled twice across the top of the door in handwritten letters, the word OUT.

"But it says we're not supposed to enter," protested Wil.

"Be'ysh safe," said Catfysh.

They climbed yet another set of stairs—these were wooden and very narrow—to a small black trap door. Catfysh pushed hard on the door, then stepped through, pulling her cloak behind her.

Wil gasped as they stepped out onto the gravel roof of the Palace of the Blazing Star. They had a perfect view of the dome of the Law Courts Building and the tower of the old Vaughn Street Jail.

And not a stone's throw from them, the two massive stone Sphinxes crouched—one looked to the East, the other to the West. A large serpent ornamented the front of each of the Sphinxes' head-cloths. Wil's heart surged at the sight of their enormous paws, their sharp claws and long, thick tails curling over their great haunches.

"The Sphinxes," whispered Sophie.

"Can you believe it?" said Wil. "We're actually on the roof, and the Sphinxes are right...they're right there! We can touch them if we—"

"Hey, what do you kids think you're doing up here?" said a rough voice. "Get down this instant!"

Catfysh evaporated away suddenly, if evaporated were quite the right word. A shimmering fog descended and she was gone, leaving Wil and Sophie alone.

Only her hoarse whisper lingered in the air. "Give'ysh your gift to the Sphinxes. *Piscis ignis nebula stella. Piscis ignis nebula stella. Piscis ignis nebula...*

Wil and Sophie turned to see one of the security guards glaring at them through the trap door.

"You could fall off the roof up here," the security guard shouted, "and then where'd be my job then? I'd be fired, that's what," he said, answering his own question. "I'd be fired because of you two. If you don't come down right this minute, I have half a mind to phone the police!"

XXX The Sphinx to the East and the Sphinx to the West

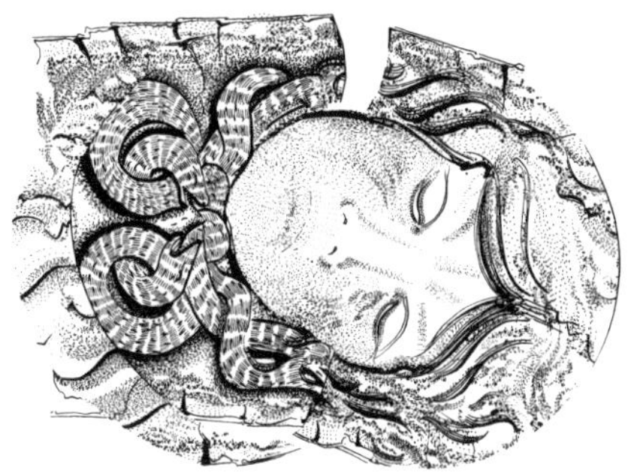

They passed underneath the head of Medusa.

VERBA DECIPERE, VERBA EDOCERE,
VERBA COGITANDA, VERBA ERRANDA
CONFUNDUNT, CONTUNDUNT, TURBANT, VEXANT.
RISUS, GEMITUS, SILENTIUS, SUSPIRITUS
NODUS, AENIGMA, NOLITE NOBIS MENTIRI.
WORDS TO TRICK, WORDS TO TEACH
WORDS TO PONDER, WORDS TO WANDER
BEFUDDLE AND MUDDLE, WORRY AND TUSSLE
A LAUGH, A GROAN, A SILENCE, A SIGH
A PUZZLE, A QUESTION, TELL US NO LIE.

The security guard escorted them grimly down the stairs, back along the corridor, through the doors, down to the second floor. He didn't say a word to either of them.

✣ ✣ ✣

The Great Hall of the Palace of the Blazing Star was filled with beautiful music. A choir stood on the landing just above the two bison; their voices quavered and echoed throughout the Hall. A small group of school children visiting from out-of-town was taking a weekend tour of the building; the guide was just starting to tell them the story of the Golden Boy.

Wil held tight onto his medallion, wondering what the security guards were going to do with them. And where was Catfysh when they needed her?

"I wish we were invisible," he whispered to Sophie.

"We could try to call Catfysh," said Sophie.

"How?" asked Wil.

"Maybe if we can get to the Pool of the Black Star—" said Sophie.

"Maybe if we make a run for it—" said Wil, taking Sophie's arm.

"That's enough out of you two," growled the guard.

Just as they reached the first floor, they heard many voices shout, "*CURSUFERRI!*"

The singing came to an abrupt halt, with just an echo lingering in the hall. Then, there was an unearthly quiet.

The mouths of the singers were still open, frozen in mid-note. The school children were frozen in place, and the tour guide had stopped in mid-sentence. He was pointing to one of the bison.

Even the guard escorting them was frozen, his face in a permanent frown.

"What happened?" asked Sophie. "Why is everyone else frozen and we're not?"

"I was holding the medallion," said Wil, "and touching your arm. The medallion must have protected both of us somehow."

"But remember when Mage Adderson found that blue egg in Stone Hall just before we started writing our exams?" said Sophie. "She froze everyone, including you. It didn't work then."

"Maybe the medallion's getting stronger," said Wil, and he grinned. "Quick before someone sees us. That *cursuferri* curse must be really, really powerful to hold everyone."

They dashed to the front door, but it was sealed shut. One of the security guards had been frozen in the moment of bending to tie his shoelace. Wil couldn't resist kneeling down and tying it for him; then he darted after Sophie, who had run down one of the side corridors.

"We can't get out," whispered Sophie.

"Let's go to the roof," said Wil. "Maybe the Sphinxes can help us."

Trying to be as quiet as possible, they snuck up the stairs and passed under the head of Medusa. Wil could not help but look up for but a moment. The Medusa's eyes were closed; and Wil remembered Catfysh's warning not to look into her eyes. Perhaps it was just the angle of light, but he could have sworn the stone Medusa had a frown on her face.

Voices were coming from the other side of the Great Hall. Sneaking from column to column they drew as close as they dared.

"—they did not comply," said a man's deep voice. "We must cleanse the building, undefiled by petty politics. We shall do what must be done."

Wil peered around the column. There were at least a dozen people standing in a circle. They were wearing long hooded cloaks; he could only see the face of one of them—a woman, who looked familiar. She had white hair and very blue eyes. It took him a moment to remember that she was one of the tourists he had seen when they took the tour with Mage Adderson. She must be part of the Serpent's Chain too.

Wil looked above their heads; embedded in the wall, there was that strange fossil that looked exactly like a human skull. And more shocking, he saw for the first time a row of sightless, horned cow skulls lining the skylight high above the Great Hall.

Trying to ignore a growing sense of doom, he whispered, "We've heard enough. Now we know for sure the Serpent's Chain is involved. Come on. Let's go."

They retraced their footsteps, ran along the corridor with the pipes and electrical wires, through the door that said NO UNAUTHORIZED PERSONNEL MAY ENTER, up the winding wooden staircase, clambered through the small trap door, and ran across the roof to the Sphinxes.

Up close, the Sphinxes' sheer size took Wil's breath away. He and Sophie were barely tall enough to reach the top of the Sphinxes' paws.

"How are the Sphinxes going to know we're here?" said Sophie. "They're stone asleep."

"Maybe we should have asked Portia and Portius how to wake up sleeping Sphinxes," said Wil.

"Portia and Portius would probably say something like, *Let sleeping Sphinxes lie,*" said Sophie.

"Or they would have gotten into an argument—you know, what was the first riddle a Sphinx ever asked?" said Wil.

Feeling foolish for trying to talk to a stone statue—and with no hope that anything would actually happen—Wil stood as straight and tall as he could. Wondering exactly how to address a Sphinx properly, he said loudly, "O, Great Sphinx to the East and Great Sphinx to the West, we, William Wychwood and Sophie Isidor…your humble servants"—that sounded good, he thought—"request your help." As an afterthought, he whispered, "Catfysh said you'd help us."

Sophie stepped forward. "We bring you a gift from your home place Egypt." She pulled Mage Tibor's vial of sand from her pocket and held it up high in the air, then took the cork out and poured a few grains of sand onto the paws of the Sphinx to the East. Then she ran to the Sphinx to the West and poured sand onto its paws too.

And as she did so, miraculously, the Sphinxes stirred. Their tails flickered—they reminded Wil of serpents—then two vast and windy sighs filled the air. Each Sphinx shook its head, stretched a leonine paw slowly, delicately, extending long, gleaming claws. Their great lips parted and they yawned and stretched again. A breeze swirled around them and kicked the few grains of sand into the air. The Sphinxes smiled, turned their faces to the sky, breathed deeply, filled their lungs, then roared, if roaring it could be called. The sound…so deep…so rumbling…so unlike any other sound Wil had ever heard in his entire life, rattled every bone in his body. The serpents on the Sphinx headdresses awoke and coiled; then they sprouted wide, outstretched wings and the shadows of the Sphinxes quivered, grew, danced over Wil and Sophie.

"Amazing…it worked!" said Wil, wondering what in snake's name would happen next.

"We Are Home," thundered the Sphinxes, their rumbling voices seeming to come from somewhere deep inside the stone. "For Years—Through Deafening Rains, Cruel Hail, Icy Storms and Blizzard Snow, Yet Have We Yearned for the Soils of Our Desert Lands."

They encircled Sophie and Wil, then sat back on their haunches, each one speaking in turn:

Words to Trick, Words to Teach
Words that Wander, Words to Ponder
Befuddle and Muddle, Worry and Tussle
A Laugh, a Groan, Here's Grief, a Sigh
A Puzzle, a Riddle, Tell Us No Lie
A Game, a Challenge Before We Ally
Answer the Riddle, Answer You Must
If No Answer Is Offered
No Help Shall Be Proffered
Your Quest Shall Turn to Dust.

XXXI The Riddle

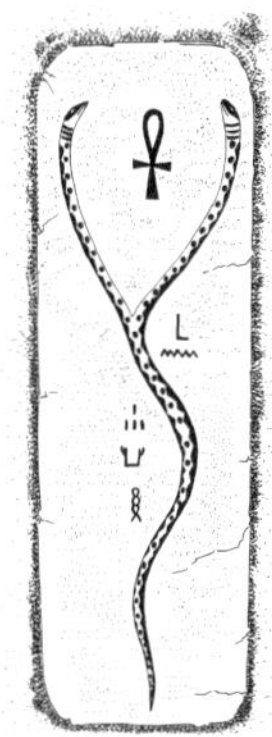

What do the hieroglyphics mean?

CONSILIUM MEUM:
AUDI ATTENTE
NE UMQUAM SIS
IN STATU SIMILI ALIQUANDO.
MY PIECE OF ADVICE:
LISTEN CAREFULLY IN THE CASE
THAT YOU EVER FIND YOURSELF IN
A SIMILAR SITUATION SOME DAY.

The Sphinx to the East spoke first, its voice hoarse, as if it tired from speaking after having been silent for so many years. "What Makes One City Strong and Yet Wears Another Away?"

The Sphinx to the West countered, "What Flows Like Water and Yet Can Be Walked Upon?

"What Takes on The Shape of Another and Yet Is Unyielding?" whispered the first.

"What Is Itself Worn Away By The Eternity Of Time? asked the second.

"We Shall Await Your Answer," they intoned together, their voices passing into whisper.

Both the Sphinxes closed their eyes and turned back to stone before Wil's and Sophie's eyes.

"Now what?" said Sophie. "What if we don't know the answer?"

"And what happens if we give them the wrong answer?" asked Wil. "Remember that old Greek Sphinx killed everyone who couldn't answer her question."

"Maybe they'll eat us. They might be hungry after being asleep for so long," whispered Sophie and she giggled nervously. "Anyway, we should stop talking about what they might do and concentrate on answering the riddle."

"Okay, it flows like water and you can step on it," said Wil. "And it takes on the shape of other things but it's hard—that sounds like pudding, only pudding isn't hard, it jiggles."

Sophie pulled out the vial she had received from Mage Tibor and smiled.

Wil didn't notice Sophie's smile. He was still muttering to himself, "Makes cities strong but it destroys them at the same time. Could be water, but that doesn't make sense, 'cause you can't walk on water, can you? I mean, not unless you're—"

"Wil, I've got it," said Sophie impatiently.

"You have?" he said incredulously.

"Yes," said Sophie, and she turned to the Sphinxes. "We have the answer to your riddle," she said loudly.

The Sphinxes opened their eyes and bowed their heads.

"Wait, Sophie, what if you're wrong?" shouted Wil.

The Sphinx to the East spoke. "The Decision Is Yours, To Answer Or Not, But Those Who Are Wrong Shall Be Forgot."

Then the Sphinx to the West spoke. "Those Who Are Right, We Sphinxes Aid And Abet, Never To Desert, Never To Forget."

"Wil, I know the answer!" whispered Sophie. "Trust me, I know the answer." She bowed to the Sphinxes. "The answer to your riddle is sand," she said. "Because you can use sand to help build a city, but sandstorms will tear a city down. The wind blows sand so that it looks like ripples on water and you can walk on sand. And sand fills whatever container you pour it into, but each grain of sand is like a solid rock, in miniature. And the winds of time wear sand down until it too turns into dust."

"The Answer Is Good," said the Sphinx to the East, and it bared its chest. Between its paws rested a cartouche carved with hieroglyphics. A circle at the top. Beneath the circle, a long horizontal rectangle with nine balls across it. And at the bottom, a large scarab beetle.

"Do You Know the Meaning?" the Sphinx to the West asked. It too bared its chest, which showed the same hieroglyphics.

"Those two look like the sun and a beetle," said Wil. Then he pointed to a circle and cross inscribed outside the cartouche. "And there's the symbol for life."

The Sphinx to the East smiled at Wil and Sophie. "The Circle Represents the *Disc of the Sun God Re. Men,* the Game Board, Means Everlasting. *Kheper,* the Beetle, meaning *The Manifestation of.* Thus, *The Firm and Everlasting Manifestation of Re, The Good God Who Has Given Life.*"

"Has given life," repeated Wil. He pulled the black medallion out. At the sight of it, the eyes of the both Sphinxes gleamed blinding gold for an instant then dimmed.

The Sphinx of the East spoke gently. "Do Not Tarry Or It Be Too Late."

"Too late? asked Wil. "Too late for what?"

"It Has Already Begun," said the Sphinx to the West.

The Sphinx to the East bowed its massive stone head, but said nothing.

"Wil," exclaimed Sophie and she pointed to the Egyptian cross. "There's a circular hollow inside the cross."

With shaking hands, Wil placed the medallion inside the indentation. It fit perfectly.

With a great scraping noise, the cartouche on the Sphinx's chest slid open…to reveal another cartouche hidden beneath—this one inscribed with a double-headed serpent. The cartouche was guarding several more hieroglyphics.

Wil stared at the hidden cartouche, not believing his eyes. He was suddenly reminded of the snake he had found at Narcisse last autumn—how, despite being mortally wounded, despite inside being ripped outside to inside, the snake had struggled to live.

"That wavy line, it's the symbol for water," exclaimed Sophie, "and the Egyptian cross—that means the key of life. I…I don't know the others."

Wil felt the hieroglyphics. He ran his fingers over the sign with one single stroke and three strokes beneath. "The one and the many," he said. "I remember learning those when we were studying Meretseger."

"Praise, For By The World Serpent, All Shall Come To Life," roared the Sphinxes. "Render Animate The Inanimate."

The Sphinxes both reared up high on their hind legs and roared, "All Creatures, To Life."

A great rumbling started beneath their feet and the air around them turned golden and sparkling, as if grains of sand had turned to sparks of fire.

Wil looked up in astonishment at the top of the dome of the Palace of the Blazing Star, for the entire statue of Hermes was aflame. A beam of light shot out from the torch he held and an enormous image of Hermes blasted high into the sky, towering over the Palace of the Blazing Star. Hermes gazed down upon Wil and Sophie and the Sphinxes.

"As Desired, So Be Done," he thundered.

The image lasted but for a flicker of the eye longer, then twinkled to bits of dust that danced in the sunlight and were no more.

"Avaunt!" roared the Sphinxes. "Avaunt!" And then they bounded away, arched gracefully into the air and leapt over the side of the Palace.

XXXII Pandemonium

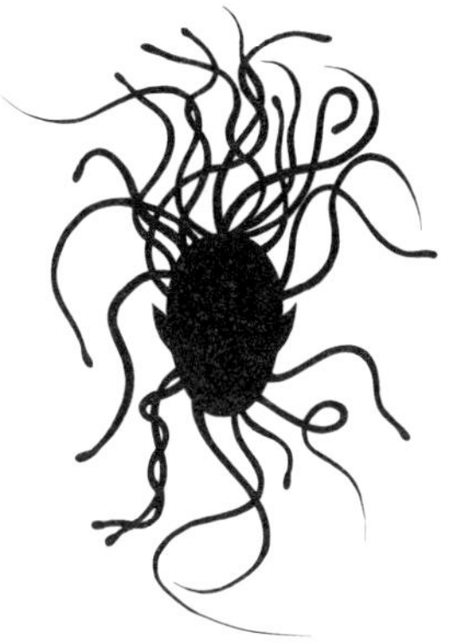

It was as if all the snakes of Narcisse had suddenly appeared unbidden.

UBIQUE PANDAEMONIUM
AND ALL WAS PANDEMONIUM

"They just jumped off the Palace," Wil said. "Did you see that?"

"Wil, we don't have time!" screamed Sophie. "Come on. They told us to go."

They clattered down the stairs as quickly as they could, Wil stumbling down the last few steps.

"Come on, Wil, come on," Sophie yelled.

They ran along the corridor, through the doors, to the third floor. Loud roars, screams and shouts greeted their ears. It was a horrifying sight.

The two bison had jumped down from their pedestals and were thundering across the marble floor in pursuit of the cloaked members of the Serpent's Chain.

The stone lions roared, tossed their great, gnarled manes and bounded up the stairs, leaving massive, gaping holes in the stone arches of the Great Hall.

Most frightening of all, Wil could hear a voice screaming high above their heads. "Serpents, Arise! They Dare Not Desecrate This Sanctuary!"

It must have been the Medusa. Wil did not look up for fear that he would look into her eyes and be turned utterly to stone.

Hissing and spitting, hundreds and hundreds of snakes—wriggling, writhing, squirming, twisting, sliding down the stone walls, across the shining marble floor, down the stone stairs. It was as if all the snakes of Narcisse had suddenly appeared unbidden.

The statues on the third floor hurled curses into the air and slipped down from their pedestals; their brawny arms grasped the railings.

The bison, hot steam pouring from their swollen nostrils, cornered five of the Serpent's Chain; they were pinioned against the stone wall at the base of the stairs. The woman with the white hair and blue eyes was one of them.

She caught sight of Wil and bowed her head for a moment. Then she smiled and whispered, "*Ein Phönix aus die Asche.*"

Although Wil did not understand her words, they sent a shiver down his spine.

The terrible bison pawed the marble floor, as if wishing they could gore their captives, while Athena, in helmet and carrying a large, bronze shield, quickly corralled the others.

The horned cow skulls from the skylight high above moaned and hovered in the air ready to give chase, if need be.

The choir was still frozen in the act of singing, even as the snakes slithered down the banisters beside them. The school children and their tour guide (who was still pointing to the now absent bison)—all were still frozen. Secretaries carrying stacks of files, the clicks of their heels stilled for the moment—frozen. There was even a camera crew at the top of the stairs interviewing one of the politicians. The politician was having his face powdered before the shoot began and was frozen in the middle of a sneeze.

Amidst the mayhem, Wil and Sophie dodged the lions and stumbled down the stairs, trying not to step on any of the snakes. Just as they turned the corner to creep down the stairs to the Pool of the Black Star, out of nowhere a great cloud of smoke exploded near the entrance. From the smoke emerged a dozen Firecatchers robed in red. They bowed to the bison and to Athena and encircled the members of the Serpent's Chain.

Not a moment too soon.

A voice at the entrance door shouted through a megaphone, "WE'VE GOT YOU SURROUNDED. DON'T MOVE!"

At these words, the bison leapt back onto their pedestals, once again guarding the entrance to the stairs. The lions returned whence they had come, each to their place on the wall. Athena returned quietly back into her rightful place above the entrance to the Great Hall. Medusa's serpents sank into the stones. The statues on the third floor clambered back onto their pedestals and resumed holding key and scroll; and the cow skulls clattered back to the skylight to stare down sightless, as they always had.

A slim wraith of smoke left from the Firecatchers spiralled in the air.

The door stormed open and dozens of soldiers dressed in khaki green and fully armed spilled into the Great Hall.

"EVERYBODY FREEZE!" one of the soldiers shouted. "PUT YOUR HANDS UP!"

"How can everyone freeze and put their hands up at the same time?" Sophie whispered.

"Isn't it funny everyone was frozen already and now they're saying freeze again?" said Wil. "We better get out of here."

✣ ✣ ✣

The tour guide looked up in surprise, as did the school children at the sight of the soldiers. The choir stopped in mid-stanza and stared blankly at this new audience. The politician (finally) sneezed. The security guards looked as if they didn't know what had hit them.

"M-M-May we help you?" stuttered one of the guards.

XXXIII Vigilance

Sharp, shiny teeth glinted as it spoke.

VIGILANTIA! IN AETERNUM VIGILANTIA!
PRAECIPUE SI NATAS NOVIS IN AQUIS.
VIGILANCE! ETERNAL VIGILANCE—
ESPECIALLY IF YOU ARE SWIMMING IN STRANGE WATERS.

Wil and Sophie scurried down the stairs and flung themselves onto the Black Star. Their small voices quavered. "*Piscis ignis nebula stella. Piscis ignis nebula stella.*"

"Nothing's happening," squealed Sophie.

"I'm sure we've got the right words," said Wil.

The sound of boots thundered down the stairs.

"Wait, we only said it two times," said Wil. "Quick, try again."

Standing in the middle of the Black Star clutching each other, Wil and Sophie recited again, "*Piscis ignis nebula stella. Piscis ignis nebula stella. Piscis ignis nebula stella.*"

The sound echoed sweetly in the chamber and flowed around them like soothing waters.

The marble of the Pool of the Black Star turned liquid black, as black as a vessel of India ink; Wil and Sophie slipped beneath its surface, just as the soldiers stormed into the chamber.

"I thought I saw two kids in here," shouted one of the soldiers. "Check outside—make sure they didn't go outside."

✣ ✣ ✣

Sophie and Wil raced through the waters without looking behind them—Sophie was convinced that the soldiers would somehow follow them—until breathless, their flared gills gasping, they darted into a cobble of large stones, from which long, green weedy fingers swayed lazily in the current.

Home, bubbled Sophie.

Where is home? bubbled Wil.

Home is where home is, burbled a deep voice.

"Who was that?" bubbled Sophie, her whiskers tingling and alert.

"It came from over there, underneath that big rock," bubbled Wil quietly.

Sophie peered out warily from underneath her stone. She couldn't see anything, but something was there...something big...something fishy. She could feel it breathing.

Home is where home is, and I shall take you where, burbled the voice.

Who...who...who are you? stutterbubbled Sophie.

A spotted brown fish, the largest Sophie had ever seen, shot out from behind the reeds. Scales covered its cheeks and the upper part of its gill covers. With its long snout and curved mouth, it looked as if it were smiling at them.

Sophie did not like the smile; she did not trust this fish. And when the fish opened its mouth to speak, Sophie recoiled. Sharp, shiny teeth glinted as it spoke.

I am Pike, burbled the fish without ceremony. *I am to escort you back to your humhuman world.*

How do we know we can trust you? bubbled Sophie.

Very good question, my girl, burbled Pike. *Vigilance! Eternal piscelistic vigilance—especially if you happen to find yourself swimming in strange waters without the proper escort.*

I have had my second breakfast already, however—a delicious, crunchy meal, I may add—Pike snapped his teeth as he burbled this, and Sophie shuddered. *I won't trouble you unduly with the boring details. You, my dear friends, are protected by Catfysh. And By the Sacred Waters of this River, I do Honour My Agreements—however tempting the circumstances to act otherwise.* Pike snapped his teeth again—this time, is if saluting them both. *A scale for a scale and a tail for a tail, that's my motto. One good finturn deserves another. And no one wants to swim afish of Catfysh.*

⁜ ⁜ ⁜

Wil and Sophie crawled up the slope of the riverbank, and sat blinking and bewildered in the noonday sun; they stared at the twinkling waters of the river. A pair of squabbling ducks swam by carried by the swift current.

They said nothing to each other for a long time, until Sophie mused, "I didn't trust Pike, did you?"

"I know what you mean. The way he snapped his teeth—I thought he was going to eat us," said Wil. "Do you think Pike would go after one of those ducks?"

Sophie didn't answer Wil's question. Instead, she said, "We won't see her again, will we?"

"We never got to ask her anything about the black medallion," said Wil. "All we know is what my grandmother said about the secret lessons and she couldn't say anything more without endangering us. And we still know hardly anything about the Serpent's Chain. Not that I really want to. But there are more than just Rufus Crookshank—"

"And Lucretia Daggar," said Sophie.

"But how did they think they could take over the entire Palace of the Blazing Star?" asked Wil. "There weren't that many of them. But that woman with the white hair and blue eyes was on that tour we had with Mage Adderson, and she was speaking some other language. So the Serpent's Chain must be growing."

"There are a lot of questions we don't have answers to," said Sophie. "We still don't know what the Serpent's Chain wants and we don't know why it's so interested in you and that black medallion. The medallion must be pretty special.

"Plus we don't know what really happened to my father or my mother. What if my father is still alive somewhere and what if my mother didn't really drown?"

"And what about my parents?" said Wil. "Maybe Gran didn't tell me the truth. Maybe they didn't die in a car accident. It's really strange that she was always the one telling me there was no such thing as magic."

"Too many questions," said Sophie sighing. "We'd better get back for lunch. Aunt Rue and Aunt Violet will be worried."

"They probably think we're with Phinneas and Beatriz," said Wil, who was gazing at the ducks. "We can't tell Phinneas and Beatriz what happened," he said sadly.

"We can't tell *anyone* what happened," said Sophie. "We've got to protect Catfysh…and besides, they probably wouldn't believe us anyway, even if we did tell them. Remember what happened to that woman who kept thinking she was a fish. We don't want to be put away somewhere."

"Secret?" said Wil.

"Between you, me and Catfysh's whiskers—all ten of them!" said Sophie.

XXXIV A Postcard

Forewarned is forearmed.

FABULAE BONAE SUNT. MELIORES TAMEN FINES INSOLITI.
STORIES ARE GOOD. SURPRISE ENDINGS ARE EVEN BETTER!

Wil sat at the kitchen table stirring his plate of baked beans, which was now quite cold. He was too excited to eat and Sophie, whose eyeglass frames were the colour of seaweed matching the deep, greenish circles under her eyes, had barely touched hers.

"Not hungry for lunch?" said Aunt Rue. "You're not coming down with something, are you?" She felt Sophie's and Wil's foreheads. "Cool as cucumbers, both of you. You're staying up much too late these days," she said severely. "Early to bed tonight."

"And no blueberry muffins for you until you finish your baked beans," said Aunt Violet.

Aunt Rue turned on the radio to catch the Saturday noonday news. A deep voice, full of urgency and tension, filled the kitchen and made Wil's stomach lurch.

"—breaking news. Early this morning, a serious breach in security at the Palace of the Blazing Star, known beyond MiddleGate's walls as the Manitoba Legislative Building, resulted in a total lockdown of the historic building. The Palace of the Blazing Star is known to magical communities around the world for its secret and esoteric symbolism. Many practitioners and scholars lament that they have yet to understand fully the knowledge embedded in the building.

"Hostages were taken and civilian troops were called in to defuse the situation. Before any arrests could be made, however, the suspects vanished into thin air. Fortunately, non-mage civil authorities in Winnipeg and Manitoba are mystified as to who the perpetrators were or what they wanted. It appears there were no immediate civilian casualties and, thankfully, no extensive damage to the Palace of the Blazing Star itself—only very minor flooding in the meeting chamber, known as the Pool of the Black Star.

"The Firecatchers are, of course, conducting an independent investigation of events and MiddleGate has been placed on a high security alert. Despite rampant rumours that the Serpent's Chain, an ancient secret society disbanded long ago—was somehow involved in the lockdown, MiddleGate officials continue to deny possible links.

"MNN was able to speak Cynthea Ciel-D'Anjou, who works in the Secretariat of Security."

The voice of a woman, sounding troubled yet soothing at the same time came on the air. "The repercussions of such hostile action against the Palace of the Blazing Star could, of course, have been very serious for MiddleGate. Our policy remains unchanged from the beginning. We must protect MiddleGate from incursion. We shall never forget The Burning Wall Revolt, in which so many of our people died and, obviously, we do not want history to repeat itself. As for public concern about the return of the Serpent's Chain, the Secretariat believes that such fears are entirely unfounded and unwarranted."

"That was Cynthea Ciel-D'Anjou speaking to us from the Secretariat of Security in MiddleGate. I'm Ashburn Goldencrantz of MNN's MiddleGateNews 91.1, and we'll have will more details for you as they—"

Aunt Violet turned off the radio impatiently. "Vanished into thin air," she sniffed. "No one vanishes into thin air without leaving a trail, however faint. What is this world coming to? Imagine the Palace of the Blazing Star being commandeered by ruffians. The authorities probably let them slip right through their fingers and now they're trying to plead ignorance to the press. I tell you, I think we never hear the half of these stories."

"I'm sure everyone's doing their best to take control of the situation… to control damage," said Aunt Rue, sounding worried. "We can't have everyone panicking after all."

Wil and Sophie exchanged glances, stifled giggles, then ducked their heads and began to wolf down their baked beans.

"What are you two giggling about?" said Aunt Violet severely. "And please don't gobble your food."

"Sorry, Aunt Violet," mumbled Wil, his mouth full of baked beans.

"The Burning Wall Revolt is nothing to giggle about, children," said Aunt Violet in a severe tone.

"But we're not," protested Sophie.

A flurry of morning mail flew in through the slot in the door and interrupted their protests. "More bills, I suppose," said Aunt Violet. She sighed and picked up the envelopes that were lying face down. "Just as I thought, nothing but—" She paused and held up a small yellow envelope.

"What's that, Aunt Violet?" asked Sophie.

Wil was amused to see that her eyeglasses had just turned the exact colour of the envelope.

Aunt Violet turned the envelope over and sighed. "Probably another bill for equipment or something." She looked guiltily at Aunt Rue, who only pursed her lips and did not say anything.

"Can I open it, Aunt Violet?" asked Sophie.

"*May* you open it," said Aunt Violet. "Yes, you *may*," and she passed the envelope to Sophie, then sat down at the kitchen table. She sighed again.

Sophie ripped open the envelope and began to read the letter. Her eyeglasses turned from yellow to the colour of juicy watermelon.

"What is it, Sophie?" asked Wil.

Sophie only clutched the letter more tightly.

"Tell us, Sophie," said Aunt Violet, her eyes widening. "It's not bad news, I hope."

"We won," said Sophie in a small voice.

"What did you say?" asked Aunt Rue.

"We what?" asked Wil.

"The prize," said Sophie.

"What prize?" asked Aunt Rue. "What are you talking about?"

"The prize. Don't you remember? The *Prize Mystery Trip*. We won!" This time Sophie shrieked and threw the letter into the air.

"But…but…that's impossible," said Aunt Violet, sounding as dazed as the day she bought the *BUZzz* ball.

"We won, we won, we won," shrieked Sophie, dancing around the kitchen.

"What exactly did we win?" asked Wil, his heart thumping wildly.

"A trip!" said Sophie.

"A trip where?" asked Aunt Violet. "Where are my glasses?"

"Are we sure this isn't a scam?" said Aunt Rue. "Here, Aunt Violet, I'll see what it says." She took the letter from Sophie and began to read aloud:

Dear Madam Isidor:

It is our great pleasure to inform you that your name has been chosen as the Winner for the Perfect Products Annual Mystery Trip Prize, an All-Expenses Paid Trip for two adults and two children.

In order to claim the Prize, you must show the original contract for your purchase from Perfect Products and answer a skill-testing question.

"You still have the contract, don't you, Aunt Violet?" asked Sophie.

"Of course I have the contract—in the wood box under my bed, where I keep all the important papers," exclaimed Aunt Violet, sounding offended by Sophie's question.

Aunt Rue frowned. "This is all a little mysterious, isn't it? What if we don't like the destination?" Her eyes skimmed to the end of the letter.

This year, the Mystery Trip Prize is for a one-week all-expenses paid trip—"

Wil, Sophie and Aunt Violet leaned forward in anticipation.

Perhaps they'd be going to China…or India…or Africa, thought Wil. Or maybe they'd have a holiday in Costa Rica. Although Wil wasn't quite sure where Costa Rica was, he knew it was an island somewhere far, far south where the world's largest butterfly, the Blue Morpho, lives—its wings were a shimmering, heavenly, iridescent, electric blue.

He had overheard Mr. Egbertine telling a customer about his holiday in Costa Rica. "An exceedingly extraordinary and exotic excursion—during which I had the exceptional privilege to witness the giant sea turtles laying their eggs on a sandy beach by night," Mr. Egbertine had murmured, his voice full of awe. "*Sans doute, une des expériences la plus mémorable de toute ma vie!*"

"Here, I'll give you a hint about where we're going," said Aunt Rue, but Wil did not hear her, nor did he see her hold up the postcard that had also been in the envelope. A postcard of the statue of a broad-chested and bearded Norse Viking, with a horned helmet. He was standing alone and resolute against a clear blue sky, his expression serious, even grim.

Still picturing himself on a beach watching a giant sea turtle lay her eggs by cover of darkness, Wil had a huge and silly grin on his face, as he gazed up at the kitchen ceiling. Now he could almost feel the waves lapping at his bare toes and the glorious sun rising at dawn and warming his face.

"Iceland!" said Aunt Rue. "Imagine that!"

All of a sudden, Wil felt the warm winds turn biting and chill. His feet felt heavy, as if weighed down by thick boots. Instead of imagining he was gazing at jewelled, turquoise waters, he was shivering at the edge of a huge glacier sparkling cruelly in the cold sun. He felt himself being rudely yanked back to the house on Half Moon Lane, to the kitchen with the same old hole in the linoleum from Aunt Rue's enthusiastic *One-Shot No-Spot Cleaning Powder* experiment.

⸭ ⸭ ⸭

Both Wil and Sophie stared wild-eyed at Aunt Rue, who was oblivious to their consternation. Had there been a contest to judge whether Sophie or Wil looked more horrified—or was it terrified—it would have been difficult to choose between them.

Aunt Rue continued reading enthusiastically:

Iceland, the land of the midnight sun and Northern lights, otherworldly landscapes desolate and beautiful as the moon, bubbling geysers, volcanoes, polar caves and black lava deserts. The Icelandic sagas live on today, heroic stories—magical and supernatural—to warm the heart and chill your bones. And with so many museums, galleries, music festivals and cultural events, rest assured you'll enjoy a fabulous trip to Iceland filled with 'galdur'—all courtesy of Perfect Products, Inc.

And remember our motto...praemonitus, praemunitus—forewarned is forearmed!

"That's quite a motto, isn't it?" mused Aunt Rue.

"But what does it mean?" asked Wil, who was still trying to grasp the awful truth that they had just won a trip to...to... He couldn't even bring himself to think it.

"It means that if you know what disasters lie ahead, you may take precautions to protect yourself," said Aunt Rue. "*Forearmed* does sound a trifle war-like; I do think, though, *forewarned* strikes just the right tone for a company that sells crystal balls."

"Hmmm, *'a fabulous trip to Iceland 'filled with galdur,'* said Aunt Violet. "I wonder what that word *galdur* means...it must be an Icelandic word." She smiled. "No matter. We can ask Mr. Bertram to look it up in one of the dictionaries." She looked up at Wil and Sophie and her smile faded. "Why, children, such long faces! What's the matter?"

"Ice…Ice…Iceland," Wil managed to stutter.

"Ice…land," echoed Sophie, her face blank. Her eyeglass frames turned clear and hard-shiny like an icycle.

Aunt Violet looked from one to the other, swept Sophie's and Wil's plates from the table and placed a large platter of warm blueberry muffins before them. "Yes, Iceland," she said brightly. "Can you believe our extraordinary fortune?"

"More good has come of this crystal ball business, Aunt Violet!" exclaimed Aunt Rue, and she handed Aunt Violet the letter. Humming to herself, Aunt Rue spread butter on her blueberry muffin and took a hearty bite. "Aunt Violet, this is scrumptious! Children, why don't you try some!" She held out the platter to Sophie, then Wil.

Wil glanced at Sophie, whose eyeglass frames still looked as hard and clear as icicles. Reluctantly, he took a blueberry muffin.

The Viking on the postcard looked dangerous, especially with those horns on his helmet. They reminded Wil of the raging bison at the Palace of the Blazing Star. *Today bites,* he thought.

With a furtive look at Aunt Rue and Aunt Violet, he secretly traced three letters on the table with his index finger, while pretending to sniff the muffin appreciatively.

Sophie nodded, cupped her hand over her lips and mouthed the words, SAVE OUR SNAKES!

Epilogue

The river floodwaters receded, and Sophie and Wil returned to the shores of the river many times, hoping against hope to see Catfysh once more, but she did not visit them again…although, one day, they did saw a large forked tail slip beneath the water's surface close by. But as each told the other, it probably wasn't Catfysh.

The security guard who had been tying up his shoelaces when the attack on the Palace of the Blazing Star began confessed to a co-worker, "I must be losing my mind. You know I bent over to tie my shoelace, but it didn't need tying. I think I'm going to buy slip-on shoes—make life a little easier."

And news of Euphemus, the man who had been speech-making in front of the two-serpents doorway near *Auntie Vi's Fortune Telling?* He decided to visit Aunt Violet's shop again one day. Briefly—and without breaching serious matters of confidentiality—she read his tea leaves and told him he was about to embark on a long journey, which would take him to far-away places. That was the last anyone heard from Euphemus in these parts.

Unfortunately, Aunt Rue never did have any definitive word on her application for the position of Assistant Deputy Minister. Minister Skelch only a short time ago mentioned that no decision had yet been made, but Aunt Rue had resigned herself to the inevitable.

Alas, Aunt Violet has still not found the perfect dress for having her portrait painted by the famous artist Ursula von Scrum.

And what of the prize trip to Iceland? Oh, dear children, much, much more remains to be told…

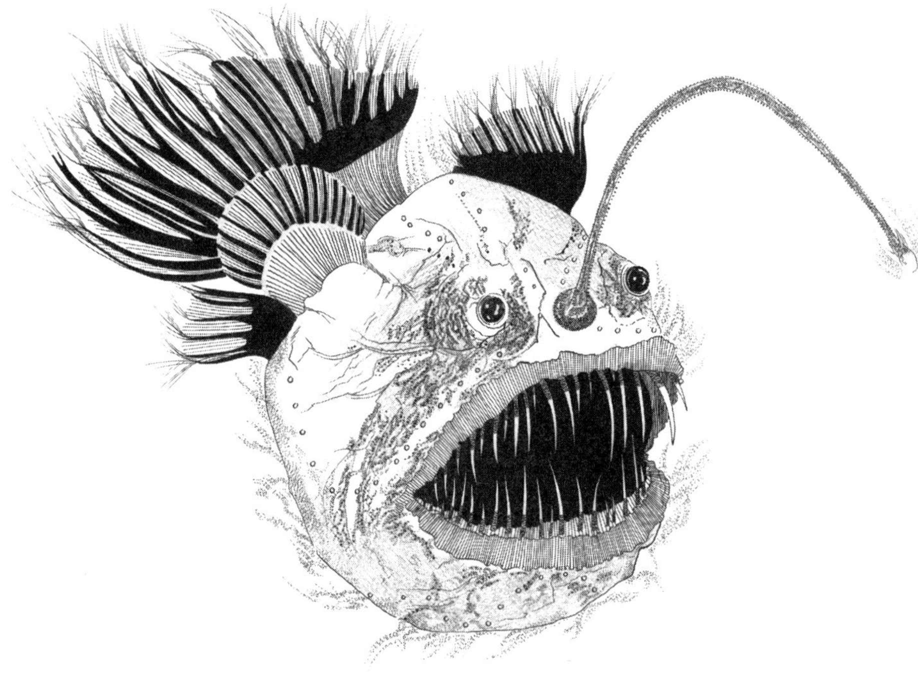